PRAISE FOR MARK OF THE LEAST

"A wildly original and magical twist on the Robin Hood narrative, Kendra Merritt's *By Wingéd Chair* is packed to the spokes with complex characters, wry humor, and flawless world building."

-Darby Karchut, best-selling author of DEL TORO MOON and FINN FINNEGAN

"With a wonderfully crafted blend of swords and sorcery and characters based on Robin Hood, Merritt tops this story off with the lead character readers need nowadays; a strong, independent, powerful female mage who also happens to be in a wheelchair. Readers will be constantly turning pages to see what happens next to this fun group of characters through the twists and turns they won't see coming."

-The Booklife Prize

"Kendra Merritt's prose is fresh, with one-line descriptions that crack like a whip, and she doesn't miss an opportunity to surprise the reader. From the first line to the last, I was enchanted with *By Winged Chair*."

-Todd Fahnestock, best-selling author of FAIRMIST and THE WISHING WORLD

ALSO BY KM MERRITT

<u>Fantasy for Kids</u>

Mishap's Heroes Series (Youth Editions)

Magic and Misrule

Death and Devotion

Trust and Treason

Illusions and Infamy

Sparks and Scales

Wastelands and War

<u>Young Adult Fantasy and Science Fiction</u>

Mark of the Least Series

By Wingéd Chair

Skin Deep

Catching Cinders

Shroud for a Bride

A Matter of Blood

After the Darkness

The King in the Tower Collection

Daybreak Colony Duology

Surviving Daybreak

Daybreak Sentinel

<u>Fantasy for Adults</u>

Mishap's Heroes Series

MISHAP'S HEROES

6

Wastelands and War

KM MERRITT

BLUE FYRE PRESS

For all the gamer girls. Keep kicking ass.

ONE

"WHAT ARE you supposed to pack for war?" Sorrel said, holding up a loose white shirt Vola had never seen her wear before. The monk always wore the same gray wrap-around tunic and loose pants tied close around her calves.

"I suppose the same kinds of things you've always packed before," Lillie said. Her lilting voice, which would have done well when paired with a lute, was distracted as she stacked books in her saddle bag. Vola was waiting for her to drop something on her foot because she wasn't paying attention.

"Knives, swords, daggers, bows, quivers, armor, two pairs of pants, boots, and new gauntlets from the vendor down the street." Talon ticked off the list on her fingers.

"That's oddly specific," Lillie said, pausing with her head cocked. "Especially for Sorrel who doesn't wear armor and fights with a glorified stick."

Talon looked up, blue eyes confused. "What's Sorrel got to do with anything? I was going through my bags."

Lillie rolled her eyes. "Sorrel was asking what to pack for war."

"I think Lillie's right," Vola said, folding her own shirts. "Just pack normal."

"Sexy underwear it is, then," Sorrel said and tossed a couple of scraps of black fabric at her bags without folding them first. "Might come in useful."

Talon snorted under her breath. "If you like to wear it for yourself, that's fine. But I think you might have to actually have sex to call it useful."

"Bleh," Sorrel said, making a face. "Whatever for?"

"Maybe because you love someone," Talon said.

"And want to feel close to them." Lillie's gaze was distant and unfocused again.

Vola scooted a stack of books closer to her reaching hand so she could grab them without having to look down.

Vola was already packed. She'd spent the night rearranging it all over and over again, mulling over what they were about to do. Heading to war wasn't something she took lightly. Too bad she couldn't repack her thoughts out of the way where she wouldn't trip over them every five minutes.

"Not sure I need to be that close to anyone," Sorrel said, shoving another shirt into her pack and sitting on it to make it close.

"Not even Renvick?" Lillie said with a sly smile.

Sorrel opened her mouth and hesitated. She and the draconic guardian had been circling the issue for a week, but they weren't any closer to defining what exactly they were to each. And with the impending conflict, they likely wouldn't even see each other for a while.

Sorrel shook her head. "I doubt we're going to be that type of couple. If we're going to be a couple at all…"

Lillie's face fell and her fair skin flushed bright red, clashing painfully with her strawberry blond hair. "I'm sorry."

Lillie's familiar, Rand, flew through the open window of their hotel room, the sun glinting from his black feathers and turning them nearly blue. He clacked his beak and dropped a shiny bit of broken jewelry into her hand before lighting on her shoulder. She smiled and stroked his head.

"It's alright, Lillie," Vola said. "We all know you're a romantic."

"Says the woman with a couple of cheap romance novels in her bag," Talon said.

Vola didn't flush the way she used to. She just shrugged. "It's research."

"For what?" Sorrel's brow furrowed. She pulled her bag off the bed. It was nearly as tall as she was.

"I'm trying to figure out how to weaponize your underwear." Vola spun for the door while Sorrel spluttered in outrage.

Talon swung her saddle bag over her shoulder and stood, the big black wolf, Gruff, flicking his ears at her feet. It was strange to see her without her cloak, so the light from the window hit her sandy-colored hair, now long enough to curl around her ears.

"Come on, Lillie," Talon said. "If the books don't fit, you'll have to leave some behind."

Lillie's mouth fell open. "No!"

"How did you even have time to acquire more? I swear your books procreate by themselves," Vola asked as Lillie tried to tighten the straps over the last couple of tomes. She winced when she heard a seam pop. "We've spent all of the last week running after dragons and putting out fires."

Sorrel sighed with a smile. "Good times. Hey, remember that day and a half when we thought Talon was dead?"

"You thought that was fun?" Vola said.

"Well, not the thinking she was dead part, but the finding out she wasn't part was great."

"I'm not leaving any of my notes behind," Lillie said, ignoring the ominous popping and trying to hoist her bag over her shoulder. "We need everything we have to go up against Anders. He has Nargilla's plans. Between those and the piece of the Broken's power he stole, I want every advantage we can get."

The others went quiet and sober for once, and Vola took the pack from Lillie without saying anything.

They left the hotel room that had been their home since they'd arrived in Firewatch and headed down the narrow, creaky stairs.

"At least now we have a god on our side," Talon said. "That should give us an advantage, right?"

They entered the common room which was patched together with a variety of woods and pieces of wagons and it was empty this time of day.

"Has Cleavah—I mean the Broken said anything to you, yet?" Sorrel asked Vola. "She likes you. A lot. And Maxim has never been the talk in your ear sort of god, so he's not saying much."

From everything Vola had heard since she'd met Sorrel, Maxim wasn't the sort of god to give his followers any sort of feedback. There'd been a time when Vola had envied Sorrel for her connection to the Greater Virtue of Strength and Courage. It had taken her a while to realize just how worthless a connection it was when the Virtue refused to use it.

"She hasn't said anything to me since we met with everyone at the museum the other day," Vola said quietly. "She might have declared war on Anders, but I'm not sure how much help that's going to be in the end."

"Why?" Lillie said, tilting her head.

Vola ran a hand over her dark braid and tried to come up with a coherent argument for what she was thinking. It wasn't just about the knot in her chest and the way she felt a little woozy every time she thought about her goddess. Vola had served the minor goddess known as Cleavah for years now. She'd grown in so many ways, some very unexpected for a paladin, all with the goddess's help.

But now Vola knew that Cleavah wasn't just Cleavah, Goddess of Vengeful Housewives. She was actually the Broken. The Greater Virtue of Righteousness. One of the greater gods and quite possibly the greatest god in the pantheon. If the others would ever agree to such a hierarchy.

"The Broken isn't exactly popular with the rest of the gods," Vola said. "She has some friends, some of the Greater Virtues on her side, I think. But there's a reason they call her the Broken."

"She was cast out, wasn't she?" Talon said. "Kicked from on high when the other gods realized that righteousness could rule all the rest of the Virtues and Obstacles."

"Yes," Vola said quietly. "She fell in flames and was missing from the pantheon for millennia while she recovered. She's still marked by it." The figure who'd broken free from her bonds and blazed her image across Vola's vision while she'd shattered Nargilla's magic tanks had been that of a woman with one arm and one leg, burn scars masking the left side of her face.

"So you don't think she's going to ride into the pantheon on a cloud and tell the rest of the gods what to do," Sorrel said.

"Actually, that sounds like the beginning of another Divine War," Lillie said. She tapped her lip. "Perhaps I should take notes the next time we see her."

"They didn't even trust her to hold Nargilla after she captured her," Vola said. The gnome was being held by the other gods.

"Yeah, but we don't have time for another Divine War," Talon said. "If the gods take it into their heads to beat their problems out of one another, Anders will have stolen all the magic of the world and we'll be better off dead."

"Maybe that's why the Broken chose a paladin for the first time ever," Sorrel said. "To convince the gods that this threat is bigger than their squabbles."

"They're gods," Talon said. "Do you think they'll recognize anything as bigger than them?"

Vola rubbed her brow, trying to smooth out the lines left by worry. Her friends weren't saying anything she hadn't already been over in her head a thousand times a night since the Broken had revealed herself. Why had she finally chosen a paladin? Why had she chosen an orc? Would Vola be strong enough to protect everyone from whatever came at them, whether that was a man who thought he could strip the whole world of magic, or a collection of gods too busy with their own troubles to notice the world they presumably ruled?

It would be nice if the Broken had explained anything to her when she'd decided she was done hiding. Anything at all.

Vola pushed through the door of the hotel. Outside, a walkway snaked up the mountains between the buildings made up of leftover wood lashed together with cords brought across the desert in caravans.

The harsh sun beat down on Vola's head, and she raised a hand to shade her face. Her green-tinted skin didn't burn as easily as Lillie or Talon's fair complexions, but she seemed to soak up the heat faster than the locals. Even without her plate armor.

There was an angry hiss, and Vola instinctively dodged as a squirt of greenish goo landed across the boards at her feet. The liquid sizzled and began to eat through the wood, throwing off a wisp of smoke.

Vola sighed. The swamp monster waited across the walkway, tied to a railing, but it had already chewed most of the way through the rope. It looked like the unhappy love child of a crocodile and a donkey. Slimy, scaled, and ugly enough that both parents had probably dropped dead at the sight of it. It oozed a bit at both ends and gave Vola a toothy glare.

"One day we will find a way to be rid of you," Vola said under her breath as she ducked the swamp monster's teeth and yanked what remained of the lead rope from the railing. She knew better than to assign the creature to one of her teammates. It was her turn, and she'd been the one who insisted they couldn't sell the thing to Lillie's mother at the field museum. "Don't make me regret saving you from dissection."

"I still think it would look ten times better inside out," another familiar voice said, and Vola turned to find a slim dark woman leaning against the wall of the hotel. Even in broad desert daylight, she looked like she was lounging in a shadow. The dark green jerkin she wore gleamed richly against her dark skin, and her black hair rose in a fluffy halo around her head.

One day Vola wanted to see Rilla actually wear the crown she was entitled to as the princess of Southglen's Dagger Throne.

"Have you been lurking—I mean, waiting long, Your Highness?" Vola said as Sorrel and Talon slung their packs over the swamp monster's back. She yanked its head around as it tried to lunge for one of them.

"Just getting some sun while I can," Rilla said, holding out a hand. Vola was surprised it didn't sizzle in this heat. "It's probably raining in Southglen. I hate soggy leather."

Vola waited till the others had strapped their bags to the swamp beast's back before slinging hers on and fastening the straps. "Oh, shut up," she murmured as it glared. "It's the only thing you're good for besides eating everything."

A huge shadow swooped over them, and they all glanced up instinctively. But the red shape swinging by wasn't familiar to any of them. Listrell and her lead guardian, Renvick, had already said their goodbyes and were presumably off collecting the rest of their dragon allies for the war ahead.

"Right," Rilla said, pushing off from the wall. "If you're ready, I'd like to get going before Anders wins this war by default." She didn't bother ducking into an alley or finding a more private spot to do this. She reached with fingers spread and ripped a burning shape in the air. The flames flickered, floating in midair for a second before spreading to form a large green doorway in the middle of the walkway. On the other side, there were a couple of intricately carved doors twice Vola's height. She couldn't see the rest of the palace that stretched above them because the portal was too close.

"You know it's hard to take your complaining seriously, Rilla, when you can open a portal directly to the front door of your castle," Sorrel said, grinning up at the princess.

"Don't take this away from me," Rilla said, her lip twitching. "Griping is my thing. It's part of my persona."

"Not taking it away," Talon said. "We like Your Grumpy Highness. Honest."

Rilla's eyes narrowed. "Just get through the portal. I can only hold it open for so long. And if we're going to war, then I have a lot of work to do to make sure Southglen stays safe before we leave."

As the princess of the Dagger Throne, Rilla was Southglen's spymaster. She kept the country safe from invasions and sabotage by being faster and cleverer than the threat. Or by throwing Vola and her team at the problem. Rilla might have first called them Mishap's Heroes as a joke, but they were really good at taking bad situations and turning them around.

All right, if Vola was being really honest, they usually made it worse before they made it better, but that was splitting hairs.

Talon gave Rilla a sarcastic salute before stepping through the fiery portal, hand on her dagger, Gruff on her heels. Knowing the ranger, she'd make sure their landing zone was clear before any of them stepped through into an ambush. The castle stood in the center of Glenhaven, and if it was under attack, then they had a lot more immediate problems than a war between gods. But Talon's paranoia kept them from making stupid mistakes, so Vola wasn't about to complain.

And there was that one time nobles had taken over the palace in a coup, so...

Sorrel trotted through next.

Lillie stopped on the threshold. "One day you really must show me how to make one of these."

"Later, Lillie," Vola said. "You literally don't have any more room for notes."

Lillie flushed and stepped through the portal.

And like a good leader, Vola brought up the rear, stepping from the hot desert afternoon into a muggy evening on the other side of the world.

TWO

THAT EVENING VOLA made her way to the All-Pantheon temple, down a couple of flights of stairs from the palace of Glenhaven. The entire city was built into the side of a cliff with terraces climbing higher and higher until it reached the palace at the very pinnacle of the whole thing.

Rilla was closeted in some meeting room with the other princesses, preparing the country for the coming war. As the kingdom's spymaster, it was up to her to work with the princess of the Shield Throne to create a good plan to protect Southglen while everyone else dealt with Anders.

Lillie was off trying to contact her father and brother who usually lived in the city but were currently away on some research assignment. Sorrel and Talon had promised to entertain themselves quietly. Vola just hoped they didn't burn down the city between them.

She stepped toward the temple entrance, but a figure coalesced out of the shadows beside the doorway. A door guard, dressed in the armor of the gods. It glowed slightly as he moved between Vola and the door.

"You may not enter here, black paladin," he said. His sharp elven features creased as he glared at her.

Vola's teeth clenched. She carried her shield with her always, the blackened surface declaring her status to anyone who saw her. But it had been long enough since she'd been in Glenhaven that she hadn't even thought twice about it. She could always ignore the whispers of the villagers they passed, and Firewatch had been inhabited by misplaced rogues and scholars who cared more for their studies than religion. She should have remembered it would be different here.

She tipped the shield so he could see the wing pattern spreading through the black of her shield. "I'm here to serve and to pray. Not to cause trouble."

He snorted. "Black paladins have forsaken their oaths. You serve no one but your own self now. Begone."

Vola lowered her chin. No law said she couldn't visit a temple. He had no right to keep anyone out, even a black paladin. And she would remind him of the fact if she had to. With steel.

An acolyte in white, face shadowed by the portico, stepped out of the doorway and put a hand on the door guard's arm.

No words were spoken, but the guard stiffened and glanced between the acolyte and Vola.

Finally, he growled under his breath and stepped back. "Watch yourself and don't touch anything. You'll sully it."

She could have spit at him, made her opinion obvious, but no. She was better than that. She raised her chin and followed the acolyte between carved columns into the All-Pantheon temple. The ceiling was open to the sky and stars winked above her.

Few people paid their respects to the gods this late at night, so the temple echoed with only the acolyte moving softly to light the candles around the edges. Little niches in the circular walls held altars to each of the Lesser Virtues and even a few of the Obstacles. There were still plenty of people who thought of the Obstacles as blessings and worshiped them as such.

Around the inside of the circle stood statues to the Greater Virtues, the upper echelon of gods, standing as pillars in the darkness.

Vola's eyes easily found the one imperfect figure among the bunch. This one balanced on one foot, the other leg missing from the knee down. She only had one arm, but she stood before a screen of flames that rose behind her like wings.

The Broken.

Vola could talk to her anywhere, just like she had with Cleavah. All she had to do was direct her thoughts toward the goddess and the goddess answered in her ear like a sister or mother standing close by to offer advice.

But it felt more official to call on her here, in a temple where Vola could see her standing with her fellow gods.

"Lady," she said in the darkness.

The air beside her remained still, but the acolyte finished lighting their candles and gently blew out the lit taper. She limped out of the shadows of the temple and into the moonlight spilling through the open roof, and Vola realized she was looking at Cleavah, Goddess of Vengeful Housewives, and a manifestation of the Broken.

The dark curling hair tumbled down her shoulders, and her skin glowed gold in the night. The simple linen shift she wore bared her shoulders and was belted at the waist. Every time Vola had seen her goddess appear as Cleavah, she'd always been dressed as a servant, working down where no one else wanted to be seen, serving those no one else wanted to serve.

"Vola," she said, her lips curling in that serene grin that made Vola feel understood and accepted.

"My lady." Vola shifted her feet. She'd spoken to Cleavah many times throughout her career. She'd spoken to her when she was just the Goddess of Vengeful Housewives; she'd spoken to her when they knew she was more than that, but not exactly how much more. And she'd spoken to her since as the Broken. But for some reason, even knowing the Broken was the same goddess she'd always called on, didn't make it any less awkward. Only more.

"Why the disguise?" Vola said, gesturing to Cleavah's form and then realizing that might be rude.

Cleavah just cocked her head to stare down at herself, but it made the goddess go cross-eyed. "I'm a little recognizable," she said, and glanced up at the statue looming above them. "The Greater Virtues don't appear to mortals often enough for them to be used to it. And…" She trailed off as she stared into the empty darkness. "People aren't as comfortable with how I actually look."

Vola's eyes flicked to the statue, taking in the missing limbs and the scars stretching across her face. "I'm the only one here, lady," she said quietly.

"Yes, I know." Cleavah cleared her throat and shifted her weight.

Vola's brows came down. Could a goddess feel awkward and self-conscious? That seemed contradictory. But Vola had known her for a few years. Maybe it was a little like Talon telling the rest of them she wasn't a boy; she was a girl. They'd known her for long enough to already have a picture in their minds. Changing that picture had taken persistence and willingness on their part and courage on Talon's.

"Why didn't you tell me who you were?" Vola said, eyes still on the statue. "From the beginning. Why appear as Cleavah at all?"

Cleavah followed her gaze, and the corner of her mouth drew up in something between a grimace and a smile. "You need to understand right now, I have always been the Broken. Cleavah is nothing more than a mask I slip on to hide the face others know. It doesn't change who I was this entire time."

"Okay," Vola said without hesitating.

Cleavah's eyes flicked to her in surprise, and Vola grinned.

"I've had practice," she said, thinking of Talon again. The ranger had always been a girl. The rest of them just hadn't known it at the time.

Cleavah hesitated before saying, "That makes things a little easier."

"I'd still like to know why. I know why Talon wore a hood—I think she still does sometimes when she's feeling vulnerable. I know why she called herself 'they' before she felt ready to claim what she really was." Vola turned to face the goddess squarely, ignoring the statue. "But why did you hide from me?"

Cleavah's eyes fastened on her face. "I have to be careful who I trust with the truth. Paladins who know who I am right off the bat tend to feel self-important. They take the prestige of working with the Broken, thinking I am the greatest of the gods, without remembering I was cast out for it. They think they are better than their compatriots who work with lesser gods. They don't realize that I am Broken. My power and my strength come because of my failures. Pride has no place in anyone working for me. And those who meet me as Cleavah? They don't want to work with a laughingstock. The ones who are willing to try it out usually find a better offer with another god before too long."

Cleavah held out her hand in a fist. "I needed a paladin who was strong." She flattened out her fingers. "But humble. Humility is as much a part of strength as courage is."

"And you never found any?" Everyone knew the Broken had never taken any mortal followers officially. She'd never given her divine blessing to anyone, healer or fighter.

"I was afraid. Anyone I chose would have to stand against the displeasure of the pantheon itself. I was afraid those prideful warriors would break before the gods. I need humility."

Vola winced. "My lady. You must know, I wasn't that paladin." She'd been as ashamed of Cleavah as all those other knights who must have rejected her through the ages.

"No, you weren't," Cleavah said with a smile. "But you accepted me, anyway. And you learned."

"So it was a test."

"Life is a test, Vola." Cleavah flung out her arms to indicate the entire world. "If you pass, you grow. Deceiving you was not supposed to be a trick. I am what I am, and I always will be. I need a paladin willing to fight for and represent those viewed as the least of the world."

A ripple of fire shook her from head to toe. And when it cleared, the Broken stood in the center of the temple under the night sky. Moonlight glinted from the puckered scars across her face. The greatest of the world. And the least.

Vola knelt.

The Broken rolled her eyes just like Cleavah. "You could have just said 'yes,' Vola."

Vola hid a smile. "Fine, it's cheesy. But I'm a paladin. If you didn't want a healthy dose of melodrama, along with my eternal loyalty, you should have gone for a cheeky monk. I know one you might like."

The Broken raised her hand to tap her lips. "There's an idea. I do like Sorrel a lot." She sighed. "But Maxim might object to my poaching on his territory. I guess we'll have to muddle through somehow."

Vola made sure to catch the Broken's black bottomless eyes and hold her gaze. "I don't know how to be your sole representative. I don't think any of this has prepared me for that. But I do know how to fight for the broken. I know how to protect the weak and the lost." Vola pulled her sword from its sheath and laid it across her palms. "Will you accept my sword in your service?"

The words weren't binding in any way. She'd already been chosen over and over. She couldn't escape the Broken now if she tried. But they had meaning nevertheless. The Broken had to know that she'd chosen this. Vola had chosen her, too.

A fierce light burned in the Broken's gaze for a moment before it was gone, hidden by that bemused smile she wore most often.

"This old thing? Certainly not." She spun to the statue of the Broken. She reached up to the stone hand that had to be at least twice as big as hers and yet seemed to shrink as she plucked the sword from the statue's grip.

It shrank as she brought her hand down until she held a long, gleaming sword. She turned her grip and moonlight flashed across the edge of the blade, bright enough to blind Vola for a moment.

She flung up her hand to shield her eyes. When she looked again, the goddess was holding the blade out to her, hilt first.

"I can't be seen with a champion with such an old weapon. Let's show them who you really are, shall we?"

The next morning, Mishap's Heroes were summoned to the Throne Room. The chamber was more than just symbolic. It held the Thrones of Southglen, yes, but those Thrones held enormous power in and of themselves. Anders had tried to siphon that power off for himself just months ago, inciting a coup by the nobles of the city to mask his actions.

Each of the fifteen Thrones embodied a specific aspect of the government and was ruled over by a princess chosen to serve that aspect. Vola and the others worked directly with Rilla, princess of the Dagger Throne and the kingdom's spymaster. But they'd also worked with War, Justice, and Shield. And the princess of Sewage Management.

Costa twiddled her fingers at them as they gathered in the center of the circle between the Thrones. She wore gaiters and a pair of goggles pushed to the top of her head.

"How's the swamp beast?" she asked, a gleam in her eye.

"Fine," Vola answered, hiding a wince. The others shifted their feet behind her.

"Not in the city, I hope?" she said. "Since there is a very specific law against creatures of unknown swamp origins roaming our streets—and our pipes."

"Um, no. Of course not."

"It's resting comfortably," Lillie added.

"Somewhere far, far away," Sorrel said.

"The prison doesn't count as within city limits, does it?" Talon muttered.

Vola elbowed her. "Yup. Not breaking any laws here."

The truth was, there'd been nowhere to stash the thing, and it wasn't like Firewatch had wanted them to leave it there either. So it was resting comfortably, as Lillie said, in the city prison just around the corner from the palace in a cell designed to hold the hardest of hardened criminals.

Hopefully, it would still be there when they got back.

The princess of Sewage Management's brows drew down in a knowing look, but she didn't pursue it.

The rest of the princesses trickled in one by one. This was only the second time they'd seen them all in one room together. Usually, they were split up, traveling around their kingdom, governing, putting out fires. Being figureheads.

Rilla sprawled on her Throne already, legs flung over the armrest. Her eyes locked on Vola standing in the middle.

Vola tilted her head in question. "What?"

"Is that new?" Rilla pointed to the hilt sticking up over Vola's shoulder.

Vola touched it self-consciously as Lillie, Talon, and Sorrel all turned, mouths open.

"The Broken gave it to me," she said. It was a greatsword, giant, and meant to be swung two-handed, but Vola was big enough that it worked more like a bastard sword. She could use two hands or one, depending on if she was using her shield or not.

Rilla flowed gracefully to her feet and held out a hand. "May I?"

Vola didn't see any reason not to let her examine the blade. She pulled it from her back and held it out to the princess.

Rilla took it and as her fingers closed around the hilt, there was a flash of light and fire limned Rilla's entire form, flickering around the edges. For just a moment, and then the flames sucked back into the sword.

"Geez," Vola said, rubbing her eyes.

Rilla remained in the center of the circle of Thrones, breathing heavily, blinking at the blade. "Well," she said as if she couldn't think of anything else to say.

"Are you all right?" Vola asked.

Rilla cleared her throat. "I'm not hurt. But let's just say it'd be better if you kept hold of it for oh, say forever."

The princess of the Religion Throne stepped closer to examine the sword as Rilla handed it back to Vola. "I had a message from an All-Pantheon priest this morning," she said, tucking her short straight hair behind her ears as she leaned toward the blade. "It seems they had a minor miracle in one of the temples last night. A statue of the Broken, which had been holding a sword yesterday, is no longer holding the sword."

"It was stolen?" the princess of Justice said sharply.

"No," the princess of Religion said, eyes on Vola. "The statue itself changed positions. It's now standing with its hand across its breast as if it never held a sword in the first place."

"You can all stop being so melodramatic about it," the princess of the War Throne said, waving a hand as if to shoo the subject away. She had her bright golden curls pinned on top of her head today. "We all know the Broken gave it to Vola, blah blah blah. I appreciate divine miracles as much as the next princess who was chosen by an esoteric throne, but can we sit down and talk about how we're actually going to use these miracles to get rid of this Anders fellow?"

Rilla muffled a snort as the princesses returned to their thrones and Vola sheathed her sword. "Yes, Your Highness," she said and plopped her butt on her throne. She didn't lounge this time, but sat forward, elbows planted on her knees and her hands clasped in front of her.

War glanced at her, unamused, but didn't say anything further.

The princess of the Shield Throne sat up straight, her long white hair cascading over the Throne behind her. "We have called up the army," she said. "They are on active duty and we are stepping up recruitment efforts as we speak."

The princess of the Health Throne raised her eyebrows. "That's a little aggressive, don't you think?"

"Anders has the power to strip the entire world of magic," Rilla said without preamble. "He already tried once, and we have no idea what else he's capable of. He needs to be dealt with. Now. Before he becomes even more of a threat."

"You defeated his lieutenant," the princess of the Education Throne said, head cocked. "That Nargilla character. Surely without her—"

"Without her, he'll have a harder time of it, yes," Rilla said.

"But he has her plans. Our operatives confirmed he possesses the spell and the plans for the tanks that Nargilla was using." She nodded to the Mishap's Heroes. "It's only a matter of time before he starts up again. We need to hit him now, while he's still reeling from her loss."

War cleared her throat, and instantly the rest of the princesses shut up and listened. They might have been a group of equals, but they were all smart enough to recognize when one of them had more expertise than the others.

"We are not debating if we are going to war," she said. "That has already been decided." She glanced at Rilla, who gave her a grateful nod. "We are here to decide how we are going to war."

Shield nodded and took the floor with a graceful gesture, her long white hair trailing behind her. "Our army is well trained but small," she said. "And possibly rusty after so many years of peace."

War winced.

"We'll need help," Vola said and almost bit her tongue. She wasn't really sure why she and the rest of Mishap's Heroes were here. These women were perfectly capable of coming up with plans all by themselves. But every single one of them turned to focus on her when she spoke.

Vola cleared her throat. "This isn't just a problem for Southglen," she said. "It's a problem for the world. Firewatch recognized that already. They've promised to send a contingent. Fighters and researchers from the museum. And the dragons will come as soon as Listrell is done waking them up."

"Southglen has many allies to call on," Lillie said, stepping up beside Vola. Vola glanced at her in relief. Lillie didn't like drawing attention to herself, but she was much better spoken, and she was a citizen. The princesses might listen to her over Vola.

"We have a little time," Sorrel said from around Vola's hip.

"Anders isn't preparing his attack yet. I'm sure Rilla would have told us by now if he was."

Rilla hid a smile with her hand. She probably had plenty of spies keeping an eye on Anders and his people.

"We will need the time to plan our defenses anyway," the princess of the Shield Throne said. "And they're right. Our offensive must include anyone else who is threatened by Anders's plan."

"Are you prepared for a diplomatic mission?" War asked Vola.

Vola blinked. "Us?" she blurted. Then she cleared her throat. "I mean, are you sure?"

"You're the ones with firsthand experience with Anders and the threat he represents. You've encountered his lieutenants and you've dealt with the areas where he's sucked the magic out of the world. You've even experienced it yourselves."

Vola grimaced. "Not something I want anyone to experience ever again."

"Which is why you are the best ones to convince our allies we need the help."

"They will need some diplomatic clout," the princess of Sewage Management murmured, scratching under the strap of her goggles.

War cocked her head. "So they will."

Rilla was already hoisting herself off her Throne.

"I suppose that's my cue."

Vola eyed her up and down. "You want to come with us?"

"Sure. If you'll have me. Can I be an honorary member or do I have to fill out an application?"

Vola glanced back at the others, who were trying not to laugh. "Well, we've had some pretty good examples of your skills," she said. "But I need to know you'll follow orders."

Rilla crossed her arms over her chest. "I know when to listen to my superiors. As long as they don't ask me to do anything stupid." She tipped her head and met Vola's eyes. "You guys get things done. I'm not about to mess with a system that works. I'll serve as your diplomatic liaison and a pair of daggers when you decide fighting is the way to go."

Vola grinned and held out her hand. "Welcome to Mishap's Heroes then, Rilla."

THREE

"So, how do you like the glamor and glory of being an adventurer, Rilla?" Sorrel asked over a week later as they climbed through the wettest forest Vola had ever seen. And they'd been through swamps before.

Rilla glared at Sorrel as the rain poured down on all sides. Her normally fluffy hair was looking a little flatter, and Vola knew from experience the wet leather of her jerkin had to be starting to itch.

To be fair, Vola wasn't doing much better in full plate armor. Water had a tendency to seep in through her neck and then drip down her spine and between her boobs. But she'd been caught once too often by an ambush while they were traveling to leave her armor strapped to the swamp beast.

Trees soared on either side of the road, their canopies lost in the near-constant mist that resulted from the rain. Vines that looked more monster than plant climbed the trunks nearest them and big ferns spread lacy leaves to collect as much of the moisture coming out of the sky as possible. Vola could make out the delicate fronds of purple and blue flowers clinging to the bark of the trees almost twenty feet over their heads.

It was probably very pretty in the one season it wasn't raining.

The swamp monster was in its element. Vola had never seen it do anything except glare and eat, but now it was frolicking. It pranced from one side of the wide cobbled road to the other, shaking its head to spray water on them.

"Well, I'm glad someone's happy," Talon grumbled. She reached as if to pull up her hood, but it had been torn to pieces back in the mountains known as the Firewall and she hadn't bothered to replace it. She paused when she realized there was nothing to pull up and wrinkled her nose. It was dripping. Gruff trudged along beside, his head and tail drooping.

The swamp monster danced ahead of them to the end of its long lead rope and turned its head up to the spray, long, slimy tongue lolling out of its mouth.

"Aw, maybe we've misjudged it all along," Lillie said. She had found a rain poncho somewhere and draped it over her head. She held up the edges like a tent.

They all looked at the swamp monster, wondering if maybe they'd been wrong about it. Maybe it wasn't as gross as it seemed. Maybe it was just misunderstood.

It lunged forward and snapped at something in the underbrush. When it straightened, a vivid purple centipede as long as Vola's arm hung from its mouth, hundreds of little legs wriggling. The swamp monster slurped, and the giant bug disappeared down its gullet.

"Nope," Vola said. "Pretty sure it's just nasty."

"How far is it to Mistvale?" Sorrel asked Rilla.

Vola hadn't thought it was possible, but the rain strengthened, pinging off her pauldrons.

"Several more miles to the edge of the forest. We'll reach the games by tomorrow, probably."

"I think what she meant to say was 'are we there yet?'" Vola said.

"What games?" Talon asked.

"The Friendship Games," Rilla said. "They're held every other year on a rotating schedule as to who gets to host them. Every nation on the continent is represented. So there should be leaders from all those Anders threatens."

"I've never heard of the Friendship Games," Talon said, Gruff trotting along at her heels.

"Yeah, but you literally lived under a rock until we met," Sorrel said.

"A cave," Talon said with a frown. "There's a difference."

"My parents competed," Vola said. "Years ago. Until they were banned because they kept winning."

"I remember. I watched Lydia Battlemane kill a minotaur with her bare hands when I was eight," Lillie said.

Sorrel gasped. "Aw, lucky. The monks don't believe in fighting for money or glory unless it's Maxim's glory. We weren't allowed to go."

"They probably knew you'd sneak off to enter and never be heard from again," Vola said.

Sorrel opened her mouth to comment and paused. "Okay, yeah. You're probably right."

"Sure, it's a good time, but it's also the best place to find allies." Rilla spoke under her breath, eyes on the woods.

"Why are you whispering?" Vola asked Rilla.

Rilla's gaze flicked to her. "There might be monsters in the rainforest. Were-gorillas and the like. Some are attracted to the magic the trees exude."

Vola glared at the trees. Rain, fog, and monsters. That seemed about right for what was supposed to be a diplomatic mission.

"As the newest member of the party, *we're* supposed to pull pranks on *you*," Sorrel said. "There is no way were-gorillas are a real thing."

"We never have to find out as long as we keep the noise down. They know better than to come too close to the road."

"Who thought it was a good idea to put a bloody great forest between Southglen and Mistvale, anyway? Especially one infested with monsters," Sorrel grumbled.

"The Graywood is far more ancient than either of the countries surrounding it," Lillie said. "It predates most forms of civilization and is home to more lifeforms than the rest of the world combined." She gestured to the canopy where even in the pouring rain they could hear hoots and howls from some of those lifeforms. Vola couldn't tell if it was a bird or a monkey or maybe some sort of plant that hunted its prey by luring it in with sound.

"Thank you, Encyclopedia Lillie," Sorrel said.

Lillie frowned. "Hey."

Talon's head went up.

Vola, instantly alert, gave them the signal to halt and hold position. They all obeyed, Rilla a split second behind the others.

"What is it?" Vola asked under her breath.

Talon gestured to Gruff, who took off between the trees without complaint, as silent as a shadow. "Listen," she said.

Vola strained her ears but couldn't hear anything. And then she realized that was because the only thing still making noise was that howler up in the canopy and a few insects that whirred through the ferns on either side of the road.

"Ambush?" Vola asked.

"Or another larger predator," Talon said. "The animals haven't minded us this whole time, but we've been sticking to the road."

"Monster?" Vola asked.

Lillie whispered under her breath, and a slight glow gathered under the ferns at the edge of the track, nothing too noticeable since it was mostly hidden under the curling fronds.

Sorrel casually strolled to the nearest tree and clambered up a vine to hang above them like a big, gray flower.

Vola drew her sword and settled her shield on her arm.

There was a growl and a short, sharp scream off to the left.

"Gruff found someone," Talon said.

"No duh," Sorrel said from above.

The wolf barked.

"They're going to go for it," Talon said. "Incoming."

Vola braced her feet. Now she could hear voices and the crunch of boots pushing through undergrowth.

The first enemy crashed through the ferns at the side of the road and a flash of light lit up the dim afternoon. A scream rang out, and the smell of burnt hair wafted toward them.

The figure staggered across the road, and Vola's gaze took in the fact that it was a human in sleek leather armor, carrying a pair of daggers. He dropped the weapons and flung his hands over his face, rubbing at his smoking eyebrows.

Vola took a firmer grip on her sword and stepped in front of Lillie as several more figures converged through the undergrowth.

Talon's bow twanged and there was a cry from their right.

Vola caught movement on the left and signaled Rilla. The Dagger Princess swept forward and knelt just as the enemy tried to clear the brush. Silent as a snake, she took his legs out from under him and he fell.

Sorrel cried out, "Death from above!" and fell on the one Lillie had blinded.

Lillie was already muttering another spell, and the area was clear enough that Vola felt all right stepping away from the vulnerable wizard. She charged for the only figure left, sword raised.

Her boots slid on the moss slick cobbles at the side of the road, and her feet went out from under her. She landed on her back, the air whooshing from her lungs.

She couldn't do more than sit there in stunned surprise for a moment or two.

Well, that didn't go well.

The enemy she'd been charging overshot her and stumbled past. She took a quick chance and grabbed his boot as it went by.

He hopped on one foot, struggling against her.

Whatever works.

She heaved and flipped him on his back.

Rilla ducked in and finished him.

Vola surged to her feet and surveyed the damage. Three attackers lay on the road, one riddled with arrows, one blackened and sizzling in the rain, and one cut into several little pieces.

Sorrel sat on top of the only attacker left alive. He lay face down, her staff pressed into his neck.

"Kept one alive for questioning," Sorrel said.

"Good work." Vola pressed her fist into the base of her spine and winced as she tried to straighten. "We'll—"

A low rumble threaded through the trees, starting low and ending as a shriek that shivered all the hairs along Vola's neck.

"Uh…Lillie, tell me that was your stomach."

"My body has never made a noise like that," Lillie hissed. "And if it did, I would seek medical help immediately."

A crack echoed across the road, like a very large tree breaking off at the roots.

"That's definitely not digestion," Sorrel said. The captured enemy beneath her heaved and tried to throw her off. Sorrel kept her feet like a sailor in a storm and shoved her staff harder into his neck. "None of that now."

Crashing footsteps raced for them, and Vola scrambled to place herself between the threat and her party.

Leaves and bits of vines exploded from the side of the road as a huge, dark shape smashed through the screening shrubbery.

Thick, fur-covered arms topped with massive shoulders

supported the thing's torso and a small head featuring strong yellow teeth and beady eyes. Its narrow hindquarters were lost behind all of that muscle.

"Were-gorilla!" Rilla shouted.

"Oh my gods, you were serious about that?" Sorrel said. The massive beast tried to take a swing at her, and she leaped into the air to avoid it. The enemy she'd caught squeaked and covered his head.

Sorrel raced at the gorilla, staff whirling.

An arrow whizzed past Vola's ear to bury itself in the creature's thick pelt.

It roared its fury and beat both fists against the ground. The road rippled like water and the cobbles surged in a wave, spreading from the gorilla's fists.

Vola danced, trying to keep her feet as Rilla charged. The Dagger princess ducked under one of its massive elbows and thrust out a hand. Green light glowed at its feet and ropes swarmed up its legs to wrap around its narrow waist, trapping it in place.

The gorilla raised its fist in the air, and Lillie shouted a spell. The monster froze, its fist creaking and turning to stone before their eyes.

Its beady gaze fixed on its disobedient limb as if in confusion. Then its brow came down, and it flexed its forearm.

Shards of shattered rock pattered on the cobbles of the road, and Lillie's eyes widened.

"Uh oh," she said.

The gorilla roared, its hot breath steaming in the moist air, and it lunged for Lillie.

The wizard disappeared in pop of cool air and reappeared at the other edge of the road.

Vola skidded forward to take her place, meeting the gorilla's blow. Her raised sword connected with the beast's arm, and there was a flash of light. Flames burst along the edge of the blade and raced up the beast's fur.

White fire spread along its limbs, unhindered by the rain that still poured around them.

The gorilla roared again, and it lurched backward. It scrambled off the road, through the underbrush, and disappeared into the forest.

Sorrel flipped to her feet while Talon crept forward, bow still drawn and trained on the bushes where the monster had retreated.

Vola stared at her sword. Nothing differentiated it from any other sword. At least, not now that the monster had fled. Its blade was sharp and shining, but the flames were gone.

"Well, that's new," she said.

"Handy, too," Talon said, finally stowing her bow.

"Aw, man," Sorrel said, standing with her hands on her hips, staring down at a smear on the roadway. "The gorilla turned our prisoner into red goo."

"Ew," Lillie said.

"Guess we won't be interrogating him then," Talon said.

"Lillie, do you have a spell for that? You've made the dead talk before."

"I'm glad you think so highly of my skills. But even if I hadn't skipped most of Myron's lessons on how to be a necromancer, I would need a complete body to work with."

Sorrel grimaced as Vola turned to Rilla. "Do you have any tricks up your sleeves?"

"All my abilities are about sneaking and stabbing people in the back. I don't tend to speak with them after they're already dead."

Vola sighed and gestured to the other dead attackers. "Well, let's search them then and see if they have anything that could identify them."

No one tried to sift through the wreckage of the one the

gorilla had stomped on. They may have been hardened adventurers, but there were limits.

"Empty pockets," Rilla said, rifling through one's clothes. "No badges or identifying markings. Not so much as a scar or a birthmark. This was a professional job. Assassins meant to fade into the background, even when dead."

"Their weapons aren't even unique enough to give any clues," Talon said, examining a dagger and tossing it aside. "Good quality but generic."

"Wait," Lillie said. She grimaced and used two fingers to pull a piece of paper from the breast pocket of one of the assassins.

Rilla's eyebrows drew down. "I swear I checked there."

"It was sticking out," Lillie said. "As if we were supposed to find it."

Rilla's jaw jutted out, and she opened her mouth.

"No, you're right," Talon said. "I checked that one, too. That wasn't there a minute ago."

Lillie passed it over to Vola and touched the band on her forehead. It had been a gift from Rilla, a long time ago. It allowed Lillie to see magic.

"Let me guess…" Vola said.

Lillie nodded. "A spell. Teleportation—a lot like mine."

Vola unfolded the paper, which was getting soggy under the rain.

"Do yourselves a favor," it read in strong, spiky handwriting. "Go find a beach and a quiet place to lie low, and maybe I won't take everything you love from you. Regards, Anders."

The ink began to run down the page, spreading as surely as the cold spread through Vola's gut.

"Geez, he really just signed his name to a threat," Rilla said. "Guy has some balls."

"He knows we're coming," Vola said. "More importantly, he knows where we are."

She glanced up and met their gazes. "Does this change anything?"

She asked it seriously. It was one thing to sneak up on an enemy. Another thing entirely to charge in head down when he knew you were coming.

Sorrel shrugged. "He still wants to suck all the magic out of the world, right? Well, then he still needs to be stopped."

Lillie nodded. "Yes, he cannot get away with this."

"I go where my pack goes," Talon said.

Vola's gaze went to Rilla. "What about you? Still want to come?"

Rilla's lip twitched. "Hell, yeah."

FOUR

MISTVALE TURNED out to be just as wet as the rainforest surrounding it. It really only rained in the afternoons, but while the mornings were bright and sunny, everything was still damp. It made for a humid city covered in green, some of which was intentional, but most of it was just mold.

Vola spent the evening they arrived polishing her armor, but she was pretty sure it would start to rust by morning no matter what she did.

She could have left it at the hotel when they left the next day, but she wanted to look as professional and serious as possible. They were asking for help to end a world-threatening bad guy after all.

Rilla led them past a market full of vendors hawking kabobs and fried cakes. Most of which were green, too. They smelled like greasy food everywhere, but Vola wasn't sure she trusted something that was the same color as swamp scum.

"Heading to the games, sir?" one called to Talon. "Don't go without your refreshments."

"Ma'am," Talon said with a growl and jerked her chin up.

"Is anyone not heading for the games?" Lillie said, shading her eyes so she could peer ahead at the massive coliseum built with light-colored stone and dark timber. Moss grew on at least half of it.

People streamed in and out of the mouth of the coliseum, which was carved to look like the head of a dragon, the low hum of their conversation echoing from the stone archway above them.

Rilla snagged the neck of Sorrel's tunic before she could join the throng.

"This way," she said. "We're not part of the common rabble today."

"Oh, fancy," Sorrel said as Rilla led them along the wall to a staircase festooned with flags. Purple and gold streamers fluttered in the heavy air.

Halfway up, a pair of knights in gold armor which contrasted directly with their dark skin and white turbans stopped them.

"Credentials," one of them said.

"Only country representatives and their retainers are allowed in the royal box," the other one said.

"Oh, for Ona's sake, Yarren. You know who I am. I spent months here getting that trade agreement hammered out."

"Nevertheless, I need your credentials," Yarren said, eyes flickering like he wanted to laugh but didn't dare.

Rilla gave a gusty sigh and dug in the front of her jerkin. Finally, she pulled out a gold circlet with rubies studded across the front. She settled it on her head.

"There, happy?"

"Enormously, Your Highness."

"You know, anyone can wear a crown." She pointed to Lillie's circlet. "See? It doesn't mean anything."

"Nevertheless, I enjoy hearing you go all growly."

Vola choked on a laugh and covered it up with a cough.

"Your retainers will have to leave their weapons behind, I'm afraid." Yarren's gaze flicked to Vola.

"Yeah, yeah. I know the drill. Hand them over, ladies. You'll get them back on the way out."

Vola reluctantly unsheathed her sword and hefted it in her hand for a second. She'd just gotten it and it already felt like a betrayal to just casually hand it over to some guard. Not to mention it might just as casually burn him up. Vola carefully placed it on the table beside the guards rather than risk it.

Lillie opened her hands to prove she had no weapons while Rand sat on her shoulder, puffing up his feathers harmlessly.

Talon unloaded her bow, her quiver, her daggers, another pair of daggers, a set of throwing knives, and a garrote Vola didn't even know she had.

"Are you sure that's everything?" Yarren said dryly.

"Her glare is certified as a weapon," Sorrel said. "But I don't think you can take that away from her."

"And what about you?"

Sorrel blinked at him innocently. Her staff had disappeared in the time it took the others to unload. Now she just had a pencil tucked behind one ear. "What about me?"

Yarren opened his mouth, but stopped and examined Sorrel again. "Very well," he said with a suspicious glance. "You may proceed."

"What happened to Maxim's Warhammer?" Rilla asked under her breath as they continued up the stairs.

Sorrel touched the pencil. "It's so much more convenient like this, don't you think?"

Rilla snorted.

At the top of the stairs, a broad box stretched at least thirty feet in both directions, situated on the first tier so the occupants had the best view.

There were a couple of wooden benches scattered through the

box, but mostly big, throne-like chairs held richly dressed personages. Closest to them was a king, lounging across his throne, beckoning a server to bring a tray of fruit. Vola also noticed a bored-looking woman who read a book hidden on her lap, a boy no taller than Sorrel, accompanied by someone who was clearly his governess, and a young woman who sat uncomfortably on the edge of her seat as if she felt like she didn't belong there.

"Princess Allellarilla," the lounging king said. He was thin and gangly and had the most unhealthy-looking skin Vola had ever seen. Which was saying something, considering she'd grown up around orcs.

"We haven't seen anyone from Southglen, yet," he said. "Did you all decide your warriors weren't cut out for the games this year?"

"Oh, come now," the woman with the book said without looking up. "We all know Lydia Battlemane hailed from Southglen. And you've never managed to front a warrior that could have bested her, Hector."

The king—Hector the Third of Mistvale, Vola assumed —spluttered.

The woman shut her book and gestured Rilla to take a seat beside her. "*I'm* happy to see you, anyway. What took you so long?"

"We're not actually here to compete, Selene," Rilla said, straddling the bench beside the woman. "Southglen isn't sending a delegation because we're busy prepping for war."

Everyone in the box sat up or stiffened.

"War against whom?" the woman asked. She tucked long black hair behind her pointed ears.

Vola didn't recognize the name, but an educated guess told her Selene was probably a representative from Elfhome.

"None of you," Rilla said. "Don't worry. But this Anders is a threat to the entire continent. Maybe even the whole world. And war is an apt description when we're mustering troops and recruiting allies to help us beat him."

"Oh." The woman, Selene, relaxed and smoothed her dress over her knees. "Well, then."

"This isn't something that can be ignored," Rilla said, brow pulling down. "Or brushed off."

"No, but it sounds like a Southglen problem," Hector said. He spit a grape seed at the floor, making a servant dance back to avoid being hit.

"I beg your pardon, Your Majesty," Lillie said. "But it's everyone's problem. Anders has the ability to steal magic out of the world itself, as well as people and objects. Even the dead."

Hector cocked his head and pouted his lips. "You're too sweet to worry about such things, honey. There are people in your own country taking care of the problem, I'm sure."

Lillie's face flushed bright red, and Vola fought the urge to come to her rescue. Instead of stammering and fading back, Lillie raised her chin. "We are those people, Your Majesty. And luckily what's in my head is more important than what's on it."

Rilla cleared her throat violently, and Lillie shut her mouth with a snap.

Hector's brow furrowed, as if trying to see the insult.

"This is probably being blown out of proportion," Selene said, cocking her head. "I've found that adventurers who encounter these things aren't all reliable when it comes to reporting their successes and failures. They tend to inflate the former and downplay the latter."

"Considering we were the adventurers to discover the problem," Vola said. "And we nearly died in the process, we're not exaggerating anything."

"The spell that sucked the magic out of the land woke a dragon," Talon said. "Firewatch nearly burned down."

"Unfortunate," Hector said. "But again, that seems like a problem for Firewatch."

"Maybe we should at least form a hearing." The other young woman in the box spoke, shifting on the edge of her overlarge chair. "I know my queen would be interested in more details."

Hector made a rude noise and picked at a spot on his nose. "The Queen of Illthane has better things to do than entertain doomsayers."

Selene gave Rilla a sad little smile. "The truth is, there's always someone saying the world's about to end or claiming some evil is about to overtake the land." The elf waved an airy hand at Vola and her party. "The adventurers always manage to deal with it before it becomes a real problem, though. So it's hard to get excited about another prophecy of death and destruction. You know all this, though, so it's a wonder you don't have the sense to ignore it."

"Maybe that should tell you something," Rilla said between her teeth even though her lips were smiling. "I'm not ignoring it, so obviously there is something worth getting 'excited' over."

"Adventurers probably take care of the problems for you because they get fed up with trying to get you to listen to reason," Lillie said. "That won't work this time. One country's stupidity will doom the rest."

"I beg your pardon, young lady," Hector said with a huff. "But you are here as a guest. I will have you thrown out if you can't be civil."

"I'd like to see you try."

"Lillie," Vola said under her breath. "Is this helping?"

Lillie flushed bright red and ducked her chin. A muscle in her jaw jumped as she clenched her teeth. But the wizard didn't say anything else.

"Obviously you all are convinced of this threat," Selene said, spreading her hands in a placating gesture as Lillie stepped back, out of direct focus. "Perhaps the delegate from Illthane is right and we should have a hearing. If you have evidence of this threat and we believe you, we will send our own scouts to assess the situation and decide if we can send aid."

"That will take too long," Vola said, trying to keep her voice even. She had one eye on the leaders and one eye on Lillie who had pulled out her spell book and was flipping through it rapidly. Either a good sign or a bad sign, depending on who she was aiming for. "Anders knows we're coming. He sent assassins to waylay us on the road here."

Selene gave her a pitying look, and Vola knew what she was about to say. That sounds like your problem. Hector wasn't even listening anymore. He was leaning forward on his throne to watch the match below. A huge brawny swordsman with mismatched plate armor faced off against a lithe elf with a bow and a fistful of magic.

"Shh, shh," he said, flapping his hand at them. "Mistvale is up against Selene's man. This is my best warrior. The most powerful swordsman in Mistvale. No way is Selene walking away with the title this time."

Selene rolled her eyes, but she also sat forward, attention on the sands below. Mishap's Heroes and their warning were forgotten.

Rilla sat beside her, jaw clenched, looking foiled and angry about it.

Sorrel planted her hands on her hips. "I don't suppose beating someone over the head with a stick ever made them see reason."

"We could just leave them to their fate," Talon said. "Perhaps the university scholars will come up with a way to protect South-glen while leaving the rest of the continent vulnerable."

Vola shivered. "As satisfying as that would be..."

"I know, I know," Sorrel said. "We'd feel bad about it later."

A tingle at the back of Vola's neck made her head snap up. She knew that feeling. "What the...?"

Talon's breath hissed between her teeth. "That's—"

Down below, the fighters had ceased circling each other and were looking down at themselves in confusion. The brawny brute dropped his sword.

Vola gasped and pointed. "There," she said. In the center of the sands, dark shadows swirled, circling the two fighters, drawing more darkness into the middle.

Vola's gut went numb. They'd seen this before.

"What is that?" Hector said, staggering to his feet. Grapes and pieces of an orange fell away and rolled across the floor.

Rilla was already on her feet. "Oh my gods. This is the draining effect. This is what we were warning you about." She spun to Vola. "Could Anders be reaching us here?"

"I don't know how..." Vola shook her head and then her eyes fell on Lillie. The wizard stood with her eyes closed, her feet braced, and her hands out to either side.

"Lillie?" Vola said.

Rilla glanced at the spell book, open at her feet. "Are you doing this?"

"Yes," Lillie said, voice grating between her teeth. "At least as far as I'm able."

"You cannot perform spells in the presence of the monarchy," Hector said, rounding on her. Selene and the other delegates were on their feet, leaning over the railing to stare down at the swirling blackness. Screams sounded from the stands around the arena, and the entire structure vibrated with the tromp of panicked feet.

Below, the fighters turned to escape the spreading blackness, but they moved as if trying to push their way through sludge. The elf fell to his knees, and the swordsman bent at the waist to catch his breath.

"You wanted proof," Lillie said. "Here is proof that we know what we're talking about. Proof that we can't wait for you to decide this is a real threat."

"Holy crap, Lillie," Vola muttered. "Next time you want to get us arrested, give me a little warning first."

"No one's getting arrested if we can get them to listen to us." Lillie cracked her eyelids to glare at Hector. "This is the spell Anders had Nargilla Pipwattle design for him. He has the ability to do this only ten times larger."

"This is an attack!" Hector shouted. "An ambush on the leaders of the coalition!"

Boots pounded up the stairs, and the two armored guards burst into the box, swords drawn. Sorrel spun and suddenly she was holding Maxim's Warstaff trained on them while Rand mantled on Lillie's shoulder.

Rilla lunged forward, her hands up. "Not an attack," she said. "This is a demonstration. An exhibition." She jerked her chin at the arena, somehow including Hector in the gesture as well. "Lillie's right. This is the least of what the world faces. You've got your best warriors down there. See if they can handle it."

Hector and Selene exchanged a glance. "This is reversible?" Hector asked.

"So far," Vola said. "We've reversed it a couple of times."

He stepped forward and leaned over the railing. "You can beat this," he called down. "Make Mistvale proud."

Selene called something to the elf in a lyrical, fluid language.

The two fighters squinted up at the box and tried to climb to their feet. The elf made it, but the swordsman didn't.

Vola cast a look at Sorrel and Talon. Talon gave a little shrug that could have meant "better them than us." Sorrel leaned on her staff in a non-threatening way but watched the guards closely. They stood, waiting for orders, their eyes trained on Lillie.

The swordsman collapsed against the sand, his chest straining to rise and fall. The elf sobbed with effort and made it another two steps before tripping.

"What's wrong with them?" Selene asked sharply. "What is this spell?"

"I told you," Rilla said as the blackness crept through the sands, turning them dark as obsidian. "Anders has can suck the magic out of the world. The land itself has no more magic. Neither does anything trapped inside."

"I know Selene's champion wields magic," Hector said, his messy eyebrows lowering in thought. "But Mistvale's champion doesn't have any. Why is he affected?"

"Every creature in the world possesses some magic," Vola said, arms crossed. "It's inherent in our design. A gift from the gods. Spell casters have more, either as a connection to the land they were born with or as something they learned." Vola gestured to Lillie. Then she placed a hand on her chest. "And some are gifted with more by the gods."

"But even if you've never been able to use it, even if it's remained dormant within you, it can still be stolen," Talon said. "And it makes you feel like shit."

"Does it kill you?" Selene said.

"Eventually," Sorrel said.

"It's not the way I would choose to die," Vola said.

The elf landed on hands and knees. Tried to crawl forward and fell face-first into the sand.

"Enough of this," Selene said. "If even our strongest warriors cannot overcome this—"

Rilla held up her hand. But Vola was already moving. She gestured Sorrel and Talon with her and vaulted over the railing to land heavily on the sands below. Oof, she'd feel that in her knees tomorrow.

She steeled herself before stepping forward into the dead spot. She'd never, ever wanted to feel this again, but she trusted

Lillie wouldn't actually kill them. And they had done this once before.

As her boots crossed the threshold between the normal sand and the black sand, a weight struck her between her shoulder blades and she staggered, falling to one knee.

There was a murmur from the royal box above them.

Vola steeled herself and fought to stand. It wasn't a feeling she'd ever get used to, like someone had taken all the strength from her limbs, a weight pressing down on her chest so she could barely breathe. But it was something she could learn to work around. And if she could stand up under full plate armor with all the strength stolen from her body, she could stand up under anything.

Vola grunted as she climbed to her feet. Sweat broke out on her brow and along her spine.

"Remind me to kill Lillie the moment we get back," Sorrel groaned from Vola's right. Vola's hypothesis was that Sorrel stood up under the draining effect much better than the rest of them because there was so much less of her to drain, but she knew in the back of her head that wasn't fair. Not that the front of her head cared right now when Sorrel was already limping across the sands using Maxim's Warhammer as a crutch.

"I thought we were fighting so we never had to feel like this again?" Talon said.

"Just once more," Vola gasped out. "Once more. Then we can rest and someone else will take over."

"You wish," Sorrel said. "You know that's not how this works."

"Just…find the anchor points," Vola said. "Lillie said this was Nargilla's spell and Nargilla's spell had anchor points. We destroy those, we destroy the spell."

"It won't destroy Lillie in the process, right?"

Vola shook her head. "Nargilla is still alive in the custody of the gods. And we didn't just destroy her anchor points, we exploded her entire system."

"You mean the Broken did," Sorrel said, but she was already trudging off, surveying the arena for Lillie's anchors to the spell.

Vola staggered to the two fighters and checked them.

"What's...what's happening to me?" the elf gasped. The swordsman was completely passed out, chest still rising and falling.

"Our royals are making an example of us," Vola said. It wasn't the whole truth, but it would work for the moment. "Just lie still. You'll be back to normal in a moment."

No healing would replace the magic he had lost, so Vola didn't even try. She just left him lying as comfortably as possible in the sand.

"Vola," Talon said. Her voice was weak, but Vola had been waiting for their signal. "The pillars...beside the combatant entrances."

Vola turned to look where she pointed. There were two entrances, one for each team or warrior competing. Pillars held up the archway and set into each pillar was a gem. Blue crystals for the north entrance. Red crystals for the south. They didn't glow, and Vola didn't have any magic to check them for spells, but little symbols crawled through them, making the back of Vola's neck prickle.

It was almost an exact replica of Nargilla's spell. Clever Lillie. She'd figured out how to set anchor points from a distance.

"Got it," Vola said. "I'll take the north, you two take the south."

Vola wanted to watch, to make sure they were good, but with her entire being drained, she could barely keep herself upright. She turned to the north entrance and trusted them to do their job.

Vola set her feet in the sand and trudged along. The distance felt doubled, tripled as if the entrance was getting further away with every step, not closer.

She took a deep breath and forced her legs to move faster. One last charge and this would be over and they could all kill Lillie together.

Using that little bit of anger helped her stir up the righteous rage in her gut. The rage that was a gift from one of the Obstacles but she used in service to the greatest Virtue.

She pounded across the sand, pulling her shield from her back, and when she reached the pillar, she swung it edge first into the crystal.

It shattered under her blow, pieces flying past her to sprinkle the arena. Vola used the last of her rage and strength to spin and smash the other crystal.

Then she let herself fall to her knees.

The first time they'd done this, they'd had the help of a goddess. And Vola had always assumed that feeling like the air had been sucked past her had come from the explosion when the Broken had shattered Nargilla's tanks.

But as Lillie's spell collapsed on itself, the air rushed past Vola again and it brought strength with it.

Vola blinked and found her limbs didn't tremble anymore. She reached deep inside and found that well of power that connected her to the Broken. A well that was cut off anytime she experienced the draining effect.

It was over. She climbed to her feet. Her strength might have been back, but she took it slowly, just in case.

Talon and Sorrel stood beside the other entrance, shaking out their limbs and stretching their necks. The crystals lay in pieces at their feet. Sorrel clearly had used Maxim's Warstaff, and Talon had managed to find another knife she'd "forgotten" somewhere on her person.

Vola glanced up to the box to see Lillie braced with her hands on her knees. She would have been ready for them to break the spell, but the backlash from all that magic pouring in and out of her had to be disorienting.

"Your Majesty," she said, as she pushed herself up straight, her voice ringing across the sands. "Delegates. This is what you face if Southglen fails to contain the threat. A very, very small piece of it."

Hector stared down at them as Vola stepped across the sand to help the two fighters to their feet. "What do you mean, a small piece?"

"I am not capable of everything Anders built with Nargilla. They have tanks that will hold much more power. Nargilla had the ability to drain entire cities. I can only manage a coliseum."

"But you're just a spell caster. We could have killed you and stopped the effect, correct?"

"You could have tried," Lillie said, eying the armored guards. "I'm a spell caster, but with this, I'm a spell caster with an infinite amount of power at my command."

Selene and Hector glanced at each other. The other delegates waited silently.

"And you were able to defeat this person once?" Selene asked, eyes on Vola.

"Nargilla?" Vola said. "Yes. But only with divine help. That's why we know how to handle the draining effect. We've had to fight past it before."

The two champions shook their heads in sympathy.

"Imagine this, but spread across the world," Rilla said quietly from between Hector and Selene. "And the more it spreads, the harder it is to fight back."

Vola and the others waited as the delegates pondered, their eyes on the sands that were still stained black.

"Very well," Hector said.

Rilla's chin jerked up.

"You will have our support," Selene said. "Perhaps together we can keep this from happening ever again."

FIVE

THE JOURNEY back through the rainforest wasn't as eventful as the first. This time they only had to fend off a pack of Change-foxes before they made it back to Southglen.

The Broken's intelligence had Anders setting up shop in an old volcano off on the edge of Southglen between the lush plains and the border to Mistvale.

"It's actually quite clever of him," Rilla commented when she'd first heard. "The area's been devastated for millions of years. It's all rock and scree. Not enough water to support plant life and not enough plant life to support game. Most people avoid it because it's just too difficult to traverse or cultivate. So he's had the place to himself for who knows how long."

"Oh great," Sorrel said. "Just what he needed. A head start."

They hurried on, racing to join the Southglen army camped on the plain just outside the desolated area.

The leaders of Southglen's allies had promised to send troops. In fact, Selene had left the Friendship games early to arrange for their march. But it took armies much longer to travel than a group of five, so they'd gone on ahead, hoping to reach the camp before Anders made his move.

They crested a hill at sundown and caught their first glimpse of the army camped below them. Tents spread across the plain and fires flickered to life as the sun went down.

It was the largest force they'd ever had to work with. But Vola couldn't help comparing it to the vast empty space beyond. The rock field lay flat and uninviting just past the last tent.

By the time they got down the hill, the sun had set and Rilla left them to get some sleep while she found the princess of the War Throne and let her know they'd returned.

In the dark, they just managed to squeeze their tent in between two others at the end of a row, and they secured the swamp beast outside, hoping it wouldn't get free to terrorize the camp before morning.

Vola slept fitfully that night, plagued by dreams of a faceless enemy that just kept running away. Whoever it was, they wouldn't stand and fight her.

She woke as dim light made its way through the flap of the tent, and she finally gave up on getting some rest. She slipped out of the tent, trying not to disturb her friends. Outside, she pulled on her boots and stood in the gray light just before dawn.

The camp was only just beginning to stir. They sat at the end of a row of tents, a trampled walkway between them and the next row. Down the way, toward the center of camp, a human in a stained apron rustled around a cookfire trying to get it lit. Across from them, someone stumbled out of their tent with a groan and shuffled off toward the latrines at the edge of camp.

Vola dug her hands into the small of her back and stretched. Her eyes still felt grainy and scratchy, but she knew closing them again wouldn't do any good.

Someone stepped up beside her, and Vola felt the air move before she even turned to see the Broken standing there. She was in her Greater Virtue shape, one leg, one arm, and covered in scars. But she'd dimmed the normal glow that seemed to emanate from her when she was being particularly godly. And Vola could barely make out the fiery wings behind her.

"Good morning," the Broken said amiably.

"Morning." Vola's voice came out rumbly, and she had to clear her throat.

"I don't sleep well before battle, either," the Broken said. "There were a lot of bad dreams in this place last night."

"And most of them don't even know what we're up against." Vola gestured to the man down the way who was returning from the latrine.

"No," the Broken said softly. "But they will soon find out. The dreams will get worse before they get better, I'm afraid." The Broken turned her head to look at Vola. "We are on the precipice. The edge before the storm."

"I kind of like storms, though," Vola said.

The Broken's lips twisted in a rueful smile. "Yes. But this one promises to be a downpour. Would you like an umbrella? Something to keep the rain off, maybe?"

Vola cocked her head. "What do you mean?"

"Come with me." The Broken beckoned and started off down the row of tents. She sort of floated, the fire at her back keeping her an inch or two above the ground.

Vola trotted to keep up.

Between one step and the next, Vola went from packed dirt and dead grass under her feet to smooth white tile. The air around her changed, the smell of musty canvas and hundreds of bodies packed together falling away and leaving fresh air that felt open and boundless.

Long white halls stretched on either side of her, opening into a chamber, echoing with soft whispers.

Vola scrubbed at her eyes, trying to rub away the grit. What the hell just happened?

"You know, I can hear when you think bad words, too," the Broken said. "Not just when you say them."

"Shi—I mean, crap."

The Broken grinned and led Vola to the center of the wide room. Vola got the impression there were no walls, just an eternal whiteness, and nothing bound them from above. No ceilings or balconies or anything.

Figures shifted and wavered around the room, indistinct shapes and colors with that endless whispering brushing against Vola's ears. She thought there might be chairs rising around her on tiers, but she couldn't exactly see them. When she tried to focus on one, she could make out edges and maybe the face of an occupant, but Vola had the distinct feeling that there was too much in that room for her to know or experience. Her mind could only grasp the barest edge of reality.

"Is everyone here?" a voice asked out of the air beside them. To Vola, it sounded obsequious, and nasally, like the speaker's nose was permanently stuffed. "Helleron? Yes, I'm afraid you must leave your party…Then bring the mutton with you, if you must."

The Broken cleared her throat.

"What?" the voice said. "Oh, all right."

An undulating figure solidified into a man, impossibly tall and slim with long limbs that had too many joints. Vola swallowed and decided not to look any closer. Besides, she recognized him from depictions in the temples and holy texts.

Vesteral, speaker of the gods. The man wasn't a god himself. He was a servant, immortal and implacable, dealing with every whim and fancy the gods could throw at him. His kind had lived many, many centuries ago, at the beginning of the world and had died out nearly a millennium before. He was the only one left.

"Sorry," he said to Vola. "We aren't used to having guests." He glared at the Broken, clearly not caring that she was one of the most powerful beings in the room.

Vesteral turned and an ebony staff appeared in his hand. He struck the foot of it against the tile floor with a clang that rang as if against walls, though there were still no walls. "Let's be official about this, shall we? I bring this summit to order."

Around the room the flashing colors of indistinct figures coalesced into individuals, men and women who sat or stood or lounged, exuding power in a way Vola couldn't quite explain to herself. They didn't glow, the way the Broken did in the real world, but something made Vola's stomach clench when she looked at them.

These were the Virtues and Obstacles that had thrown the Broken out of their ranks. These were the gods themselves, sitting on their thrones discussing mortal and immortal affairs as if they ordered breakfast.

The Broken touched Vola's shoulder and led her to an unoccupied side of the room. Vola stuck close to her.

It was one thing to serve the most powerful Virtue down in the real world. It was quite another to sit in the same room with the gods and see them as real people.

The Broken leaned toward her and gestured to a woman dressed in bright pink and orange. Her robes were cut wide and flowing but still managed to show off her graceful movements without tangling anything. Smile lines were etched around her mouth.

"Bierhel," the Broken murmured. "Greater Virtue of Joy. We can corner her later if you like. She does this joke of the day thing that really annoys some of the others but it always makes me laugh."

She pointed to a tall woman with straight white hair and a

gray gown. "Ona, Greater Virtue of Honor. She's a popular one with the paladins." The Broken gave her a sidelong smile.

"And you know a little bit about Maxim from Sorrel, I expect." She jerked her chin at a man dressed in shining plate, standing as if at attention across from them. He'd removed his helmet to reveal artfully tousled black hair and a mouth pulled in a hard frown.

"Ah," Vola said. "Yes. He's, er, a bit hands-off when it comes to his followers."

The Broken sent a sad smile toward Maxim that he didn't notice. "Don't judge him too harshly," she said. "He cares…very deeply. And mortals are, well, mortal. You don't stick around very long compared to us. It can be very painful to care for someone who has such a short existence. Even knowing it is coming. We've all learned to live with the pain in different ways. Maxim has chosen to distance himself. He chooses many followers and allows many to choose him, but he doesn't allow himself to get close to any of them. It hurts him too much when they eventually leave."

Vola blinked. That wasn't something she'd ever considered before. To her, the years she'd spent with Cleavah and then the Broken had seemed long and fruitful, but her life was fleeting compared to the goddess.

"How do you live with the pain?" Vola asked quietly.

"I learned to make the most of every moment I have." She flashed a smile at Vola. "And I'm very picky about who I spend my time with."

Vola fought down a tingle of pride. "I'm honored, my lady, but…what exactly are we doing here?"

The Broken's smile thinned. "The same thing you were doing in the world. Gathering allies."

Vola's breath caught. "I thought…I thought they wouldn't listen to you."

"Not usually," the Broken said. "But this problem is anything but usual."

Before she could elaborate, the Greater Virtue of Honor stood.

"Right," Ona said, tilting her shoulder to let her fall of starlight-colored hair cascade behind her. "Shall we get on with it? I have some paladins that need looking after."

"What is this even about?" Maxim said. "I thought we all agreed the Broken could pursue this…" He waved a hand. "Quest with the mortals of this realm. Why must we concern ourselves with it as well?"

"You weren't at all concerned by the fact that this mortal enemy managed to strip me of my power?" the Broken asked into the silence. "Let's not pretend," she said sweetly as Maxim spluttered. "You all know who I am. You chose to cast me out because of it. And yet, this *mortal* managed to drain even me. He is a threat to all of us."

"Some of us recognize that, at least," Ona said and cast a glare at Maxim.

The Broken raised her chin. "I asked you here to this summit to establish what we intend to do about it. Practically."

"Fun," a voice said from the back. "I love strategy games. They're so much fun at parties."

Vola strained around the Broken to see who had spoken. A man lounged across his chair, skin slack as if he'd once been rotund but lost a lot of weight recently. He examined a leg of mutton in his hand before taking an enormous bite.

"Helleron," the Broken whispered. "Greater Obstacle of Debauchery."

Vola whipped around to stare at her. "The Obstacles are here?"

"This concerns them, too. Their power is as much at risk as

ours. It's nice actually. I haven't seen us all together in one room in…quite some time."

Vola decided to take her word for it. Working with Obstacles had never really appealed to her, especially not as a paladin. She'd spent most of her adult life trying to get away from one in particular.

Her eyes searched the crowd for him, but she'd only ever heard his voice and fought his representatives. She didn't recognize him in the sea of faces.

"We could give the Broken over to this enemy," Helleron said, still munching his mutton. "While we all run and hide. That seems about right for us. Since we cast her out once already."

The gods chuckled, and the Broken flashed him a sharp smile. "I don't see that working for you this time around," she said. "Maybe if you'd taken the chance to flee when I was caught the first time."

"Now, he knows he can drain the gods," Vola said without thinking. "He'll be coming after you directly."

Vesteral's eyes narrowed at her.

Oof, had she just opened her mouth in front of the entire pantheon? She swallowed and tried to look like she wasn't completely freaked out.

"Ah yes," Maxim said. "Your mortal representative. How long has it been since you chose one?"

"Since my fall," the Broken said quietly. "I thought it was past time to choose another. This is a problem for all the world and therefore all the gods."

"You keep saying that," Maxim said, creases deepening around his mouth.

"I trust the Broken's judgment," Ona said. "In this and in all else."

The words fell like slabs across a stone floor, echoing with their own weight.

Vola swallowed. The gods hadn't wanted to risk being ruled by the Greater Virtue of Righteousness so they had cast her out. They'd only let her return when she promised not to try to rule them, to allow them to go their own ways. And she'd stood apart ever since. Was that changing?

Could it change? The pantheon was the pantheon. The war between gods was ancient history. Vola had never thought of it as something that was still happening.

"Very well," Maxim finally said. "Speak to us, representative. Tell us, what the mortals are doing."

"We're gathering our strength and our allies outside Anders's stronghold," Vola said. "We have other nations joining us for the assault and friends that we've gathered along the way who are lending their support." Or at least Vola hoped so. They'd sent all sorts of messages, but so far there'd been no replies.

We only just got to camp, she told herself. *Maybe there was a flood of people while we were gone.*

"That sounds promising," Maxim said.

Vola steeled herself to disagree with a god, but the Broken had brought her here for a reason. Clearly, she was supposed to help convince them. "Thanks, but I'm not sure it will be enough," she said.

Maxim tilted his head.

"Anders has the power of the world at his fingertips. Power to rival the gods."

Several of them shifted uncomfortably.

"We're going to need all the help we can get," she said. "More than mortals can provide." *Come on, take the hint.* They couldn't be dense enough to miss her meaning, could they?

Maxim frowned. "You have already taken care of his lieutenants, have you not? That seems plenty capable to me. Or are you saying that was a fluke?"

"Not a fluke," a familiar voice said from the back row. "Unless you doubt *my* power, Maxim."

A shudder went down Vola's spine. She'd heard that voice often enough this last year. And off and on before that. She still heard it occasionally, whispering in the back of her mind, urging her to lose her temper and destroy everything that stood in her way. She'd learned to work with it. She'd learned that losing her temper wasn't always bad. Righteous anger differed from straight up rage.

Vola lifted her chin and found Mulgash in the back row. Now that he'd spoken, she could match the voice with the face.

The man sprawled across a large chair looked nothing like an orc, which was disconcerting, since he was sort of their patron god. He was as pale as moonlight, with stark black hair and a straight nose. The only thing about him that indicated he was the Greater Obstacle of Rage was his round, bloodshot eyes.

Those eyes met Vola's, and his lips twitched in a tight little smile.

"Volagra and her team trounced my mortal representative. Spectacularly. If you'd like to dispute their might, you can talk to me. Convince me that I'm a weakling."

Maxim waved a hand. "We all know what you're capable of. I'm not disputing anything with you."

"Good." Mulgash crossed his arms and sat back. "Because if this threat has Mishap's Heroes worried, we should all be worried. Although, Volagra, I will expect a rematch when this is all over."

Vola glared up at the god of rage, trying to come up with a witty comeback, something scathing. And utterly failed. He'd just complimented her. In a room full of gods. And the Obstacles were here and ready to listen. She couldn't ruin that just because she'd fought with her rage her whole life and with Mulgash specifically.

But she'd also thrown his follower out a window, so she couldn't imagine his smile was entirely genuine.

As he said, they'd have to hash out their differences later.

The Broken didn't seem to have anything to say about this. She just watched them with amusement.

"Well, if that's the case," Maxim said, recalling their focus. "I suppose we can provide some backup."

Vola sucked in a breath. They'd won? After a divine war and millennia of ignoring the Broken, they were finally going to listen to her just like that?

"Some blessings here and there," he said. "Perhaps some holy weapons. That should do the trick."

The triumph drained from Vola's veins. "What? We're...the world is at stake and that's all you're going to give us?"

He was the god of Strength and Loyalty. You couldn't get much more warlike than him, and he was going to pass up the opportunity to actually go to war?

He gazed at her with sad eyes and spoke like he was explaining things to a recalcitrant puppy. "We are perfectly willing to help," he said. "But it sets a bad precedent to actually descend from on high and get involved personally. Obviously, there are some who do so anyway." He cast a look at the Broken. Her eyebrow twitched "But we will not bend the rules even for this."

"But..." Vola stood there, brow furrowed trying not to clench her fists. "We need more than that. A couple of blessings are not going to be enough here."

"Mortals do not grow if we don't allow them to solve their own problems. And there are...consequences even to us if we interfere."

He wouldn't meet her eyes.

Vola glanced at the Broken, seeking help.

The Broken's jaw clenched, and she stood. "Vola's right," she said quietly. "This is too big for them to handle. We need to do more."

"And are you forcing the issue, Broken?" Maxim's words snapped out.

The Broken glanced between him and Ona, who stiffened. There was a long pause where the Broken remained frozen, considering. "No," she finally said.

"Then we reserve the right to say no." Maxim turned with that final word and his image fuzzed and faded.

Many of the gods faded as well, following his example.

If the gods weren't led by anyone, then there should be some who were free to say yes as well, but it was clear to Vola who set the tone for the rest. They would follow where Maxim went.

Ona and Bierhel cast Vola and the Broken worried glances before they faded away as well.

Vola surveyed the pantheon as they disappeared into the air. There at the back of the pack, Mulgash remained, staring at her.

He tilted his head and gave her a sly smile. As if plotting something. Then he, too, faded and fuzzed away.

Vola turned to the Broken, who stood straight and tall. Unbowed by their opposition.

"It won't be enough," Vola said.

"I know."

"The consequences he was talking about," Vola said. "Did he mean caring? Is he worried about caring for mortals?"

"Sometimes the fear of pain can be greater than the fear of not doing anything."

"If they don't do anything, we could all die. Wouldn't that hurt more?"

The Broken's lips thinned. "Right now, he doesn't care enough about you for it to hurt. The gods will go on, even with all mortals gone. But if he intervenes…"

"Then he has to meet us on a personal level. He has to care about us and the fact that we might die."

"Yes," the Broken said, simply.

Someone cleared their throat, and Vola realized Vesteral was still there, looking at the ground at her feet. "I can show you out now, ladies," he said.

He walked off on his oddly long limbs. Vola caught a hint of regret in his eyes before he turned. Maybe he sympathized with a mortal species about to face extinction.

Maxim was their problem. The Broken was powerful, but even she'd admitted they needed the help of the rest of the gods. But Maxim and his fear stood in the way of that.

Then they would have to do something about that. They would have to make Maxim care. Care enough to help them and that would convince the rest of the gods.

And Vola had thought recruiting mortal allies was going to be the problem.

SIX

BETWEEN ONE STEP and the next Vola was back in camp, with the bare packed earth beneath her feet and the smell of burned porridge in her nose. She swayed, and a hand caught her elbow.

Vola blinked at Talon, the ranger's face drawn in concern.

"Are you back, now?" she said in her gravelly voice.

Lillie and Sorrel sat at their feet as if they'd been waiting for something. They stood when they saw Vola rub her face.

"What? What do you mean? Of course I'm back, I'm right here."

"Yeah, but you were right here this whole time without actually being here," Sorrel said, brushing off her backside. "You were just standing there staring off into space. It was a little creepy, to be honest."

"Oh," Vola said. "I didn't realize…the Broken took me somewhere. I didn't know it was only my mind that had gone. It felt real while I was there." She held out her hand, examining her greenish skin to see if it had changed somehow.

"That's the conclusion I drew when I couldn't find any sort of magic on you except for a sort of divine buzz," Lillie said. She picked up the towel she'd been sitting on. "We decided to guard you while we waited for you to return."

"Thanks," Vola said, cracking her neck. She might not remember it, but she felt stiff, like she'd been standing in one place for an hour. "I was probably safe enough; the Broken wouldn't have taken me otherwise. But it's nice to know someone's watching my back, anyway."

"Always," Talon said. She ducked into the tent and returned a moment later with her bow.

"First, tell us what was so important the Broken had to abduct you," Sorrel said. "No, wait. First, Rilla wanted to see us at the command tent. No, first the story."

Talon pushed her out into the lane between tents. "Walk and talk."

"We should also grab breakfast," Lillie said, following. "I have the feeling it will be a busy day."

Vola tried to describe the summit of the gods while they passed by the cook tent, but since she still wasn't sure how much her mortal brain had grasped, she had a hard time describing it.

"Ona seems to be on our side. Or at least she agrees that they need to do more than just sit up there and look pretty," she said, juggling a hot roll filled with cheese and sausage. "Maybe Bierhel, too. I get the impression they're my lady's friends in spite of everything that's happened between the gods. Mulgash even had some good things to say."

"Mulgash!" Sorrel yelped. "He was there?"

"All the Obstacles were. He…sort of defended us."

"Didn't we kick his ass?" Sorrel skipped out of the way of a soldier carrying a crate of weapons on his shoulder and hopped over a tent stake.

"That might be why," Vola said. "He saves face if a group of mighty heroes beat him, rather than…you know, us."

"Speak for yourself," Lillie said. "I am a mighty hero." Then she tripped over a guy wire and fell on her face.

"Very mighty," Vola said as she picked Lillie up. "My point is, this is going to be harder than I thought. Maxim…" She glanced at Sorrel, unsure of what exactly she should say about the halfling's god.

"Isn't exactly breaking down doors to come and help us," Sorrel said with a resigned shrug. "I'm aware."

"The Broken says it's because he cares too much. He doesn't want to get hurt. But we might need to get him to care more. At least enough to come down and do something."

"How do you get a god to notice what's going on?" Talon said. "They've been watching everything since the beginning. What can we do to get things to change?"

"I don't know," Vola said as they stepped between the last of the tents into the wide, open space at the center of camp where the princess of the War Throne had set herself up.

It might have been clearer here than in the ranks, but the open space bustled with soldiers visiting the quartermaster, boys running messages, and captains arguing at the edges of everything.

Vola skipped aside to let a runner through and found a large tent at the edge of the space with its front flap thrown open, either to welcome them in or to take advantage of the breeze.

A familiar figure in a dusty robe was bent over a table in the back with glassware and tubes stretching all over the interior.

"Myron?" Vola said.

The figure started, knocking over a rack of glass phials that poured their liquid contents into the dirt.

The tall, gangly elf blinked at the puddle, which rapidly turned the dirt into mud that smoked and steamed.

"Oh, that's probably not very good," he said.

"Should we, um, do something to clean it up?" Lillie asked.

The elf grabbed an empty bucket and flipped it over to cover the puddle. "No need," he said. "I've fixed it."

He finally looked up to see who had interrupted them. His straw blond hair had escaped its tie and fell in lank strands around his wan face. His eyes watered as he blinked.

"Oh, it's you," he said, brightening. "My first enemies. That was fun, wasn't it?"

Myron Vidal. Necromancer and researcher for Anders, providing him with power stolen from the dead. Vola was glad he didn't seem to have any hard feelings about the way they'd destroyed his lab or unleashed the army of undead that had turned on him to inflict their revenge.

"Hi, Myron," Vola said. "What are you doing here?"

"Trying to find a cheaper and more effective substitute for coffee," he said, gesturing to his glassware. "Something to keep the men alert without having to be brewed." He gazed ruefully at the bucket. Smoke drifted out from under the edges. "I have the alert part down. But I think most people will object to the way it eats their insides."

"Probably," Talon said, eyes on the smoke.

"I meant what are you doing in camp?" Vola said. "Last I heard you were still in a lab working for Rilla."

"Oh, I'm still working for her," Myron said. He pushed back his hair and leaned over to squint at the bubbling glassware. "She thought it would be good to have me along on the campaign. Anders is still using techniques he appropriated from me to store the power he steals."

"That makes sense." Sorrel crossed her arms and leaned against another table. Then she stepped back in alarm when something in a beaker hissed.

"Oh, yes. I don't generally do things that don't make sense. It's sort of a personal creed." He brightened. "Since you're here, would you like to try my coffee substitute? I still need test subjects—"

"Nope, nope, nope," Sorrel said as she disappeared out of the tent.

"Um, I think we'll pass, Myron," Lillie said. "Perhaps on a later version. When you have more data."

Vola shuffled backward, keeping herself between Myron and the rest of her party. "See you around, Myron. Be good."

"That's ambiguous," Myron muttered as they left. "I am good at many things. But which applies in this case?"

"Phew," Sorrel said as soon as they'd escaped. "That was close. He's as bad as he was when he was on Anders's side."

"I mean, he's not making zombies anymore," Talon said. "Or stealing their magic. That seems better, right?"

There was a crack and an echoing boom from behind them, and they jumped. Vola spun to see a column of smoke rising from Myron's tent.

"Yeah, better," she said weakly as soldiers and onlookers raced for the tent.

They hurried across the open space, ignoring the chaos behind them.

The command tent stood on a little hillock making it taller than the rest of the camp, and the flag of Southglen flew from its peak, two swords crossed over the crest to indicate that the Princess of the War Throne was in residence.

A group of gray-clad figures milled in front of the tent, sending nasty looks at another group of people dressed in armor and hoods.

Sorrel perked up. "Hazel," she cried.

The lead monk, a dwarf with thick brown hair and sharp blue eyes, turned at the sound of her name. Her face brightened when she saw Sorrel.

"Sorrel! We got your message calling for aid. Didn't bother sending a reply because we figured we'd beat it here."

Sorrel threw her arms around Hazel. The dwarf was only a foot taller than her, unlike most of the world.

"Good to see you, Hazel," Vola said.

The abbess of Sorrel's monastery nodded to Vola, Talon, and Lillie. "Likewise. We brought nearly everyone after Master Bao told us what happened in Firewatch. I hope we can help."

"Where is Master Bao?" Sorrel asked.

"Holding our place in camp," Hazel said with a glare at the group in armor and hoods. "Guarding our site against poachers."

"Poachers!" A man stepped up and pushed his hood from his head, revealing bright gold hair and a sour expression. "We need that space to be close to the command center. Battlemages are integral to the functioning of this army—"

"And we require a space close enough to the temple tent so we may continue our devotions." Hazel planted her hands on her hips. "Besides, we were there first."

The battlemage stepped forward, and Hazel dropped to sweep his legs out from under him.

"Whoa," Vola said as both sides of the argument surged forward. Monks and battlemages clashed as Vola thrust herself between Hazel and her target. She held the monk back by the collar and used her palm to keep the lead battlemage from advancing. She'd left her armor in the tent, but she was big enough to serve as a bulwark between the two factions.

"We're on the same side," Lillie said, hauling on a battlemage's arm.

"Ouch!" someone cried, and Talon danced away looking smug.

Vola exchanged a glance with Sorrel, and the monk gave her a grim nod. Vola let go of Hazel and let Sorrel drag her friend away while Vola concentrated on the battlemages. She put both hands on the leader's breastplate and shoved him back a step. He stumbled and crashed into his fellows. They went down like a faulty tower.

"Now," Vola said. "Maybe we can talk about this like adults and not like children."

"Causing trouble, Lightless?" a voice said behind Vola. "Why is it, every time there's a ruckus, a black paladin is involved?"

Vola stiffened as the voice reached deep past who she was now and pulled out the angry, helpless teenager she'd once been. She turned slowly, feeling like every joint and muscle had locked up in protest.

Lined up across from them, five men stood, armed and armored to the teeth. The one in the middle stared at Vola with light gray eyes.

Vola couldn't help noticing that Knight Commander Imralen still had a full head of thick white hair. If there'd been any justice in the world, he would have gone bald. Painfully.

Vola hadn't seen the paladin council or Knight Commander Imralen since they'd stood in the All-Pantheon temple in Glenhaven and stripped her of her rank, using holy fire to blacken her shield.

Something in her posture must have given her away. Lillie's breath caught in alarm, and Sorrel stepped up beside Vola to lay a hand on her forearm. Talon's leather creaked just over Vola's shoulder.

"You all right?" the ranger said.

Vola realized she wasn't breathing, and she forced air into her lungs. "Fine," she grated out between her teeth.

Knight Commander Imralen's gaze flicked over her shoulder, fastening on her shield. Even when she wasn't armored, she still carried it slung over her back. Not just because it was a rule—all black paladins had to declare themselves by carrying the sign of their disgrace—but because it was a significant part of who she was now. Her story was written in the blackened metal.

"Shouldn't you be curled up in a bar somewhere?" Imralen said, brushing imaginary dust from his arms. "That's all black paladins are usually good for."

"I decided to go the exterminator route," Vola said, crossing her arms. Her blood sang and the rage Mulgash was so fond of coursed just below her skin, but she'd had loads of practice holding it in check by now. This man had helped with that. "I take care of pests. If you decide to become a nuisance, I'll have to treat you like a pest, Imralen."

Imralen's face went a vivid red under his stark hair. "That's Knight Commander, if you please."

Vola raised her eyebrows. "Not to me," she said. And turned her back on him.

Holy Broken, that had felt good. She'd never brought herself to talk back to him before or to any of the masters. They'd held her career in their hands, and she hadn't dared jeopardize it. But with her shield blackened, she had nothing left for them to take away.

"Don't ignore me, black paladin," Imralen said, his voice ratcheting up a notch.

She smirked. "Now, where were we?" she asked the monks and battlemages. "I think we can settle this like professionals and not like squabbling children, can't we?"

Vola deliberately met Hazel's gaze first since she knew her personally.

Hazel sighed and removed her arm from Sorrel's grip, catching Vola's drift. "I can do that," she said. "Maxim applauds strength and courage, and he knows that negotiation requires both."

The head battlemage inclined his head after only a brief hesitation. "I'm willing to listen to anyone who's willing to insult the Knight Commander," he murmured.

The flap of the command tent flipped back with a slap of canvas, and the princess of the War Throne stepped through, Rilla close on her heels.

"Where are Mishap's Heroes? We need to get this—Oh, there you are," the princess of the War Throne said as she caught sight of them between the three factions.

When the War Princess was being official, she piled her gold curls on her head in an elaborate up-do that showed off the long graceful curve of her neck and downplayed the sharp angle of her nose. Today she'd pinned her tight braids back, ready for business, and her profile reminded Vola of a hawk eying its prey.

"Your Highness," Imralen said, taking a step forward. "We have brought the paladins you requested. The entire council and our troops are at your disposal."

"Great," War said without even a glance. "We'll see you on the battlefield."

Imralen spluttered. "Your Highness. We expected a more personalized welcome."

War's eyes narrowed. "What? You need a commendation for doing your jobs? No, sir. I'm not here to babysit you. What? What are the rest of you here for?" She glared at the monks and the battlemages.

"Er, there was a dispute over camping spaces, Your Highness," the battlemage said, quite bravely Vola thought.

"Like I have time to manage that. Lightless, you and your team are up. Let's go."

She spun and let the tent flap close behind her.

Vola glanced at the two factions.

Sorrel caught her look. "You go. I'll handle this." Her gaze slid to the paladin council. "And those."

"But the meeting…" Lillie said.

"You can fill me in later. I'm not much for decisions, anyway." She walked backwards still talking. "I'll go wherever you need me."

"Your Highness," Imralen said, voice going sharp.

"Come on, buddy," Sorrel said, taking his hand like he was a big child. "You had your chance. You blew it. Now retreat gracefully."

Vola bit her lips hard to keep from laughing as she turned her back on the council and led her party into the command tent.

Inside the central space, a large table held a map and strategic markers. A rumpled cot stood along the back wall, partially obscured by a curtain.

Rilla strode to the edge of the table and stared down at it with bleary eyes.

"Did you sleep at all?" Vola asked. The princess hadn't returned to the tent last night, and Vola hadn't been sure if it was because she didn't feel welcome or if it was because she hadn't found the time to go to bed.

Looked like the latter.

Rilla shook her head absent mindedly.

"You know, technically you're still under my command." Vola spoke while staring down at the map, too. "I could order you to rest."

Rilla snorted, then rubbed her eyes. "You sound ridiculous," she said. "But technically…you're right. And I will sleep as soon as this is done. I'll need the rest for what comes next."

Vola opened her mouth to ask for more details, but the War Princess stepped up to the table from the other side and cleared her throat.

Lillie and Talon stared down at the table, waiting patiently.

"Right, we're in as good a position as any," War said. "The Shield Princess is on alert back in Glenhaven. She will hold the line if anything gets past us. But it's our job to be sure nothing gets past us."

Vola nodded and surveyed the map and the tiny troops arrayed across it. The army camp rested on the very edge of the arable land surrounding an ocean of dark rock barrens. The volcano rose in the middle. Anders's stronghold.

"We haven't exactly been stealthy up to now," War said.

Rilla snorted.

"All right, not stealthy at all. But we also haven't been telegraphing our plans. Anders knows we're here. But hopefully that's about all he knows. And if we strike now, we may catch him scrambling to gather his own defenses."

"Are we ready for that?" Vola asked. "Do we have enough people?" She couldn't help thinking of the gods that should have been helping but weren't.

Rilla's lips twisted. "There are still some trickling in. But War is right. We need to make our move."

Vola took a deep breath and looked down at the map. "All right, then. Where do you need us?"

War took up a marker carved to look like an angular orc. "As front and center as anyone's gonna get. I hope you're ready for some action."

SEVEN

"I can't decide if this is a step up or a step down," Talon said, moving smoothly over the rough lava rock that blanketed the hills. Trees still stood, breaking the monotony of the burned plain. They were scraggly and twisted, burned long ago when the mountain had erupted and lava had flowed over the land. But their preserved corpses still marked the party's path.

"You were the one who seemed excited about scout duty," Vola said. "I just kept nodding my head and now here we are."

"Scouting for an army is pretty important," Sorrel said, clambering up a round outcropping of black stone. "And technically we're still working directly for a princess as well as directly *with* a princess." She grinned back at Rilla.

Rilla looked much better today. The six-hour nap she'd taken directly after their planning session had probably helped. Vola was rather proud the princess had trusted them to get the party's gear from the quartermaster and everything kitted out. She knew Rilla was particular about that sort of thing.

The princess had ditched her simple yet elegant jerkin for a leather cuirass, tight enough Vola couldn't see how she could actually move, and thigh-high boots lashed in place. She was lined with more buckles and straps than a packed-up tent, each one holding a knife or dart or vial of something deep and black.

Vola didn't ask the spymaster what she kept in her pockets. She was better off not knowing.

Scouting wasn't exactly glamorous. But it got them out of camp where people were starting to pick fights and step on each other's toes just for the fun of it. An army could only sit in one place for so long before it started to fall apart from the inside.

Gruff ranged out in front of them while Lillie's familiar, Rand, kept an eye on him from above.

The eerie cry of a gull a million miles from any body of water echoed across the rocky terrain and they angled themselves toward the spot where the War Princess wanted to stage the first assault.

"Hazel's team is keeping up well," Vola said. The abbess and her monks were out there supporting them from either side. Since no one knew what Anders was capable of with the power he'd already stolen, Vola hadn't wanted to advance alone. And both Rilla and the War Princess had agreed.

"Of course, they are," Sorrel said. "An abbey full of monks could take on an entire army." She paused at the top of a small rise and glanced back. "Er. They won't have to take on a whole army. Will they?"

Vola hesitated and shared a look with Rilla.

"There are reports of troops moving across the old lava field," Rilla said. "They aren't ours."

"So, Anders is gathering his own troops," Lillie said quietly.

"Who would be fighting for him?" Sorrel raised a hand to shield her eyes. The day was hazy. No fog, but with low-hanging clouds that reflected enough light to disorient them and still keep everything rather dim. "And why? He's the bad guy."

"Bad guys always have minions," Talon said. "Don't they?"

"Yeah, but what is he promising them?"

"Maybe some of the power he's been collecting," Lillie said. "That would be a temptation to a lot of people."

"Either way, it's a good thing we've got the monks along," Vola said. "I feel better with them around."

"Me, too," Sorrel said cheerfully and hopped off the rise. "Oh wait. You mean for combat. Yeah, that too."

Lillie smiled at her. "Have you been catching up, then?"

"Well, I mean, I did sort of send them all off with a slap on the wrist and an admonishment to be good for Hazel. It's nice to see that they're actually following her. I knew she'd make a good abbess."

"Did you get them to make nice with the battlemages?"

"That was easy. They all wanted the same spot, so I told them none of them could have it. I gave them spaces that were equidistant to everything, right next to each other. Now they have to learn to live with each other."

"What about the…the council?" Lillie asked, glancing at Vola.

"Well, I figured Vola didn't want to be running into them every other hour so they're on the other side of camp."

Vola winced. "It's fine. I don't actually resent them."

Talon gave her a look. "Yeah, right, try another one."

"I don't," Vola said. "I still think they're terrible old men with more power than is good for them, but they don't have any power over me anymore. And what's funny is they were the ones who made it that way. They freed me. I have all the support I need between you guys and the Broken."

Lillie gave her a sappy smile and Talon snorted.

"Aw, that's so sweet," Sorrel said. "But I still put them downwind of the latrines."

Vola choked on a laugh.

"Not only do they have to smell them constantly, they'll be awake all night as everyone and their dog traipses past to pee."

A short bark interrupted their laughter, and Gruff came bounding over the rough terrain and skidded to a stop beside Talon. He wound himself around her, whimpering.

Instantly, the rest of them circled up, keeping their backs to each other, surveying the terrain.

"What's wrong?" Vola said. "What did he find?"

"I'm not sure. He says it's a wall. But a regular wall wouldn't have spooked him this bad."

"Lillie, you want to check with Rand?"

Lillie's eyes were already closed, and Sorrel moved to cover her while she connected with the raven.

"Gruff's right," she murmured. "It's a wall. Of light. Right across the spot where War wanted to stage our assault."

"Is it an ambush?"

"I don't believe so." Lillie shook her head as she broke her connection.

"Then we should check it out," Rilla said. She glanced at Vola. "That is, if you want to. I'm still following your orders out here."

Vola's lip twitched. "And I take suggestions from my team. Move out."

The War Princess had designated a spot in the bend of an old river. The meandering stream bed had been completely destroyed when the mountain erupted, but you could still see the edge of its course where the rest had been blown away.

"Geez," Sorrel said, prodding the lava rock, which had broken down into gravel-shaped pieces. "What happened here?"

"Steam," Lillie said shortly. "When the lava hit the river, it exploded in steam. It's quite spectacular, I'm told."

"As spectacular as that?" Rilla said and pointed ahead of them.

A shimmering barrier cut directly through their target area, straight, smooth, and slightly opaque. It glimmered like the surface of a pearl or those lights that floated in the sky far to the north. Mostly white but shot through with bits of blue, green, and purple.

It stretched higher than Vola was tall and disappeared somewhere in the low clouds above them.

"What is that?" Vola said.

"A wall?" Sorrel suggested.

"That's like no wall I've seen," Vola said.

"It reminds me of the wards around Glenhaven," Rilla said. "Only…"

"Only what?" Vola said.

She smiled ruefully. "Only I'm not keyed to these. I have no idea how to get past."

"Are we sure it's really blocking the way?" Sorrel said.

"How about you run at it and tell us?" Talon said.

Sorrel tilted her head. "Fair point."

"How far does this go?" Rilla asked. "Our previous scouts haven't seen it before. Gods, how many are trapped on the other side? I have to contact War." She stepped back and pulled a palm-sized mirror from one of her many pouches.

"Sorrel, can you signal the monks?" Vola asked, still staring. "Warn them if they haven't found it already, and if they have, ask if they've found the edges."

"Can do." Sorrel scrambled up a ridge parallel to them and cupped her hands around her mouth to cry like a gull.

Rand circled over them, angling his wings to keep an eye out on all sides.

Lillie shook her head. "Rand says this goes as far as he can see on either side. It circles the entire lava field with the volcano directly in the center."

Vola's lips thinned. "Seems likely to be Anders's work then."

Gruff crept forward a couple of steps, his nose snuffling toward the glowing wall.

"Stay back from it, Gruff," Talon said. "We don't know what it does."

"Lillie, do you have anything for that?" Vola gestured helplessly toward the wall. "Something that would tell us what it is, what it does. How to get rid of it."

"I'm not sure…" Lillie started. "Well, I guess there is one thing."

She whispered under her breath, and above them, Rand gave a sharp croak. He spun on his tail feathers and arrowed straight for the wall.

He struck the surface with a brief, blinding flash of light and a surprised squawk. Singed feathers fell around them.

"Holy shit," Vola said. Lightning cracked against the rock at her feet.

"Oh my gods, he's dead," Talon said. "Did you just kill Rand on purpose?"

"I didn't! I just asked him to test the solidity," Lillie said.

"And he couldn't think of a better way?"

"Well, I needed him to touch it in order to try something."

"Does it really count as murder if he's a familiar she can summon over and over again?" Vola said.

Talon's face screwed up. "That doesn't make me feel any better about it."

"I'll have him back as soon as I can sit down and cast the spell," Lillie said. "In the meantime, I learned several things."

"Like what?" Rilla said, stepping back over the rough ground.

"That barrier is stronger than anything I've ever seen," she said. "And it stretches at least two stories up which is where Rand was when he hit it."

"Is it even stronger than the wards Rilla was talking about?" Sorrel asked, sliding down a ridge to rejoin them.

"I think so," Lillie said. "I tried to dispel it through Rand as he struck." She shook her head. "I'm not a battlemage or anything but the way it just absorbed my power…Nothing got through. This is…I think this is what he's been doing with all the power he's collected so far."

"Hazel says the monks have found the same thing where they are. They're within calling distance, so not far, but no one's been dumb enough to touch it."

Talon glared at Lillie, who winced.

"So this is made up of all the magic Anders has managed to steal so far?" Rilla said, eying the barrier up and down.

"Yes," Lillie said. "I can do more tests to confirm but…if I had to guess from what we've encountered so far, it's made up of more than one kind of magic."

"The living, the dead, and the land," Talon said.

"And the Broken," Vola added. "The piece he got away with."

Lillie bit her lip and tilted her head back to examine the barrier. "Which will only make it stronger."

"And the only way to get to Anders," Vola said. "Is to break through."

EIGHT

As THE REST of them stood there staring at the barrier in dismay, Sorrel stooped to pick up a rock and bounced it off the rough ground so it flew at the ward.

The barrier crackled and then shimmered for a few seconds.

Sorrel shaded her eyes. "Could anyone see if that went through?"

Vola started to shake her head and then froze. The air around them wavered, and fog seeped up from the ground. Fog that hadn't been there two seconds ago.

"Form up," Vola said and drew her sword. The others centered on her, backs to each other as they watched the fog warily.

"Lillie, is this harmful?"

Lillie touched the circlet on her brow. "It's not elemental or poisonous, as far as I can tell. It's…an illusion?"

The fog drifted upward and clumped into large lumps, forming bulbous figures. The figures solidified, gaining weight and detail.

It was a little like watching the gods meld into reality, except way less colorful.

Vola blinked at the new terrain.

Instead of the endless black lava rock, there were now fields. Green grass and yellow wheat waved under a summer sun and a blue sky. Ahead of Vola, a barn stood beside a picturesque little farmhouse.

Nearby, a boy of about fourteen or fifteen raised a hoe over his head and brought it down, striking the ground in time to the off-key tune he was humming.

Vola felt a little pang. He looked a lot like Finn, although Finn had grown up in the city and picked pockets for his living rather than digging in the dirt.

Other forms worked out in the fields, a man and a woman and another girl at least.

"You're all seeing this, too, right?" Talon said.

"Idyllic farm, almost too perfect for words?" Rilla said. "Yup."

"What in Maxim's holy name is this?" Sorrel said.

"Lillie?"

"It's…definitely magic," Lillie said, touching her circlet.

Vola rolled her eyes.

"No, really? You think?" Sorrel said. She'd pulled the Warhammer from her back and held it out as if the farm boy was about to leap on them, teeth bared.

"Does anyone else feel like this is vaguely familiar?" Talon said.

"Yeah," Sorrel said. "Me."

"It's just like Lord Arthorel's manor," Vola said. "He had rooms full of immersive illusions just like this. Where you'd swear you were in a place." She glanced at Lillie. "Can you dispel it?"

"I can try. This might be above my pay grade."

"I guess you'll have to apply for a raise," Rilla said. She also watched the surroundings warily.

Lillie raised her hands to start a counterspell.

"Anders!" one of the distant figures called. "Time to come in for dinner."

Vola reached out to stop Lillie, but the wizard froze, her mouth hanging open.

"Anders?" Talon hissed. "As in our Anders?"

"Do we really want to claim him?" Sorrel asked.

"Shh," Vola said. "What's happening?"

The fifteen-year-old Anders propped his hoe on his shoulder and started for the house and the barn. But before he'd taken two steps, a scream rang out from the buildings.

Flames spread across the fields and licked up the sides of the farmhouse, faster than was physically possible. Vola had the disorienting sensation of skimming through time.

"Mama!" the boy cried. "Pa!"

He raced across the fields, his hoe held like a weapon.

Dark figures swarmed the scene, faceless shadows wielding torches and grisly weapons.

Vola's heart leaped.

"What do we do?" Talon said. "This is…this is just a spell, right? A memory or…something."

Vola exchanged a glance with Sorrel as the dark figures cut through the door of the farmhouse. Sorrel's brow was set and her lips thin.

The boy lifted his face to the sky. "Please, help them!" he cried, as if praying. He swung his hoe at the nearest enemy and was struck down.

Vola's mouth twisted in a grimace. "In Lord Arthorel's manor, we dispelled the illusions by fighting them. Or confronting their realness."

"You want to do the same here?" Rilla asked.

Vola drew her sword. "Yes. And…and I can't just stand here."

"Me neither," Sorrel said. She sprang forward, staff swinging.

Vola signaled Rilla and Talon to flank as she followed Sorrel into the fray. Lillie stayed behind, weaving a spell through the air.

"Are we really helping the enemy?" Talon said, but she moved into position, anyway.

"He's a boy," Lillie called. "An illusory boy."

"Yeah, he's not tall enough to be our enemy, yet." Sorrel leaped at the first wave of faceless fighters and disappeared between their legs.

"That has nothing to do with it," Vola said. "Nargilla was shorter."

"I wasn't actually going to stop you," Talon said. "I was just pointing out the irony."

Vola smashed aside an attack with her shield and swung her sword around in an arc that cut one of the dark shadows from neck to knee. It dissolved in a swirl of smoke.

Definitely illusions.

Vola spun and dropped to one knee to avoid a blow to her head and brought her blade up to block another swing. She swung her shield around and bashed the shadow so it stumbled back. Straight into Talon's daggers.

Rilla ducked a blow and came up under the shadow's guard, twisting her blades into its neck. It dissolved into black smoke.

Vola winced. She'd never enjoyed staring at a man's face while he died on her blade, but faceless enemies were somehow worse. You couldn't look them in the eye. You couldn't look for clues about their actions or motivations. Even monsters were better than this. A wyvern defended its nest; an ogre needed to feed its family.

These were just shapes that fought and advanced like a thinking creature but wore the blank aspect of a shadow.

Vola whirled and chopped, surrounded by writhing bits of black fog both solid and not. Impossible to keep track of her people. It was her duty to protect them, but they were swallowed by the miasma, torn away from her as she fought.

Was this Anders's story? Had he really lived through this attack? Or was this the foggy recollection of a terrified boy? Blown out of proportion by fear and confusion.

Maybe it was both.

Vola shouldered her way through another shadow, throwing it to the ground and planting her blade so deep in its chest the point stuck in the soft earth underneath.

And the rest of the shadows faded away around her.

Sorrel stood nearby, leaning against the side of the burning farmhouse, panting. Blood trickled into her eyes from a cut at her hairline. Rilla crouched in the dirt, blades up and crossed, as if waiting for the next blow. Talon spun, looking wildly around the empty farmland, her daggers searching for more enemies.

Lillie stood where they'd left her, staring at the spell stretched thin and glowing between her hands.

In front of the house, Anders knelt, his face streaked with sweat and soot, his hands curled around a bloody hoe. Figures lay crumpled on the ground around him as tears streamed down his face.

"Why?" he croaked, voice hoarse from shouting or from the smoke. It billowed thick and black above them. "Why didn't you save them?"

Vola wasn't sure who he was talking to until he tilted his head and aimed a glare at the sky.

Boots crunched in the gravel of the narrow road that passed in front of the house.

Vola raised bleary eyes to see a man with midnight skin and dark eyes kneel beside Anders. He wore a set of mismatched armor, chainmail shirt under a leather cuirass with plate pauldrons, and rusted metal greaves. But he made it look good. Well-used by someone who knew what they were doing.

He reminded Vola strongly of Henri.

"The gods can't do everything," the man said, voice low and steady. "And you weren't strong enough to do it yourself. Not yet."

Anders stared up at him, the bodies of his family in the dirt around him.

The man extended a hand, and the boy took it.

Light flashed as their palms touched and the scene around them smeared and dissolved into the earth.

Vola was left kneeling on the rough lava rock, her sword piercing the stone as little fissures snaked away from the blade.

The others remained in their positions, just breathing the damp cool air, eyes still wide with shock and exhaustion.

Beside them the glowing barrier still rippled, flecks of green and blue and purple streaking its surface.

A rumble shook the earth at their feet, and the wall of light shimmered.

Then slowly, it pulled back, gliding over the rock away from them, shrinking towards the center where Anders's stronghold stood.

It slowed and stopped another seven hundred yards away. Just far enough that they could still see it standing there. Waiting.

"All right," Sorrel said, using the staff to push herself upright. "I'll say it again. What the hell was that?"

"Anders's memory?" Talon said.

"An illusion," Rilla said.

"Yes, but an illusion can still depict something real. Or remembered," Vola said. She picked herself up off the ground and yanked her sword free of the rock. Little flames licked through the fissures before dying out completely.

"But why…" Sorrel waved a hand at the distant barrier. Blood still trickled down her face. "Why did that move?"

"They're connected," Lillie said.

Rilla and Talon finally relaxed and gathered themselves. "What?" Rilla said.

"The illusion was connected to the barrier. That's what I was doing inside it. I was trying to see what it was anchored to. You were right. It is just like Lord Arthorel's manor. We broke the illusion, either by fighting the shadows with Anders or by completing the story he was trying to tell. And breaking the illusion broke its hold on the barrier."

Vola stared off at the glow on the horizon.

"But it's not gone completely."

"No."

Vola sighed. "So there are more illusions. More keys to break to get to the stronghold."

Lillie chewed her lip. "That does seem to be the case. I sensed at least four more anchor points while we were in there. We will have to break them all to get to the stronghold."

"Of course we do," Vola muttered. "You can never just walk up and storm the castle. There always has to be something, someone who thinks they're so clever."

"We're sure Lord Arthorel is put away, right?" Sorrel asked.

"He's serving his time in jail," Rilla said.

"Anders must have learned a trick or two from him before he was arrested," Talon said.

"I'll send word to put him under heavy guard, just to be sure," Rilla said.

"I take it we're going to have to see the rest of Anders's life story," Sorrel said. "In order to advance."

"Seems likely," Vola said. "There's obviously something he wants us to see."

"Typical," she said with a sniff. "Why are all bad guys narcissists?"

NINE

They returned to camp by a straighter route this time, not having to be so careful to avoid Anders's attention. Clearly, he was prepared for them already.

The monks came, too, filing in beside them as if they'd just appeared out of the rocky landscape.

Around them, the army packed up, breaking down tents and camp furniture, loading everything onto the mules that would carry it or into the packs of individual soldiers. The War Princess must have assumed they'd either have good news, and they could advance, or bad news, and they'd have to retreat.

The cook had packed up his fire, wood, and all since there was little fuel to be had out on the lava field and a line of angry soldiers stretched away from his site. All of them had waited just a little too long to collect their lunches.

Myron puttered around, collecting his glassware and packing it carefully in sawdust-filled boxes. The sides of his tent were still a little blackened from his coffee-substitute explosion the day before, as were his robes, but on the bright side, the flames had given his hair a trim for him.

The command tent had already been struck by the time they got there. War stood by, dressed in gold-tooled leather, her hair pinned close to her head as she surveyed the packing of her maps and cot.

She caught sight of them and raised her chin. "Tell me," she said.

Vola wasn't sure how much she could read from their expressions, but she started at the beginning.

"We can advance to the location," she said. "But there's a complication. Anders erected a barrier miles and miles around the mountain. He's effectively penned himself in, and it won't be easy to get to him."

War rubbed her brow. "Always another thing."

"Hey, that's the same thing Vola said," Sorrel exclaimed.

"Why did you say we can advance?" War asked. "If that barrier is keeping us out?"

"We know how to take it down," Rilla said, crossing her arms. "Though it's annoying and circuitous, we can eventually get the army to the mountain. Or whatever is waiting for us in his lands. We still have those mystery troops to deal with."

"How?" War apparently wasn't one to waste words in a crisis.

"We found the anchor keys to the spell," Lillie said. "He's hidden them within illusions around the barrier. As long as we continue to break through them, we can push back the barrier, bit by bit."

"You were right," War said. "Tedious in the extreme. But I suppose we don't have a choice?"

"We can get someone in from the universities to study the barrier," Rilla said. "Maybe they'll have some better ideas for removing it. Sometimes a battering ram is better than a lockpick."

War placed her hand on her chest, as if surprised. "I never thought I'd hear you say that."

"Yeah, well, enjoy it while it lasts. If I get the chance to stab Anders in the back without warning, I'm taking it."

"You have my blessing," War said with a smirk. "It would save me a lot of trouble. Right, Mishap's Heroes. I guess this means you have a job to do. You'll ride out ahead of us and make sure we have somewhere to march to."

"A bad idea, to be sure," a voice said.

Vola's spine stiffened. Sorrel might have put them at the far end of camp, but of course, that didn't mean the man couldn't walk in order to make her life miserable.

"Excuse me?" she said, turning to glare at Knight Commander Imralen. "I wasn't aware you had a say."

"I should," he said. "I should have more of a say in the operations of this company than a black paladin with no rank. That's exactly why I requested a meeting with you, Your Highness."

"Which I couldn't duck out of," War muttered.

"The paladins have always been a cornerstone of Southglen's martial might. We are the ones people turn to, the ones people trust when there are bandits or robberies or anything requiring honor and strength. We are essential. Which means we should be a part of your war council. We should be making decisions alongside you as our monarch."

"When I need the opinion of a war council, I will ask for it," War said.

"And yet you continuously consult this black paladin, who was publicly stripped of her rank and thrown out of our sacred order for her actions."

War lowered her chin. "I am aware of the allegations against her. I'm also aware of how she's held herself, both before her demotion and after."

"You see the surface," Imralen said. "You see what she wants you to see."

"You know the best part about being a black paladin," Vola

said, examining her fingernails. "Is that I don't actually have to stand here and take your hatred anymore. I can fight back."

"Is that a threat?" Imralen said, looking down his nose at her. He had to tilt his head back and squint to do it. "Do you see how your animal is threatening me?" he asked War.

"Watch your tone," Rilla said.

"I meant," Vola said with a glare of her own. "That if you don't like me, if you really have a problem with what I'm doing here, I'll meet you in fair combat. We'll let the gods decide."

War snorted. "That's hardly fair." She turned to Imralen and cocked her head. "You know, the gods chose her as their spokesperson. She represents the Broken. You really want to argue with the Greater Virtue of Righteousness?"

Imralen's mouth twisted and thinned.

"Or if you're afraid to go up against her," Sorrel said. "I'll happily fight you. I've served as a champion before. Come on. You wouldn't be afraid to fight me? Would you?" Her grin held far too many teeth as she tipped her head back to meet Imralen's gaze.

"Or me?" Lillie said.

"Do Rilla and I have to volunteer, too?" Talon said, exchanging a look with the Dagger Princess. "Or can we just assume you two will flatten him so he never gets up again?"

"Or I can just make it official and say no one is fighting anyone," War said, her hands planted on her hips. "Duels and honor fights have no place in a camp that's marching to war. In fact, I'll court-martial any party who pursues this conflict past today." She huffed and crossed her arms. "That's my official edict. My personal one is this…" She stepped up to Imralen, nose to nose. "Leave Volagra Lightless alone. You enacted your punishment upon her. And that's the end of her relationship with you. She is more essential to this war effort than you are, and if you go after my people again, I will kick your ass so hard you'll land back in Glenhaven. Do I make myself clear?"

Imralen's teeth crunched as he clenched his jaw. "Yes, Your Highness."

He spun and left the clear space which was rapidly transforming into trampled mud as soldiers and assistants packed out the last of the tents.

"Well, now that we're all friends again," War said, and Vola snorted.

War narrowed her eyes at her. "You and your team have a job to do. Do whatever you have to do to get us through that barrier. Take those illusions down. We'll be advancing behind you, so we're counting on you."

Vola straightened and gave her a sharp nod.

"Vola," War said as she started to turn with the others. "I don't blame you for wanting to bash his teeth in. But I meant what I said. God's representative or not, I'll kick you out of here if I find you've engaged with him in any way. Keep yourself out of his way and we won't have a problem."

"Understood, ma'am." There had been a brief moment where she'd thought she could finally pay the Knight Commander back for all the hurt he'd caused her during training. But even if she was a black paladin, she was still a paladin. And defending her reputation was not a good enough reason for violence.

She jerked her head at the others and they trotted back through the dissolving chaos of the camp. They still had to pull down their tent and load up the swamp monster. Then they'd have to find someone brave enough to wrestle with the creature while the army moved and Mishap's Heroes went on ahead.

On the other side of the quartermaster's tent, which was half packed away already, a hand shot out and gripped her elbow, hard enough to pinch the skin in the gap of her armor.

She reacted, twisting around and throwing her attacker over her hip.

Imralen landed on his feet with a glare.

Vola held up her hands. "I'm under strict orders not to kill you," she said. "Are you trying to get me kicked out?"

Imralen's face hardened. "Yes."

Vola rolled her eyes. Ask a stupid question…

Imralen stepped close, and Vola refused to retreat from him. She raised her chin, stretching to her full height. Imralen didn't seem to notice.

"You are a beast," he sneered. "A beast of burden. You don't fool me. That veneer of civilization will crack, and then everyone will know you for what you are."

Vola rubbed her nose. "Your words don't mean anything to me anymore, Imralen. You lost your chance to earn my respect."

He shook his head. "An animal's bleating. Know this, I will defy the princesses to expose you. I will go up against the gods themselves to show everyone that you're not fit to carry that shield."

He spun on his heel and strode off through the camp.

"Well, that'll be fun," a voice said.

Vola cocked an eyebrow at Sorrel. "How long have you been standing there?"

"Does it matter? I think I could feel his hate from a mile away. You gonna watch out for him?"

Vola shrugged and started walking, catching up to the others. "I don't have much of a choice. War doesn't want me to play his game so I won't play."

"There are lots of other things he can do to hurt you other than fighting you directly."

"Then I'll have to deal with them when they come up, won't I? I can't engage."

"Maybe *you* can't," Sorrel muttered, hurrying to keep up.

Vola didn't blame the monk for wanting to fight back. Her skin crawled knowing Imralen was out there working against her somehow. And she knew nothing she said would keep Sorrel from watching her back, officially and unofficially. She just hoped her second in command was patient enough to keep it under wraps.

Mishap's Heroes led the army to the spot where they'd relived Anders's memory, and War declared they camp there until Vola and the others had pushed the barrier back some more.

Rilla insisted they set up their tent near the command tent this time. Maybe she suspected Imralen would try something less official, too. Or maybe she figured it would be easier to keep an eye on War from there. The Princesses of Southglen got along better than most siblings and War was perfectly capable of taking care of herself, but Rilla's nature made her suspicious and she tried to situate herself so she could protect her fellow royalty when she was able.

They had their tent up in ten minutes flat and Lillie hung her robe in the corner to give it a homier feel. Vola couldn't help remembering how long it took them in the beginning. How much cursing was involved and how many times they'd slipped and fallen into the swamp.

Not only did they work faster now, they could divvy up chores without even exchanging a word. Vola and Lillie pitched the tent while Talon took care of the swamp beast, making sure it was tethered as far away from the horse picket line as possible, and that there were enough turtles to satisfy it and keep it in one place for the night. Rilla had procured the beast's feast. And Sorrel had trotted off to the mess tent to look for some food for the rest of them.

On the lava field, the command tent sat on the same level as everything else, a little more understated than before. Probably a tactic to ensure that War didn't attract Anders's attention. Vola doubted an assassin could make it all the way through their camp *and* Rilla, but it paid to be careful.

Of course, that meant, she was harder to find in general.

"Excuse me," a soft-spoken voice said. "We're supposed to report to the Princess of the War Throne, but we seem to have gotten turned around. All these tents look the same."

The voice was familiar enough that Vola straightened with a frown and turned to find a short plump human wringing his hands behind her. He'd trimmed his graying hair since she'd last seen him, but the shape of his face still strongly reminded her of Lillie.

"Lord Ephyra," Vola said. "I wasn't expecting to see you here. What brings you?"

A young man poked his head out from behind Lord Ephyra. He was slim with reddish hair and Lillie's eyes. Her brother, Kellan.

"Volagra, correct?" Lord Ephyra said, his eyes lighting up with recognition. "Good to see you again, young paladin." He thrust his hand out to shake Vola's as if he were a common merchant. "We came with the university scholars." He gestured to the six or seven men and women behind him who stood shifting their feet, glancing around nervously.

"Hey, Lillie," Talon called through the tent flap. "Get out here."

"What is—Father!" Lillie cried, untangling herself from the tent. She lunged across the space and threw herself into her father's arms.

"Welcome, Lord Ephyra," Rilla said, with a smirk. "You'll forgive me for not throwing myself on you."

Lillie drew herself away with a flush and turned her attention on Kellan.

"You're forgiven, Your Highness," Lord Ephyra said with a chuckle. "We were on our way with the results of our research on Anders's spell when we received word that there was a new complication. A barrier of some sort? We decided to spend the resources to portal the rest of the way rather than waste the time traveling."

"I appreciate it," Rilla said. "War gets cranky when people tell her to wait. So the faster we can get her moving forward again, the better for all of us."

"I've known quite a few knights that fit that description."

Vola's breath caught at the familiar voice. It sent a little tingle down her spine and made her feel all awkward and proud and in awe at the same time. Henri had always had that effect on her, but it seemed like it was worse now she hadn't seen him in so long.

A stocky man with silver-colored hair, spiky from being under a helm all day, gazed at her from behind the scholars. The corner of his mouth rose, pulling at the long scar that stretched between the corner of his eye and his neck.

Lord Ephyra bobbed his head at the man. "Can I introduce you to Knight Henri? He's been keeping us safe along the road."

"Not a knight, my lord," Henri said. "Just a trainer."

"They know each other already," Talon said.

Vola wasn't the kind of person to fling herself at her old mentor, and neither was he. The feeling in her chest when he gave her a proud little smile was enough. It had always been enough.

There was a time when she would have turned her shoulder to hide the shield he'd given her and keep him from seeing everything she'd done to it. But she wouldn't do that now. Not with the Broken's wings spread across the black, telling their own story.

Henri stepped forward to clasp her shoulder, and Vola's breath hitched.

"I've missed you, Vola," he said quietly, while the others murmured their own greetings. "Glad I got the chance to see you in all this." His gesture indicated the camp, the war, everything that had happened since she'd rescued him from a slave ship and he'd gifted her with his own shield.

Vola cleared the lump from her throat. "It's good to see you, too." The words weren't nearly accurate enough, but what else could she say? Henri's simple presence, his acceptance, and pride wiped away every hateful word still lingering from Imralen's tirade.

"I brought someone else who'd like to see you."

Vola caught sight of the gangly youth behind him. The boy had filled out a bit, put more muscle on his limbs so he actually fit the leather armor he wore. But he still had a spray of freckles across his nose and carrot-colored hair.

"Finn," Vola said, the strange feeling in her chest twisting. The pride was still there, but instead of the awkwardness of youth, it was mixed with a little shame and regret. Shame for not protecting him better. Regret that she hadn't been able to finish his training herself.

This time she did want to reach out and bundle him into a hug. But he'd grown more than she'd thought possible, and she didn't want to embarrass him. Instead, she held out her hand.

He clasped it gratefully, his eyes shining.

"Gods, what has he been feeding you?" Vola said. "You're nearly as tall as me."

"Bacon," Henri said. "All the bacon, all the time. Kind of like you."

"No bacon anywhere in camp," Sorrel said, popping up between them, holding a tray full of bread and cheese and dried meat. "But there's some undefined jerky. Hiya, Henri. Finn."

"Sorrel," Henri said with an amused smile.

"Look, Vola. More people to watch your back."

Vola winced as Henri raised one eyebrow. "Yeah, I should probably warn you—"

"The paladin council is here," Finn said, rubbing the back of his neck. "Henri said they would come. We planned to steer clear of them."

"Probably a good idea. Hopefully, they'll be so distracted with me, they won't even notice you."

Finn licked his lips. "I, um. I know what you did for me, Vola. Back in Glenhaven. Shielding me from the council."

"Oh," Vola said, voice going flat. She glanced at Henri.

"He was ready," Henri said.

"I know what they did because of it," Finn said, his eyes going to her shield. "And I know why you didn't tell me, but...I kind of wish you had. So I could thank you. Before this."

"You don't have to—"

"I know I don't, but I want to."

Finn glared at her fiercely, and Vola blinked. Henri hid a smile.

"I'd say you taught him well," Henri said. "But I'm not sure you meant to teach him stubbornness."

Vola grinned ruefully. "Not intentionally."

"We should get to the War princess," Lord Ephyra said. "I'm worried that our information is of a time-sensitive nature."

"I can help you with that," Lillie said quickly. "And I need to look over your results from Anders's spell as well. I have what I gleaned from Nargilla, but I'm sure you've made some progress I haven't seen yet."

"I'd say you already have enough on your plate," Rilla said. "But you are the foremost expert on everything Anders is doing so far."

"If the barrier continues to give us trouble, we'll be back in camp a lot anyway," Vola said. "She can work with the scholars anytime we're here and not racing out to fight more things."

"And War will appreciate a representative from the scholars who can explain things to her using small words," Rilla said with a toothy grin.

TEN

Wʜᴇɴ ᴛʜᴇʏ ʟᴇꜰᴛ the next morning to find the next key to the barrier, Lord Ephyra and the scholars gave Lillie a list of conditions and parameters to check. Ephyra would have come with them himself, except War didn't want to risk civilians so close to the barrier. But Lillie knew plenty about the barrier and Anders's work already, and she had all of Mishap's Heroes to back her up.

They set out directly from the army camp and walked a straight line to the glowing, undulating barrier in the distance. War had commandeered Hazel and the monks to serve as scouts, looking for Anders's mystery troops.

"He can't have put the second illusion directly in line with the first," Talon argued as they trudged across the lava field. "He knows we're going to be working through them to break down the barrier, so he'll make them hard to find."

"That is, if his goal is to keep us from breaking through," Lillie said.

Talon's brow furrowed. "What do you mean? Of course he wants to keep us from getting to him. What else would he want?"

"Maybe he's just delaying us," Vola said. "Making sure we

have to jump through his hoops so he has time to do…whatever it is he's doing in there."

Sorrel glared at the barrier suspiciously as they came up next to it. "He seems like the kind of narcissist to make us go through his story and use it to stage an ambush."

Vola glanced at Rilla, who had been quiet most of the morning. "What do you think?"

She gave them a sly grin. "A very wise mentor once told me, 'always assume ambush.'"

Sorrel whistled. "Catchy."

"Whatever Anders is planning," Rilla said. "We're following his rules, playing his game. He has the power. We have none. Unless we can find a way to surprise him, we're at a disadvantage. So…" She shrugged.

"Always assume ambush," Vola said. She stopped just feet from the barrier and glared up at it. "In that case…" She cupped her hands around her mouth. "We're here! What did you want to show us?"

Talon rolled her eyes. "We didn't even want to try for subtlety?"

"We don't have all day!" Sorrel called. "There's a war to fight, in case you didn't notice."

Vola tapped her foot and looked around at the bare lava rock.

Nothing. No wisps of fog or shadowy illusions. No ethereal figures ready to take them into the depths of Anders's mind.

Rilla raised an eyebrow. "I suppose it was worth a try," she said.

"So, what do we do?" Talon said. "Just wander around the edge until we find it?"

Vola noticed Lillie hadn't said anything in a bit, and she turned to find the wizard with one hand raised toward the barrier, the other holding a notebook.

"Lillie?"

She closed her fist. "Sorry, just taking some readings for the scholars." She jotted something down with her pencil. "What were we up to?"

"Do we just wander around until we find Anders's illusion? Or is there a way we can force his hand somehow?"

Lillie blinked and peered up and down the barrier. "I imagine we just wander. I don't have nearly enough information to force his hand yet. And I want to play by his rules a little longer to get more data we can use against him."

"Wander it is," Sorrel said, thrusting her fist in the air. "North or south?"

"I vote north," Rilla said. "That seems intuitive to me."

"North," Lillie said, absently.

Vola glanced at Talon.

"I literally don't care," Talon said. "Just so long as someone picks one."

"North then," Vola said.

They traveled along the edge of the barrier, taking care to keep far enough away that no one accidentally stumbled into it. Lillie had re-summoned Rand when they'd gotten to camp the night before, but he'd ruffled his feathers and shuddered as if he remembered what had happened when he'd disintegrated.

The wizard had had to bribe him with cheese and bits of sausage before he would hop back on her shoulder and clack his beak in her ear the way he did when he was feeling affectionate.

Now he flew above, monitoring their surroundings, but also steering well clear of the barrier.

"You know, if Anders is so into illusions, he could at least provide some more interesting scenery," Sorrel said as they trudged along. "I think I'm gonna die of boredom before anything else manages to kill me."

They had been walking for nearly an hour already with no

sign of Anders's next illusion. And the barrier still encompassed a massive amount of space.

A shadow flickered beyond the shimmering opaque surface, and Vola hesitated. "What was that?"

"What was what?" Lillie said.

"I thought I saw something."

Sorrel reached for her staff, but Lillie looked blank.

"Was I the only one to see it?"

"You aren't the only one," Talon said. "Something's moving around back there. I'm just not sure what."

Vola stared hard at the surface, but everything seemed still now.

"Whatever it is, didn't seem very fast," Talon said. "Just very deliberate."

"I don't think that word is as reassuring as you meant it to be," Rilla said.

"Who says I meant to be reassuring?"

"Heads up," Sorrel said.

Wisps and bits of fog crawled out of the ground at their feet, gathering together into now-familiar figures.

"Well, I mean, this is what we wanted, isn't it?" Lillie said as the gray sky and black earth around them dissolved into an entirely new landscape.

Sawdust shifted under Vola's feet, cushioning them almost like the real thing, and light shone from mirrors set along the edges of a wide, open room. The late afternoon sun poured through high windows, illuminating racks of weapons lined up between mirrors.

Vola raised her eyebrows. She'd gone to one of the more prestigious paladin academies on the continent and their practice ring was only a little nicer than this.

Lillie immediately began muttering, her hands glowing with

magic, and Vola assumed she was digging into the spell surrounding them.

Scarred fighters in worn leathers lounged around the room, watching the boy standing in the middle of the ring. His black hair had grown and now hung in his eyes. He'd shot up a few inches, the way teenagers often did, and he sported a fading black eye.

He faced the older mercenary they'd seen at the end of the last illusion, a dark man with short gray hair cropped close to his head.

"Pick up your sword," the mercenary said, gesturing to the blade on the ground at Anders's feet.

"No," Anders said, his brow lowering. "I wanted to learn magic, Master Johnson."

"You wanted to learn to defend yourself," Johnson said.

"Why can't I do it with magic? Everyone has magic. Everyone in the whole wide world. Rangers, and bards, and berserkers, and even paladins. They all get little spells here and there. Why do I just have a sword?"

The man met Anders's eyes squarely. "Everyone is born with a little magic, yes. Enough to connect us with the world. But it is one of life's greatest injustices that some are born with less than others."

"Can't I just learn more magic?"

"Some can," the man said.

Anders's shoulders drooped. "And some can't."

"You can spend years beating your head against that wall until you're bloody. Or you can pick up your sword."

Anders grimaced and knelt to grasp the blade.

"Why do you want magic so bad?" Johnson asked as he stood.

"It's closest to what the gods have. That divine power that can change the world. If I had that, I'd be able to do anything. No one would ever have to die again."

The man pointed his finger at Anders's face. "Magic is a tool, no more special than that blade. If you learn to use that, you'll be as powerful as any spell-caster. Now. Defend yourself."

The other fighters around the ring straightened up and closed in.

"Now?" Sorrel said, keeping her eyes on the fighters.

"Now," Lillie said, dropping her spell.

They sprang forward.

The boy, Anders, had clearly learned some things in his time with the mercenary already. He defended himself well enough to hold off two of the attackers, but Vola cut in and took down the closest one, who wielded a heavy mace.

Step and slash, shield up to block the blow, cut under, and step again.

Anders almost seemed to mirror her, as if echoing her earliest lessons. If this mercenary was half the teacher Henri was, Anders had been in good hands.

Sorrel hurtled by, staff swinging in an arc. Rilla ducked in behind Vola, guarding her back before reaching to slash another attacker.

Vola assumed this illusion was like the last one and they just had to finish the fight to break its hold on them and on the barrier. She counted as she fought.

"Six. Seven. Eight."

"Nine, ten!" Rilla said, taking down the last illusory fighter.

"Hmm," Sorrel said, gazing around as if disappointed. "These guys weren't very exciting."

"It was just a practice bout," Talon said. "I don't think it was supposed to be exciting. It was supposed to prove a point."

Sure enough, the man stepped up to Anders, where he stood panting. "Learn to use this," he said, lifting the tip of Anders's sword from the sawdust. "And you can defend anyone from anything."

"Aw, that's sweet," Sorrel said as the illusion dissolved around them. "But when you use it to become a bad guy, that's when you get people like us coming after you."

Vola blinked to clear her vision, but the world still blurred.

"Shh," Talon said. "I'll bet he'll make us watch that part next. Don't spoil the end—"

Vola gasped as a shape lunged from the shifting colors and latched onto Talon.

"Oh, shit," Sorrel said and whacked at the shape. But then a wall of bodies came at her, and she had to swing her staff around to defend herself.

Vola spun, sword ready, and caught a grayish figure on her shield. The edges of everything still fuzzed, but her reflexes saved her and she shoved the shape away.

A snarl ripped through the air, and Gruff flung himself on Talon's attacker to help her struggle free. She pushed the figure away and its arm came off in her hand. She stared at it for a moment.

"Zombies," she said and spat.

"They're everywhere," Vola said, using her shield to thrust the line of undead back. "They must have been waiting for us." Those were the shadows she'd been seeing through the barrier.

"I knew the arrogant pig would use his ego to trap us," Sorrel cried.

"Is this Anders's army?" Talon asked. She slashed with her daggers, cutting down the zombies ahead of her, forming a little wall the rest had to climb over. "You said he was moving troops around."

"I sure hope not," Rilla said, grimly. "Otherwise, we're screwed."

Army or not, they were pinned on all sides. The lava field was mostly an open plain, but Vola couldn't see past the wall of dead soldiers.

She concentrated on her sword, her grip creaking against the leather-wrapped hilt, and the blade burst into flames. Fire licked up the edge, reflecting in the zombie's eyes.

She swept it out in an arc, setting three undead on fire with one blow.

"Shield your eyes," Lillie said. She stepped back into the center of the circle they'd made and raised her hands.

"Oh, shi—" Vola flung her arm over her head just as Lillie's fist burst into flame and she punched the ground.

A wave of heat blasted out, and flames licked past Vola's ears.

The fireball swept around them, leaving them untouched but knocking over three ranks of zombies. The next wave fell over their brethren and writhed.

Sorrel straightened up and wiped her brow. "Hey look. Breathing room."

Rilla patted herself down and seemed surprised to find herself in one piece. "Angels, demons, and all the pantheon warn a body next time."

"I did warn you."

"I mean warn me that you can do something like that."

"Oh, yeah," Vola said. "Lillie can pocket some of her more explosive spells. By the way."

"Thanks, so much."

"Guys, this bought us time, but there's still a *horde of undead* between us and the rest of our army," Talon said. She still stood alert, Gruff beside her, ears pricked forward, his lip raised to reveal teeth.

She was right. The zombie horde was already picking itself up and climbing over the crisped corpses in their way.

"Lillie, can you port us out of here?"

She shook her head. "I have to be able to see where I'm going and all I can see is zombies. And the camp's too far. Rand, go for help," Lillie called to the familiar, who circled above them. The bird croaked and wheeled away toward camp.

"Looks like Anders learned a few tricks from Myron as well," Sorrel said. "He is still in custody, isn't he?"

"Last I checked," Rilla said.

"Okay, we need to pick a direction," Vola said. "Camp is that way. Theoretically, there should be fewer zombies between us and it, so we can try to punch through."

"Great," Sorrel said. "I always wanted to die fighting dead guys."

"We're not gonna die—"

"Less talking, more punching!"

And the horde was on them. Vola didn't have much of a choice except to protect herself and her team. But the enemy was endless, or at least what they could see of it, and she gave them about ten minutes before they were overwhelmed.

A screeching cry rang out across the sky, drawing their gazes up.

A giant shape blotted out the hazy sun and dove earthward. The great eagle fell on the undead, ripping and clawing a path through the horde before sweeping back up to the sky once more.

There in the space he'd created, a tall, slim figure in blue strummed a lute. The zombies in earshot went slack and fell to their knees. The simple little melody finally reached Vola's ears. A bawdy tavern song twisted into a soothing lullaby.

"I can only hold this for so long," the figure sang out in a melodious voice. "Shall we get the hell out? Or wait until I keel over from hoarseness."

The zombies lying at their feet began snoring.

"What the actual fuck?" Rilla said.

Vola just laughed.

ELEVEN

Vola and the others surged forward to meet the bard while the eagle covered their retreat.

"The day you stop talking is the day I hang up my shield for good," Vola said with a relieved chuckle.

The bard kept up the soothing melody, plucking out the notes on his lute. He wore a blue-dyed leather tunic and black pants that left little to the imagination and he'd look like a complete fop if it weren't for the rapier hanging from his waist.

"Well, then," he said with a charming grin. "What a happy little reunion. But that's funny, I don't hear any gratitude."

"Thank you, Cyrano," Lillie said and darted in to give him a peck on his cheek.

Cyrano took a break from strumming to clutch his heart. "Oh, adoration from beautiful women is the best thanks I could hope for."

The eagle shrieked above them.

"But of course, I won't accept it because I have all the love I need," the bard said loud enough for the eagle to hear.

"Rilla, I don't think you ever met Cyrano and Raven," Vola

said, gesturing between the bard and the eagle. "The friends who helped us defeat Inga."

"How do you do? And let's get the hell out of here," Rilla said. "How long will your sleep hold?"

"I like a woman who knows her own mind. About thirty more seconds and then we're on our own."

"Right," Vola said. "And how many more times can you do it?"

"Maybe once. It doesn't always work though. I got lucky this time."

"Then draw your blade. Lillie, I want as much fire as you can make in a line going that way." Vola pointed toward the army camp. "Sorrel and Raven, go in under cover of the flames and keep the area clear for the rest to advance. Rilla and Cyrano, protect our backs. Talon and I will keep Lillie moving forward. Go."

They weren't exactly an army. But they also weren't completely useless. Zombies didn't last long between Lillie's fire and the rest of them working in concert.

Even a horde of moaning undead was smart enough to recognize a formidable threat, and by the time they popped out of the mass of bodies, the undead army had begun shuffling back, disengaging from the fight.

Mishap's Heroes stood on a bare bit of lava rock and panted as the giant eagle swooped down and landed. His outline shifted and flowed until a young man stood before them, brown hair a bit long around his ears, all sharp elbows and knees, and a pointed chin. Not to mention he was completely naked.

Cyrano pulled a silk robe from the pack on his back and handed it to Raven. Then he stood between them and the shapeshifter to block their view.

"Eyes off," he said. "I'm the only one who gets to stare."

Vola rolled her eyes.

Raven held out his arm, draped in a blue and silver fabric that shimmered. "Silk?" he said. "On a battlefield? Really, Cyrano…"

"It was the only blue I could find, and silk packs down really small."

The gray clouds above seemed to press down on them and Vola squinted up, wondering if it would rain.

"Thanks for the rescue," she said. "It was timely. But what are you doing out here?"

"We came to join your army, of course," Cyrano said. "But when we got there, some princess pressed us into immediate service as scouts."

Rilla rubbed a smile from her lips, and Vola could imagine her telling War about the "some princess" comment later.

"She told us to find Mishap's Heroes and lend you support. Apparently, you're supposed to be dealing with this barrier thing."

Vola glanced over. She hadn't noticed it before while fighting zombies, but sure enough, the barrier had retreated after they'd dealt with the illusions.

Lillie's familiar drifted down from the clouds to land on Raven's outstretched arm. "Rand here led us to where you were," Cyrano said.

"I'm glad he's working out for you," Raven said as the familiar clacked his beak.

"Yeah, we've only killed him the once," Sorrel said.

Vola cleared her throat.

"Why did War think we needed support?" Rilla asked, eyes narrowing. "We hadn't discussed sending reinforcements before we left."

Cyrano and Raven exchanged a look. "There have been some…developments since you left apparently," Cyrano said.

"Spit it out," Vola said. The bard could dance his way around meaning for ages if they let him.

"Lord Arthorel escaped from prison," Raven said flatly. "She said that would mean something to you."

"Geez," Vola said and rubbed her forehead.

"Escaped?" Sorrel said. "That weasel? I would have expected him to stay put, considering they fed him and gave him clothes and a place to sleep. All he has to look forward to outside is being broke."

"Not to mention being an escaped convict," Talon said.

"That won't mean much," Lillie said, a stubborn set to her lips. "He's nobility. He believes he was entitled to sell those people. They were his tenants, and they belonged to him."

"And there will be plenty of others in Southglen who agree," Rilla said. "We didn't root out every malcontent in the coup last year."

"Still, Arthorel was an illusionist," Vola said. "How did he escape?"

Cyrano held a hand out, palm up. "He had help. They're not sure who or how, but he didn't break out alone. But who was this guy?"

"One of Anders's lackeys," Vola said, waving to the mountain barely visible past the undulating barrier. "You know how Inga was sending people to Anders?"

"Yeah. Brainwashed them so they'd be docile as he drained their magic, or so we assumed."

"Same thing. Lord Arthorel was broke and sold off the bandits and villagers on his lands."

Sorrel kicked a loose piece of lava rock so it went clattering away over the ruined plains.

"And now he's out," Lillie said, golden brows drawing down. "Free to do it all again."

"And that's not the last of the news," Raven said. "Someone went after Myron Vidal as well, right in the middle of the camp."

"What?" Rilla said, straightening.

"They tried to abduct him."

"Tried?" Vola said.

"Yeah, some knight named Henri and his student stopped them. Unfortunately, there wasn't a lot left to question after they were done, even for a necromancer. Myron himself doesn't know anything, at least as far as War can tell."

"Knowing Myron, he really doesn't," Vola said. "He was never that interested in being evil. Even if he is a necromancer."

"We are going to have a little chat about Anders and his undead army, though," Rilla said. "If I find out he's been moonlighting for Anders on the side…"

Lillie shook her head. "He's not."

"How do you know?"

"Who else would try to abduct him? It has to be Anders. He helped Lord Arthorel escape from prison, and he's trying to bring Myron back, but Myron chose our side. And luckily we have the people who can enforce his decision for him."

"Why would Anders be trying to bring them back?" Talon said. "He already has their illusion magic and the power to raise an undead army."

"Maybe he needs more," Lillie said quietly.

"Or maybe he just wants his old gang back together," Sorrel said.

"Whatever it is, he'll want the others back as well," Vola said. Then she exchanged a smile with Sorrel, Lillie, and Talon.

"What?" Cyrano said.

"Well, he'll have a hard time with that. Lillie's brothers are serving out their exile in another plane, Inga's dead, and Nargilla is being held by the gods."

"We were there for one of those," Cyrano said. "And I find myself perturbed by the fact that it sounds like the least exciting story in the bunch."

"Lesson one," Rilla said, holding up a finger. "Don't piss off Mishap's Heroes."

TWELVE

By the time they returned to the War Princess, she stood at the head of a column of warriors with her arms crossed and her toe tapping.

"About time," she said, as they finally came into view. "I assume the way is clear?"

"If by clear you mean there's an army of undead between you and your goal, then yeah, sure," Sorrel said with a shrug.

War's face froze before she finally glanced at the sky as if asking for patience. "Say again?"

"We cleared the illusion, and the barrier pulled back again as we expected," Vola reported. "But the risen dead ambushed us. There're hundreds of them, maybe thousands between us and the barrier now."

War set her mouth in a thin line and raised her hand to signal her commanders. "Move out, slow march. Let's make this slow and steady, people. Lancers ahead. Archers mid-ranks."

"You're just going in?" Lillie asked, brows raised. "Even with—"

"An army of undead?" War said and chuckled. "You forget.

We're an army, too. Why do you think I bothered to bring them? Besides, I don't want to wait and give Anders another chance to steal back Myron. He's already got Lord Arthorel."

Vola winced and didn't argue.

They marched at the head of an army with a War Princess looking for a fight. Mishap's Heroes had already seen action this campaign. Now it was everyone else's turn.

Vola and the others led them across the lava field on a direct line to the barrier. The sun rode low in the sky behind the flat gray clouds, but they should have been able to reach it in a couple of hours of steady marching.

However, only an hour in, a rumbling under their feet interrupted them. The calvary's horses danced and bucked, and War reined her mount in with a firm hand.

Vola glanced at Sorrel and Talon and Lillie.

"Uh oh," Sorrel said.

Talon stepped forward and touched her fingertips to the ground.

"What is it?" War said, hand raised, ready to signal her commanders.

"Brace yourselves," Vola said. "Here come the dead."

Cyrano drew his rapier, and Raven morphed into his great eagle shape.

"Where?" War said, whipping around, trying to pinpoint the source and completely failing.

"Look down," Talon said. Just then the rock at her feet crumbled and mounded until a ragged head popped through the surface to look around.

Talon took the zombie's head off its shoulders before it had a chance to get its bearings.

"First division," War called. "Forward. Second division, hold the line." Then she leaped down from her horse and caught the next zombie to emerge with a kick to the head.

Undead erupted from the ground all around them. Long gangly figures held together by stringy tendons and half-rotted muscle moaned and lunged for the living that they could reach.

Raven dove from above, knocking a head off. Cyrano caught it on instinct.

"Whoa, ugly." He batted it away.

Vola caught it with the flat of her sword, and it burst into flames as it flew off into a line of undead. It exploded on impact, showering the advancing dead with bits of burning zombie.

"Vola wins that round," Sorrel called.

"It's not a competition," Vola said, blocking another zombie that lurched for Lillie. "Just stay alive."

"Stay alive and look as cool as possible," Talon said.

"Well, I can play that game," War said and uttered a blood-curdling war cry as she raced for a clump of zombies over-whelming Rilla. Her greatsword swung in an arc over her head and she spun, her blade a blur.

The zombies all froze, as if in surprise. Then, one by one, their torsos tumbled to the ground, leaving their legs standing free for a moment longer.

"Hey," Rilla said. "It's my job to protect you."

War raised her eyebrows. "You're welcome," she said.

"All right, the Princess of War is in the running," Sorrel said.

"What did you expect?" War said.

"It's. Not. A. Competition," Vola yelled. "Sorrel, watch your back."

"I can multitask." Sorrel knocked three zombies off their feet so she could bash their skulls in. They each popped with an alarming squish. "Ew."

Rilla glanced around the battlefield and heaved a huge sigh. Then she darted back through the ranks of the army.

"What the—Rilla?" Vola called.

Moments later the Princess of the Dagger Throne pushed

through the lancers, keeping the horde at bay, dragging a figure in a long, stained robe.

"Fix this," Rilla said and shoved Myron forward. "Anders learned this from you."

Myron grumbled. "I was just in the middle of some very delicate experiments. I knew I should never have agreed to travel with an army."

"Experiments in the middle of battle?" Vola said. She spun to keep a zombie from creeping up on the necromancer.

"Of course." He surveyed the fight before him. "What an inefficient way to solve a problem."

"Do you have a better one?" Vola said.

"Probably." He tilted his head, eyes unfocused. "Sloppy work. Anders might have an awe-inspiring amount of power but he's only just learning how to use it."

Myron waved his hand over the field as if blessing it, and suddenly, all the dead fell, like puppets with their strings cut.

"You just had to ask. You didn't have to drag," he huffed at Rilla and then turned on his heel to push back through the ranks.

The fighters stopped, glancing around in confusion while the enemy went from undead to very dead.

"Of course," War said flatly. "We travel with a reformed necromancer. Why didn't I think of that?"

"Your strength is meeting an army head-on," Rilla told her. "Mine is avoiding direct confrontation."

War scowled and kicked the nearest corpse. "This was hardly an army. Barely even a division."

"That's probably why Myron was able to manage the whole field," Lillie said. "That and Anders's inexperience."

"You said there were thousands. So where are the rest of them?" War asked, swiping a hand across her brow. The sun hid behind clouds, but it made the light a flat featureless spike in their eyes.

"This must have been a graveyard once," Talon said, kicking at the crumbled lava rock. "Before the mountain exploded. And Anders used the dead to slow us down."

"We'll find the rest of the horde at the barrier, I expect," Vola said. "Or beyond it. They may be able to pass through freely while it kills those of us who try to get through."

"Hmm," War said. "Then we'd better leave this little distraction behind as quickly as possible."

She swung back on her horse, and ignoring the dead strewn in her way, she urged it forward.

Another rumble shook the ground underfoot.

"Now what?" War snapped.

Ahead of them, the lava rock fell away abruptly, like a vast canyon opening at their feet. War's horse reared and danced back in alarm. Corpses rolled over the edge and plummeted hundreds of feet before going splat.

Vola and Talon leaped back, dragging Rilla and Sorrel with them.

The rumble died away, leaving nothing but a jagged cliff of lava rock and empty air between them and the barrier.

"What. The. Hell?" Rilla said.

Vola crept forward again to examine the sudden cliff. The ground dropped off like a giant cook had taken a cleaver to it. Far, far below, Vola could make out the splattered remains of some of the undead they'd just fought. She raised her head and squinted, but couldn't make out the other side. Only the barrier shimmering in the distance.

"Lillie," Vola called. "He knows illusions now. Is this real? Or just a trick?"

Lillie pulled her hands apart and started delicately sifting through the air as if pulling a set of fine strings. "This is…definitely not an illusion." She blanched. "It's real."

"All right, so which of his lieutenants did he learn that from then?" Rilla said.

Vola shook her head. This wasn't illusions or necromancy. It wasn't the power of the Thrones of Southglen or mind control. What kind of magic could change the landscape itself?

"I think this is something from the gods," Vola said. "He still has some of the power he stole from the Broken."

War rubbed her face. "What does he think he's doing? You can't just rearrange the world any time you want. There will be consequences."

"Maybe he's not ready to fight us yet," Talon said. "This is another delay."

"Not ready—" War said, then looked like she bit her tongue. "This is war. Not a first date. He's had plenty of time to primp in front of the mirror if he wanted."

War reined her horse around. "Find a way over," she said, speaking to Vola and Rilla. "I don't care how. I have to go come up with contingency plans. And find a place to camp tonight if we can't make it across."

She withdrew to the front ranks of her army to consult with her commanders, leaving Mishap's Heroes at the edge of the canyon with Cyrano and Raven.

They all stared to the south. Then they all stared to the north. The canyon stretched as far as they could see in both directions.

"Well," Sorrel said, fists planted on her slim hips. "What now?"

Vola blew out her breath. "We find a way across."

"Can we climb down?" Lillie said.

Sorrel stepped up to the edge and frowned down. "Talon and I might be able to manage without breaking our necks, but it's very smooth. We'd have to use ropes. And even then, we'd have to get the whole army down the cliff. Mounts, pack animals, and wagons alike."

"And then, once down there, we'd be stuck," Rilla said. "No way up."

"I don't like it," Talon said. "If he can just rearrange the landscape anytime he likes, what's to stop him from swallowing us up into the ground."

Cyrano stared at her. "What a bright and cheerful thought," he said. "I'm so glad you shared with the rest of us."

"I figured if I had to suffer, the rest of you should, too," Talon said.

"Okay, so we're agreed. We don't want to go down," Vola said. "And there isn't going to be a bridge across, nor any way to make one that wide. So how do we get to the other side? Magic?"

Lillie shook her head. "Even if we get all the battlemages and university scholars on board, we wouldn't be able to do it. We have to be able to see where we're going to teleport. Or know the area well enough from memory."

Vola sighed. No physical way across. No magic. That really only left one option.

"My lady," Vola said quietly. The others heard her anyway and went silent.

The Broken coalesced out of the air at her shoulder, wearing her Cleavah aspect, all tumbling curls and dark golden skin.

"I see," the Broken said without preamble. She stared at the chasm, her lips pulled tight in thought. "Well, that's unsettling."

"Don't say that," Cyrano said. "Geez, she's as bad as you." He jerked a shoulder at Talon. Talon glared.

The Broken raised a dark eyebrow. "Because I feel the need to share my distress? Burdens are lighter when they're passed around." She winked at Talon.

Cyrano gulped as Raven morphed out of his giant eagle shape beside him. "You were listening."

"Rule number two," she said, gesturing to Rilla. "Always assume someone is listening."

"I like her," Rilla said. "Have I mentioned that I like her yet?"

"Yeah, Vola has the best goddess," Sorrel said.

"Careful," Lillie said. "That's the sort of comment that starts divine wars."

"Can you help?" Vola asked Cleavah, gesturing across the wide expanse.

She heaved a sigh. "I could…"

"But?"

The Broken gave her a rueful look.

"But the others wouldn't like it," Vola said for her. "They still don't think the gods should be involved."

Rilla glanced between them. "So this is political."

"It's political," the Broken said. "Imagine you knew something had to be done, but all your fellow princesses thought they were already doing enough. How would they feel if you went and promised another country troops and supplies and began feeding them inside information?"

"I'd be hung as a traitor," Rilla said flatly.

"Exactly," the Broken said.

"Then let me do it," a different voice said.

Vola wasn't the only one who jumped, even though they stood at the edge of a cliff. The deep, insidious voice was very familiar, but she'd only heard it outside of her head once before.

Vola whipped around to find another god standing between their little group and the rest of the army. Round, bloodshot eyes stared back at them.

"Who…?" Rilla said, obviously trying to figure out how this man had gotten behind her.

"Mulgash," Vola said. "Greater Obstacle of Rage."

"Thank you, my dear," Mulgash said, tilting his head.

"Ho, boy," Sorrel said.

Cyrano growled and took a deliberate step to place himself in front of Raven.

Mulgash's dark eyebrows twitched. "You needn't worry. I have no need for a familiar. And I have no need for Inga anymore, who was the one who wanted one."

"Great," Raven said over Cyrano's shoulder. "Then you won't mind if I stay over here, while you stay over there."

Mulgash's lips curled. "As if distance mattered."

Raven looked as if he might have flung himself off the cliff and changed on the way down if it weren't for the way Mulgash turned away from him, dismissing him as inconsequential.

"What are you offering?" the Broken asked.

"I'm not bound by our fellow gods' prejudices or strictures. I believe in your cause. I could help without the hindrances you experience personally."

Vola's eyes narrowed. "Why would you want to?"

He put a hand on his chest. "Just because we've been on opposite sides before doesn't mean we don't have the same interests at heart now."

"Do you even have a heart?" Talon muttered.

Vola cleared her throat over her. "Inga was working for Anders. And you were using her. Seems like you might still be wrapped up in all of it."

"Like you said. I was using Inga. What she did with my power was her business. But the moment this Anders started thinking he could take what belongs to me, that's when things changed."

Vola glanced at the Broken, but she didn't look angry or implacable. She looked calculating.

"I have no intentions of sharing my power with a mortal I didn't choose," Mulgash said, hand slashing through the air. "And since this is a problem for all of us—" he turned the gesture into a wave between himself and the Broken. "Then it seems like we should work together to get rid of it. Before we can't any longer."

Vola exchanged a look with the Broken.

"Do you trust him?" Rilla asked, not even bothering to lower her voice.

"No!" Cyrano said. "He helped Inga capture Raven and enslave him."

"Not to mention us and a whole bunch of innocent villagers," Sorrel said, eyes narrow and cold.

It was so similar to the look she'd had when Mulgash had taken over their minds. Vola had fought them in order to get her friends back to their normal selves. It wasn't something she ever wanted to see again, even in memory.

But…Mulgash was right. This was a problem for all the gods, not just the ones she liked. It was what she and the Broken had been trying to convince them of this whole time.

The Broken still looked at her. The goddess might have been the guiding wisdom for Vola, but Vola was the one who'd been hurt directly by the Obstacle in front of them.

Still, she was a paladin. She'd spent her whole life trying not to give in to the Greater Obstacle of Rage. What kind of holy warrior would she be if she gave that up now?

"Fine," she said.

There was a unified intake of breath behind her.

"You're going to trust him?" Talon said.

"No," Vola said, eyes locked with Mulgash. "I am going to use him, though."

Mulgash's lips stretched in a proud smile. "That's my girl."

"I don't belong to you," Vola said. "I'm spoken for already."

The Broken didn't say anything, just chuckled deep in her throat.

Mulgash shrugged. "Fair enough." And he stepped to the edge of the cliff.

The others moved to make room for him, giving him a wide berth, Cyrano and Raven especially. Rilla was the only one to remain a little closer, watching his movements carefully.

Sorrel and Talon looked between Vola and Mulgash, each with their own expression of confusion and doubt. Vola kept waiting for them to ask "what are you thinking?"

Instead, Lillie leveled a rueful smile at them. "I don't know why you're surprised," she said. "This is the same woman who forgave Ella for all those hurtful things she said when they were children. Even though Ella didn't deserve it."

Vola winced. That was different. Vola had needed to forgive the girl she'd grown up with. Without that hate, she was finally free to forget about all the hurt. It was more for Vola's sake than for Ella's.

"I'm not forgiving, Mulgash," she said, instead of arguing. "I'm just recognizing this is bigger than our differences. As soon as Anders is gone, we'll go back to hating each other, I'm sure."

Lillie stepped up to her and tucked her hand into the crook of Vola's elbow. "Sure you will."

Vola frowned at her. "Why do you say it like that?"

"Because I'm not sure you actually know how to hate. You've spent your whole life fighting against others who see you as violent and aggressive. You only know how to be gentle."

"I carry a sword and bash people in the face when they make me angry. Gentle is definitely the wrong word."

Lillie just smiled to herself and turned away.

Another rumble made them turn back to Mulgash, who knelt at the edge of the cliff. He had his hands buried in the lava rock as if it were thin mud and the muscles in his arms strained. Little bits of rock danced across the ground, their clatter completely lost in the all-encompassing grumble from the land itself.

War ran back to them at a dead sprint and skidded to a stop, sending a cascade of stones over the edge of the cliff.

Cyrano watched, his jaw set so hard his lips had gone white. Raven stared at the ground.

The chasm that had dropped out from under them now rose,

like sea water pulled by the inevitable tide. Land surged back into place, lining up with the ridge where they stood.

The ground shuddered so badly, several of them staggered and fell to their hands and knees. Vola stumbled and planted her feet wider, putting a hand under Lillie's arm to keep her upright.

Behind them, the army murmured and clanked as soldiers tried to keep their feet.

The rumbling stopped, and the land fell still, though Vola could still feel a buzz under her boots.

The lava field stretched ahead of them exactly as it had been, and they had a clear shot to the barrier.

Mulgash stood and dusted his hands off. "There. If he wants to play with a god's power, he can play with some real gods as well." He shot a glance over his shoulder at Vola and War. "Do let me know if you need anything else, Vola dear. You have only to ask."

He disappeared into thin air in a shower of black and purple sparks.

"Do I want to know who that was?" War asked.

Vola winced. "Probably not."

THIRTEEN

The army camped close enough to the barrier that its undulating light and colors lit up the canvas tents that night.

Talon was off, setting up their campsite and making sure the swamp monster didn't eat any more pack animals. The camp hostlers had threatened mutiny if it did. Rilla was closeted with War, planning the next day's push. And Lillie had disappeared to work the last few hours of the day with the scholars.

Vola and Sorrel had a rare moment to walk together and check on the different factions Sorrel had settled. The monks and the battlemages seemed resigned to living in peace with each other finally. Vola wondered if it had something to do with each group being close enough to see the others fight.

They definitely caught Hazel asking the leader of the battle mages for tips on avoiding magical attacks, and the leader responding politely to ask for some physical exercises that would increase his mages' speed in their heavy armor.

"Did you do that on purpose?" Vola asked under her breath as they left the two groups to their polite discussion.

"Do what?" Sorrel said with a grin.

Vola just shook her head.

Several more groups had joined the army as they marched through the lava field. Vola caught sight of a contingent camped under the Mistvale flag, and she suspected the large force of graceful elves in matching leather had been sent by Selene.

But there were also other smaller groups, villagers from towns and hamlets she recognized. Three spaces down the row, Cyrano helped a group of halflings from the village they'd saved from Inga. Sorrel trotted over to say hi to Sandry, who had grown much more proficient with the staff she carried. Sorrel had given her some preliminary lessons, but apparently the girl had taken them seriously and found another teacher to continue the lessons.

Vola half expected to turn a corner and find her parents, but so far she seemed to be the only orc in the camp.

She drifted toward the other side of the row and caught a familiar redhead with broad shoulders. He wore a set of practical leathers and carried a sword strapped to his back.

"Braydon?" Vola said.

The man looked up and gave her a friendly smile. "Volagra Lightbringer," he said. "It's been a while."

"It has," Vola said, not bothering to correct him on her name. She didn't really feel the need to get into it with a man she'd counted as a rival once. Though they'd managed to settle their differences. Really, they'd just had to save Braydon and his team over and over again until he'd finally admitted that maybe she wasn't a monster and was actually pretty good at what she did.

"I haven't seen you since Water's Edge," Vola said. It was the town where Vola had first met the others.

"Yeah. We got word that Mishap's Heroes was calling for help. After you saved most everybody in the village, it wasn't hard to convince some of them to come with me to fight. I even brought my old team. Had to drag Obron out of retirement."

All Vola remembered of Obron was a wizard swinging from a

tree by his ankles, his robe around his ears. And it was more than she wanted to remember about the old man, if she was honest.

"That's great. Do you need anything?"

"He doesn't need anything from a black paladin," a voice said. Another figure joined Braydon, a tall, slim woman who carried two swords. Vola vaguely recognized her as one of Braydon's people. In fact, she'd gifted Vola with the hand axes that hung from her belt even now.

"Hey," Braydon said. "What are you talking about? That's our savior, remember?"

"You haven't heard? It's all over camp. This is Volagra Lightless. The black paladin."

Braydon opened his mouth as if to refute her claim, but his eyes flicked to Vola.

She steeled herself. "I don't make it a secret," she said and turned so her blackened shield caught the torch light.

"Oh," Braydon said, voice going low and flat.

"She lost her shield, Braydon," the woman said, turned so she could talk in his ear. "And they say she consorts with the Obstacles."

"Now where did you hear that?" Sorrel asked, coming up next to Vola.

"Does it matter?" the woman said. "It's true, isn't it? She's changed since she helped us."

"Yeah," Sorrel snapped. "She represents the Broken, now. That's why War trusts her."

Braydon blinked and his mouth fell open.

Sorrel yanked on Vola's arm and hauled her away down the row of tents and campsites before he could say whatever he was thinking.

Whispers followed them. Sideways looks and wards against evil. Vola tried to convince herself she was imagining it, but Sorrel's eyes flicked toward the looks, too. People she knew.

Soldiers she'd talked to and joked with the day before stepped back and dropped their eyes as she passed. The cook's gaze locked on her blackened shield. And for the first time in a long time, Vola considered hiding it.

"This is Imralen's doing, isn't it?" Vola said. Even with her long legs, she had a hard time keeping up with Sorrel's determined pace. "Gods, why didn't I think of that before? He's doing exactly what he said he would do. He's making everyone see what I really am."

Sorrel stopped. "And what are you?" she said. "A paladin who was wrongly accused? A paladin who is doing everything she can to keep the world safe? A paladin who managed to convince a Greater Obstacle into helping people? Let them see all of that." She flung her arms out to encompass the entire camp. "Let them see who and what you really are, Vola. The things Imralen says about you behind your back aren't true." She poked Vola hard in the gut. It was as high as she could reach. "You know that. I know that. Lillie and Talon and Rilla and War know that. That's. All. That. Matters." She punctuated each word with a poke.

"Ow, your fingers are like little daggers."

"Let them see you, Vola," Sorrel said again. "And they'll be as proud of you as we are." The monk spun around on her heel and strode toward the center of camp where the command tent had been pitched.

Vola hesitated, feeling the looks burning into the back of her neck. It was the same. It felt exactly the same as it had her whole life. Walking down the street and hearing the whispers of "orc," "monster," and "obstacle-worshiper." Enduring the insults and the hazing while she'd been in training. Seeing the disbelief when anyone saw her shield and realized she wasn't just a paladin, she was an orc paladin.

She'd felt this her whole life, and she'd dealt with it for just as long.

What did she always do? She took a deep breath and kept going. She kept her shield up. She treated the people who insulted her with politeness—if not kindness—and she kept fighting for the weak and the oppressed. She kept doing what she'd been chosen to do, trusting that eventually it would pay off. Eventually, people would see her. The way she really was.

She trotted to catch up to Sorrel. "How is it I always forget that you're wiser than all of us combined?"

Sorrel rolled her eyes. "I work very hard to cover it up. Do you think it's easy to be this perky all the time?" She flapped her hands over her head.

Vola ignored her antics and leveled a gaze at her. "Thanks," she said.

Sorrel shrugged. "I'm your second, right? First job for a second in command is to support their leader. Whether that means doing what they say or making sure they're strong enough to give the orders."

They were close enough to the command tent now that Rilla must have heard their voices through the canvas. She poked her head through the flap.

"What's wrong now?"

"Nothing," Vola said as Sorrel slipped inside the tent.

"Imralen's just making Vola's life difficult," she said. "Which we knew he would. So we're not letting him get to us." She gave Vola a significant look.

"I don't know what that man's bitching about," War said, bent over her map table. "It's not like you're even in charge of anything. I decide when we move, where we go. And if I choose to do that based on your opinion, what does it matter to him?"

"He thinks I'll corrupt you," Vola said, willing to see the humor in it.

"Even if you do work with Obstacles, which isn't a bad thing in this war, they're not evil. They'll make us stronger."

Vola hadn't realized War was one of those who believed the Obstacles were a blessing, but then, she was the princess of the War Throne.

"You could just ask the Broken to manifest," Sorrel said, hopping up onto a pile of crates in the corner. "That would shut him right up."

"No," Vola said but didn't elaborate. She didn't know how to explain the surge of panic that thought brought her. The Broken had chosen her to be the one who fought for the weak and broken. So maybe it was as simple as she didn't want the goddess to feel like she'd chosen wrong. After all, in this instance, Vola was the one who was broken. And who would fight for her if she wasn't strong enough to fight for herself?

Her gaze went to Sorrel, who swiped an apple from one of the crates and examined its surface before she bit into it.

Vola smiled.

FOURTEEN

When they left camp the next morning, War had set up divisions around the perimeter to defend against the army of undead that must still be out there somewhere. Raven and Cyrano were trying to find the main body of the enemy supported by the monks while Mishap's Heroes slipped out the back and started trekking across the lava field around the edge of the barrier.

According to Lillie, there were still three key points anchoring the barrier that they had to get through and it seemed like the perfect time to strike since they'd messed with Anders's time-line the day before. Mulgash had enabled them to move ahead when Anders had wanted them to stay put. It made sense to push ahead now and catch him further off balance.

Lillie scanned the area carefully, using a couple of different spells Vola didn't entirely recognize. The whole point today was to not get ambushed.

Though Sorrel had pointed out that should be their goal every day. Mishap's Heroes. Purpose? Don't get ambushed.

Vola had the feeling they'd find this anchor point equidistant around the barrier as the first two. That seemed about right. If you wanted to anchor a circle, it made sense to do it from all sides.

"There," Lillie said and pointed.

"I don't see anything." Sorrel shaded her eyes, though the day was as foggy as the one before. It seemed like an ashy layer of clouds permanently covered the sun here.

"I can see the magic tied to the land. Almost like a knot. When we follow the illusions through to their conclusions, we untie the knot. This must be the next one."

"All right," Vola said. "But we're not getting caught the same way again. If he ambushed us once when we came out, he's probably just going to do it again."

"We should set a watch," Talon said. "We don't all have to go into the illusion. The fights haven't been that bad so far."

Vola nodded. "Three of us will go in. Two can stay here and keep anyone from creeping up on us. They can warn us if they see anyone setting up an ambush." She gestured to the flat plains. "That shouldn't be too hard."

"I'll stay," Rilla said. "The Dagger Throne is good at traps and defenses."

"Gruff and I can stay as well," Talon said. "We're used to standing watch."

"And you'll let us know if anything's trying to sneak up on us," Sorrel said.

"We can hold anything back until you return," Rilla said.

"Let's get it over with then," Vola said, drawing her sword. "The sooner we get in there, the sooner we can get back and deal with whatever Anders throws at us."

They slunk toward the area Lillie had indicated. Rilla and Talon stayed far enough back to remain clear of the illusion, watching for movement across the open lava field.

Between one step and the next, fog figures began rising from the ground. The bland, mostly gray and black surroundings blurred into the more vibrant colors of a temple yard in the fall. Several trees shaded them from the bright sunlight, their leaves a mosaic of yellow, orange, and red. Above them, the temple's stained-glass windows reflected little bits of blue and purple onto the vivid green grass.

Vola glanced around, immediately trying to get her bearings. Lillie and Sorrel flanked her. But Rilla and Talon hadn't come along. As planned.

Vola sent up a quick prayer to the Broken. *Watch over them while I can't.*

She recognized Anders's mentor, the dark man in the mismatched armor, lounging in the grass at the base of a tree. Anders, grown tall and muscular, stood beside him, watching their surroundings with wary eyes.

A stranger knelt beside them, flipping through a spellbook.

"Sit, boy," Johnson said. "You never know when you're going to get another chance to rest."

Anders shook his head, eyes still on their surroundings. "Brindle the Butcher's men could be hunting us even now. An ambush is always a possibility. So if you're not watching, then I will." He said it without rancor, like they'd agreed to disagree long ago.

Johnson snorted. "That's why I hired you for this. You keep us safe."

Anders's lip twitched.

"Aw, Vola," Sorrel whispered. "He's just like you."

Vola didn't laugh. The comparison gave her a strange twinge in her chest. This was the man they were fighting? This strong intense fighter who just wanted to protect his party?

"Ah," Johnson said and pushed himself up off the tree roots. He stood and dusted himself off. "Here she is."

The temple door had slid open, and a woman stepped out. She

wore a breastplate of solid steel over a lilac-colored gown that fell to her feet in delicate waves.

"Oh, I like her," Lillie breathed.

Anders seemed to agree. He stared at the dark-haired woman as she locked the temple door and walked toward them.

An arrow struck the tree behind Anders's shoulder.

"Shit. Ambush!" he cried. "It's the Butcher's men."

Vola spun to see a line of archers in matching uniforms taking aim at the edge of the temple yard.

Anders raced past her to engage.

"Is this our cue?" Sorrel asked.

"It seems likely," Lillie said. "We've had to fight in all of the others so far."

"Right, you two focus on the archers," Vola said. "I see a problem."

Four fighters were creeping up on the temple yard from the other direction. Vola charged them, shield down. She struck one with a thump, and he fell into his fellow.

These were faceless enemies, just like the first shadowy figures that had attacked Anders's home. Was that because he just hadn't bothered to create a more detailed illusion? Or was this how he remembered the altercation? Faceless shapes that threatened his people.

Vola managed to take out the first three fighters, but one got through her guard. But instead of attacking her, the figure darted forward to strike at Johnson, who had his back turned, dealing with the archers.

Anders turned in time to see the blow coming. He cried out, but he'd never reach the old mercenary in time.

Swirling light surrounded the enemy's feet and swept up his body, freezing the shadowy man's hand in place.

The woman from the temple stood halfway down the path to them, her hands raised and her eyes intent on the frozen enemy.

Glowing lines snaked up her breastplate, illuminating the symbols etched into the metal.

The enemy's outline flared, and Vola had to fling her hand over her eyes. Then it fell into dust, a pile of pale ash gathering on the green grass.

Anders cut down the last archer and hurried across to Johnson. "Are you all right?"

The man raised an eyebrow. "Perfectly," he said.

The woman crossed the rest of the distance to them. "Well, that was an exciting beginning." Her smile fell just short of a grin.

"Mariel," Johnson said with a nod to the woman. "Thanks for joining us."

"Master Johnson." She returned his nod. "Of course. It will be a pleasure, I'm sure." Her gaze flickered over Anders.

Anders flushed a deep red.

The third man who'd sat under the tree snorted. His features were bland and generic. As ill-defined as the woman's were crisp and stunning. Clearly, Anders's memory was very focused when he set up this illusion.

"Mariel Stillwater is a cleric," Johnson said. "A spell caster and a healer. She'll be keeping us safe—"

"That's my responsibility," Anders said with a sharp glance between Johnson and the new woman.

"And I'm sure you do a wonderful job," Mariel said. "I'm not here to step on your toes. I'm here to provide more divine protection."

"Oh," Anders said. "The gods."

Her lips twitched at his tone of dismissal. "Yes, the gods. You don't believe you need their protection?"

"I…I've never had much luck in getting them to give it to me."

"Ah. Well, that's what I'm for." She used her toe to nudge the pile of white dust at their feet.

Anders blanched.

"Between the two of you, we should be well protected." Johnson glanced between them with a gleam in his eye. "I expect you to work well together."

"Yes, sir," Anders said automatically, as if used to obeying without question.

"We'll need it if we're going to take down Brindle the Butcher. There aren't enough curses in the world for that man."

Johnson and the third man started down the lane.

Anders hesitated for a moment while Mariel hid a soft smile. Then he extended his arm to her.

The scene dissolved as they followed the rest of their party.

"Aw, they're kind of cute," Lillie said.

Sorrel gasped. "Do you think that's what all this is for? To get us to feel sorry for him?"

"What else would it be?" Vola said, shaking her head to clear her vision. "Aside from sheer arrogance. Obviously, there's something in his story he wants us to see."

The lava field came into focus around them, the first few feet growing clearer as the illusion faded. Vola noticed Rilla immediately, crouched on the ground beside them, blades ready in her hands. Little creases around her eyes deepened as she sought Vola's gaze.

"Are you out now?" Rilla asked, voice tight and worried.

A bit of ice trickled down Vola's spine, and she searched for Talon. The ranger had her bow strung and an arrow notched, though she held it pointed at the ground.

"What is it?" Vola asked sharply. "What's wrong?"

Talon jerked her chin, and Vola squinted into the distance. Her vision wasn't entirely back to normal yet.

Her ears picked out what her eyes couldn't tell her yet. A low shuffling and moaning came from about twenty yards away.

She blinked and the blurry distance finally came into focus, as if the last of the illusion fell away.

The undead horde shifted just beyond a green line drawn in fire across the lava rock. Rilla's handiwork. They'd seen her lay traps before, even for the undead. Vola was impressed her magic could hold so many at once. Though maybe she shouldn't be. Rilla held all the power of the Dagger Throne, after all.

"Well, that's not unexpected," Sorrel said.

"Though I had hoped they would be more divided between us and the army," Lillie added.

"That's not the worst part," Talon growled, her voice as gravelly as it ever got.

Vola glanced between Talon and Rilla.

Rilla used two fingers to touch the rock at her feet. Ahead of them, the green fire broke in the middle and forced the horde apart, like a wave parting around a rock. The zombies shuffled and groaned, but Rilla cleared a path between them.

Smack in the middle of the horde, the lava rock rose in a hummock, and Rilla's fire cleared a path to the hill.

As the zombies roiled out of the way, Vola's breath caught.

On the small rise, a man stood dressed in full plate armor, a crimson cloak fluttering at his shoulders. He leaned on a greatsword, its tip scratched into the rock at his feet. His sleek honey-colored hair was tied back in a tail, revealing delicately pointed ears.

"Oh my gods, I thought he was exiled," Vola whispered.

His hair didn't have the same red tints, and he was a lot less soft around the edges, but the shape of his features still echoed Lillie's perfectly.

"Xavier," she whispered.

FIFTEEN

"Hello, sister," Xavier said. He heaved his sword over his shoulder and started to pick his way down the rise between the zombies. Like a king descending to greet his subjects.

Lillie gulped so hard Vola heard it from six feet away. "What—How are you here? You were exiled. Banished."

He chuckled, though his smile didn't reach his eyes. "Yes, to a lovely little summer home in the Outer Plane. Thank you so much for that."

Lillie's jaw hardened. "I did what I had to do. You were going to destroy the Thrones. Topple our entire government."

"So you exiled your own flesh and blood without trial."

"Her decision still stands, Ephyra," Rilla said. "You're a traitor to Southglen. And now you're an escaped convict."

"Yes, funny how that works out."

"Where's Innis?" Lillie asked.

Xavier shrugged, making his plate clank. "Innis didn't have the stomach to do what needed to be done. He's not with me anymore."

"What did you do to him?" Lillie's voice went shrill.

"You ask as if you care."

She pressed her lips together. "I do care," she said quietly.

"Not enough, apparently," he said, just as softly. He raised his chin. "I thought you were soft. I thought you were the baby, coddled until you were useless. You ran away instead of facing the things you'd done. I thought the ruthlessness of our noble line had skipped you completely. I underestimated you." His eyes narrowed. "I won't make that mistake again."

He snapped his fingers and Rilla's spell holding back the undead horde broke in a shower of green sparks.

The dead surged forward just as Xavier charged his sister.

Lillie disappeared in a pop of empty air, and Vola lunged into the space where she'd been, catching Xavier's double-handed blow on her shield. The force of it rang down her arm and sent numbness zinging toward her elbow.

She heaved, making him stumble back. Vola swung her sword to take advantage of his unbalance.

Instead of trying to meet the blow, Xavier ducked, avoiding her altogether.

Lillie had reappeared behind Vola. She couldn't go very far with the undead pressing in on all sides.

Xavier sprang for her, completely ignoring Vola.

Three new figures coalesced, each one identical to the wizard, down to the blue-green eyes and the way they stood.

Xavier growled, eyes flicking from one image of Lillie to the other.

Talon, Rilla, and Sorrel held back the horde, cutting down the front ranks to form a barrier around them that the rest would have to climb over.

Vola struck Xavier from the side, long enough to distract him so the real Lillie could summon a wall of fire. It snaked between them and the undead horde, making the zombies hiss and moan and shuffle back.

"Get off me!" Xavier flung himself away from Vola, and he slashed at the nearest image of Lillie. It burst into a shower of light motes as his sword parted the illusion.

Well, those wouldn't last long. He'd cut through them like paper, and sure enough, he disintegrated the next one even while Vola was recovering her footing. There were only two figures left that could be Lillie, and even Vola wasn't sure which one was real.

She threw herself at Xavier, slashing at his face. He had to defend himself or be blinded.

Xavier stepped back to avoid the blow, but then immediately planted his feet and swung for an opening in Vola's defense. Vola raised her shield, deflecting the edge of his greatsword, which slid off the metal, slicing through the elbow joint of her armor.

She hissed and stepped back, her shield arm hanging limp at her side.

"Vola!" Lillie cried.

"I'm all right," Vola said, sweat standing out on her brow.

Xavier's eyes flicked between the last copy of Lillie and the one who had cried out, and Vola could see him make an educated guess.

He went for the real one. Lillie raised her hands, and a whirlwind sprang up between them, knocking Xavier flat on his back.

The others had their hands full keeping back the zombies that were brave enough to risk the flames. Heat made Vola's skin feel tight and stretched, and the air around them shimmered with it. The smoke sat heavy in her lungs, but she didn't dare cough. Xavier might have been focused on Lillie but he was too fast and too strong to give him any sort of opening.

He'd already rolled to his feet. He hesitated, and Vola thought he was glaring at Lillie, catching his breath. But she caught the movement of his lips and blue fire flickered across his blade, dripping onto the ground in little splatters of sparks.

Vola's eyes narrowed. What the hell? Xavier had never shown an aptitude for magic before. But then he was related to Lillie, Kellan, and Lord Ephyra, all accomplished spell casters.

A breeze touched her cheek, clearing the air around her head for a moment. "It's a wizard killing poison," the Broken whispered in her ear. "Don't let it touch Lillie. He's keyed it to her specifically."

"Great," Vola muttered. "Our enemies learn new tricks as fast as we do."

Lillie flickered and reappeared in another spot, but she was hampered by her own flames now, and the zombie horde beyond them.

Xavier anticipated her move and lunged in the opposite direction to catch her just as she was reappearing.

Vola lurched between them, but her arm ached and stayed limp, and she couldn't get her shield up in time. His blade sliced across her breastplate with an unholy shriek, spitting blue sparks everywhere. She stumbled and fell to her knees.

"Eyes." Lillie's voice came into Vola's head, calm and implacable, and Vola flung her arm over her face just as a brilliant orb of light sprang into existence above them.

Through the flames, the zombies shrieked in pain.

Vola waited for another blow from Xavier, but none came. She cautiously peeked around her arm and found him on the ground, rubbing at his face.

Vola climbed to her feet, her shield scraping against the lava rock.

Xavier cast around for his dropped sword, eyes streaming.

"Now, Vola," Lillie said, face hard and set.

Usually, Vola offered mercy when she could afford it. But there came a time when you'd used up all your chances, and Xavier had run out of mercy from all sides.

Vola stepped forward and raised her blade, ready to lop his

head from his shoulders in one clean stroke. But he turned his torso at the last minute and the blow glanced to the side, leaving a long gash in his neck.

Xavier scrambled aside as Vola advanced, one hand dragging his sword, the other pressed to the blood spurting under his jaw.

Vola lunged for him and Xavier managed one more turn to take the blow on his back. Vola's blade left a gash as long as her arm in his plate and deep enough that blood seeped through the torn metal.

Xavier grunted and hesitated before he flung himself through the fire. He rolled across the rough rock on the other side, snuffing the flames that had caught his hair and cloak. Then he hauled himself to his feet.

He snapped an order at the remaining zombies. There weren't nearly as many as there had been before. Many had disintegrated from Lillie's sunburst or succumbed to the flames. Or piled high under Rilla, Talon, and Sorrel's attack.

Xavier glared through the fire, hand still pressed to his neck. He coughed like he was trying to say something scathing, but the smoke or his own blood choked him.

Vola wanted to leap after him, to finish what he'd started back in Glenhaven. But her legs trembled, and she still couldn't raise her left arm.

Finally, Xavier whirled and limped away, dragging his sword.

The undead horde shuffled and followed him, leaving the lava field clear except for the burned bodies of the fallen.

SIXTEEN

THEY WAITED in silence long after they couldn't see Xavier or his army before Lillie finally snapped her fingers and the walls of flame died down and smothered themselves, leaving plumes of smoke in the air.

Vola fell to her knees, clutching her arm.

Lillie knelt beside her, lips white and eyes tight with worry.

"Don't," Vola grated out, voice hoarse with strain and smoke. "Don't touch. I still have that poison all over me." The blue flames still flickered at the edges of the gash in her armor, threatening destruction to Lillie.

"What poison?" Lillie said. She ducked to get a good look at the gash, blue reflecting across her face. She went pale and gasped.

"It's keyed to you," Vola grated out. "I'll be fine once I catch my breath."

Lillie drew back, tucking her hands under her arms. Her expression closed off, as if her thoughts followed the brother who'd just done his best to kill her. Even during the coup, he hadn't really targeted her seriously.

Rilla and Sorrel knelt to help Vola instead, while Talon kept an eye on their surroundings. Xavier had pulled back, and Vola felt confident that he was hurt worse than they were, but that didn't mean he couldn't turn around and send more troops back their way.

"He's working with Anders," Vola said quietly.

"Makes sense," Rilla said as Sorrel gently slid Vola's shield from her arm. "He has combat experience. He was trained as a commander, though I hear he wasn't a very good one. Anders is probably using him to lead his undead troops."

"That's not the worst bit though, is it?" Sorrel said, placing Vola's shield aside carefully. "Xavier and Innis were exiled. To another plane. They shouldn't have been able to escape."

"Not without help," Lillie said.

"Yeah," Sorrel said. "And Anders has already helped Lord Arthorel escape."

"If Anders has the power to reach across planes and free Lillie's brothers," Talon said, "then we know who he's going after next."

"Inga," Vola said. "And Nargilla."

"Isn't Inga dead?" Rilla said.

Sorrel gestured to the bodies littering the lava field. "So were all those guys. How dead do you have to be to avoid getting brought back as a zombie?"

Rilla and Sorrel helped Vola remove the damaged breastplate, keeping the sharp edges and the poison away from anyone who might accidentally touch them.

Vola breathed a sigh of relief when the weight left her shoulders. She rubbed her face with her good hand, and it came away streaked with sweat and soot. The others were covered in ash as well.

Vola reached deep inside to the well of magic that connected her with the Broken. Divine power swelled at her fingertips, waiting for her bidding.

"Lady bless," she said and pressed her palm to the wound on her arm.

White light flashed and sharp pain indicated that the skin was knitting a hundred times faster than it did naturally.

Vola coughed and Sorrel handed her a water skin. She took a swig to rinse her mouth out, then passed it around to the others while she examined the wound. A fresh scar stretched from the back of her elbow over the crook of her arm and down to the seam where her armor gaped a little to provide freedom of movement. She flexed her fingers to test the healing. Everything seemed in order.

"Anyone else?" Vola asked.

Sorrel shook her head. "Just some scrapes and burns. Nothing a little salve won't fix. I think we'd better save your healing for bigger things from now on. Who knows when we'll get jumped again?"

"I agree," Vola said. "Same with Lillie's spells." She glanced at the wizard. "Save them for battle."

"I don't exactly waste them as it is," Lillie said. She reached out to take Vola's arm and examine the fresh scar. "Thank you," she said quietly.

Vola shook her head. She'd barely done anything. "I know this isn't easy," she said. "We thought we were done with it. You weren't supposed to have to see them ever again."

"We don't get to choose what the world throws at us," she said. "Only how we will act when it happens. I'll be fine. Eventually. We should be preparing ourselves for what comes next."

Vola shook her head and pushed herself to stand. "I'm not worried about Inga."

"She had the power to control minds. She took us over, turned us against you. And…" Lillie ducked her head. "She knew you.

Better than you knew yourself. Knew what you were going to do even before you did it."

"All right, so I'm a little worried about Inga." Vola gave her a rueful smile. "But she didn't know me well enough to keep me from getting you all back. And in the end, she's not the one who's the key to Anders's plans."

Lillie's mouth went round. "Nargilla."

"If Anders can help Xavier and Innis escape…"

"Then he might be able to steal Nargilla right out from under the gods' noses," Sorrel said.

Rilla's lips went thin while Talon and Lillie exchanged a look.

"I have to warn them," Vola said. "The gods need to know what they're up against."

They were gods. They should have been watching. They should have been all-knowing. The Broken certainly stuck her nose in often enough that Vola knew she had to be watching pretty much constantly. But the others hadn't proved themselves all that attentive. Maxim was revered for his strength and loyalty, but his followers all admitted he didn't really look in on them very often.

They would need a nudge to get them looking in the right direction. Even after the one she'd already given them about Anders.

So far, wrangling gods was more work than it was worth.

"You guys get back to camp and tell War to keep moving forward. The more we can drive forward while Anders is scrambling, the more we can keep him off balance," Vola told them. "Sorrel's in charge while I'm away."

Sorrel gave her a solemn nod.

"Get them back safely. I'll meet you there."

"You're going now?" Lillie asked, eyes wide. "Alone?"

"Not alone," Vola said as a little puff of displaced air told her someone had appeared at her shoulder.

"Never alone," the Broken said.

The others took her armor with them. Hopefully, the army blacksmiths could burn away the poison and repair the damage for her. Besides, she wouldn't need it where she was going.

She watched until her people disappeared into the distance, back toward camp. It hurt to watch them walk away. More than she'd thought it would.

They're heading for safety, she told herself. *And I have to do this now. If I wait, Anders could slip Nargilla right out from under their noses and we'd be fu—I mean, screwed.*

She glanced at the Broken out of the corner of her eye to see if she'd caught that slip.

"Ready?" the Broken said, catching her glance.

"As I'll ever be."

"Then walk with me."

Vola stepped alongside the Broken, the gravelly lava rock shifting a little under her feet until the next step she took landed on stable marble. The long bright hallway stretched ahead of them. A long gangly form was silhouetted against the white chamber at the end.

Vesteral, speaker of the gods, watched unblinkingly as they approached.

Vola glanced at the Broken, but she just gave a serene nod.

Vola cleared her throat. "Speaker," she said. "We need to speak with the gods that hold the mortal traitor Nargilla Pipwattle."

Vesteral arched one curved eyebrow.

The chamber echoed. No bits of color or whisper of voices indicated the presence of the gods this time.

"They aren't here," Vesteral said, correctly interpreting her glance. "The gods have many duties. They have their own lives which they spend ruling over mortals. They do not…hang around here waiting for a summons."

"Oh." Well, of course not. But it wasn't like she was familiar with the personal lives of the gods. Only what they showed to select mortals.

"I think what my representative means," the Broken said, with her own eyebrow tilt. "Is would you be so kind as to request Maxim's and Dierdre's presence? It's a matter of some urgency."

Vesteral sniffed. But he couldn't disobey a direct order from any of the gods. Much less the Broken, who stood apart from the others because of her power.

"Very well," he said. "Wait here."

"Where does he think we'll go?" Vola asked as his form faded and he disappeared. "It's a big empty room."

"You're in the realm of the gods here. This is a hub between every realm of the Greater Virtues and Obstacles. If you were determined enough, you could enter any of the realms you chose. Even without invitation."

Vola blinked at the vague outlines of the room around them, trying to figure out where the openings to these other realms were. Did the Broken have one? Did she live there when she wasn't hanging over Vola's shoulder? For some reason she couldn't imagine the goddess lounging on a couch eating grapes out of the hands of an attractive server.

A flicker of dark color and movement drew her eye, and she turned to find Mulgash coalescing on one of the tiers, his feet up on the bench beside him.

"What are you doing here?" she said, without stopping to think.

He shrugged, unperturbed. For a god of rage, Mulgash rarely showed any temper as far as Vola had experienced. He was always the calm voice in the back of your head, urging you to more and more violence.

"Keeping an eye on you," he said, examining his nails. "I did tell you I would be looking out for you, didn't I? Don't mind me. Keep doing what you're doing."

Vola's brows drew down, and she opened her mouth to protest, but Vesteral reappeared along with two other figures.

Maxim, in his golden armor, manifested first. With his deep ebony skin and even darker hair, he looked particularly statuesque in the sunlight that suffused the room. The woman with him had close-cropped steel gray hair and eyes a milky white that meant she should have been blind. But her gaze fixed on Vola without stuttering.

Dierdre, Greater Virtue of Justice. She had nearly an army of paladins who followed her as well as judges, lawyers, and the odd criminal who thought sucking up would improve their chances.

These two were the ones in charge of Nargilla and keeping the clever gnome imprisoned. At least until Anders was dealt with. Then she'd face her own trial before the gods whose power she'd tried to steal.

"Why do you call us, representative?" Dierdre said, her voice snapping like the strike of a gavel.

Maxim remained silent, staring.

Vola wanted to glance at the Broken again, let her take the lead. But the goddess was in an odd position politically. She couldn't give the others commands, and even suggestions would be met with disdain. It was up to Vola to ask and nudge.

Vola bowed her head. "Lady Justice," she said. "Lord Strength. I have a warning. The traitor Anders has more power and skill than we originally anticipated. He's collecting his former lieutenants from their various imprisonments, and he's even managed to help one escape from planar banishment. If he can do that, it's possible he could storm the realm of the gods and take

Nargilla by force. And if he has her…he has the key to stealing the rest of your power."

Vola stopped to take a deep breath.

Maxim and Dierdre exchanged an indulgent look.

"It was good of you to come to us with this warning," Dierdre said. "Thank you."

Vola's mouth worked. "Then…you'll take precautions? Make sure he can't take Nargilla back? She's the key to all his plans. If he gets her, we'll have no chance."

"We are aware of all this. You warned us of her role when the Broken entrusted us with her imprisonment."

"Okay," Vola said. She still wasn't getting the response she'd wanted or expected. On the bright side, they hadn't dismissed her. But they didn't show the alarm she felt like the situation warranted.

"We appreciate the warning," Maxim finally said and placed his gauntleted hand on Vola's shoulder. It weighed her down and burned her shoulder through her shirt. "But you needn't worry, little one."

No one had called her 'little one' since she was ten and had grown taller than her father.

"There really is nothing Anders can do against us," Deirdre said. "Not while the Virtues and the Obstacles stand united."

There was a snort, and Vola glanced at Mulgash, still lounging on one of the tiers.

She wasn't the only one to notice him.

"You have something to add?" Maxim said, coldly.

"You're underestimating her again," Mulgash said in a singsong voice. "If Volagra Lightless is worried, you'd do better than to brush her off."

"Noted," Maxim said in a voice that told them he was just trying to shut Mulgash up.

Mulgash shrugged. "There's a part of me that just wants to say screw it and let you do what you want. It will be so much more fun when you see the truth. But if Anders gets Nargilla, he gets you. And if he gets you…" He spread his arms wide. "He gets the whole pantheon."

"That will not happen," Dierdre said with a cold glance. "Anders would have to get through both the goddess of Justice and the god of Strength and Loyalty in order to get to Nargilla. We're no mere Obstacles," she said with a sniff. "We're Virtues."

Mulgash surged to his feet, jaw tight. His knuckles went white, and Vola held her breath. Was she about to see an Obstacle actually strike a Virtue? It would certainly be interesting, but maybe she should find some cover.

Mulgash took a deep breath and visibly reined in his temper. Vola had to admit to a grudging respect. She knew first hand how hard that was and it had to be even worse for the god of rage.

He flashed a grim smile at Vola. "Now you see what you're up against. They'll discount anyone different from them, no matter their value or wisdom." He gave the Virtues a mocking little bow and sank into the floor, disappearing with a puff of warm air.

"Such dramatics," Dierdre said. She smiled at Vola and the Broken. "Hardly necessary and hurtfully untrue. We regard all with the same level of care. There's really nothing to worry you, my dear. Anders cannot move against us as long as we're united."

She turned, and Maxim went with her. Together, the two faded as if they walked through the wall.

"I trust the Broken can show you out?" Vesteral said, and bowed himself away as well.

Vola stood, clenching her fists. She had the distinct feeling she was standing behind a wall of glass shouting that a monster was coming while the people on the other side chuckled and pointed out her antics to their neighbors to share the joke.

She glanced at the Broken to ask if they were really overreacting. But the Broken stared at the wall where Maxim and Dierdre had disappeared, her eyes tight and sad, scarred mouth drawn down. The mixture of pain and longing and regret on her face was clear, and Vola looked away, embarrassed to be a witness.

If she were a mortal, Vola would have said the Broken missed her god siblings desperately. But there were far more layers here. The goddess missed them, yes. But she seemed proud and ashamed of them at the same time, and Vola knew there were deeper wounds there that she couldn't even begin to guess at.

The Broken was her goddess, not one of her teammates. But still, there was the pull to fix this. To say something that would fix what was broken. But how did you fix a broken goddess?

"It's good to see them working together at least," Vola said quietly. "Maybe one day, they'll be willing to work with you again, too."

The Broken cast her a rueful glance, and Vola felt like she'd missed the point.

"Don't let them fool you the way they've fooled themselves. They are not united. They might be working together, but they are not united."

The Broken turned and started down the hall. "And until they are, they are just as broken as I am."

Vola kept quiet. She didn't know how to fix what was wrong. She barely even knew what was wrong between the gods, other than a political rift. And patting the Broken's arm and saying "there, there, it will be okay" didn't seem fitting. Especially since she wasn't sure it would be okay.

She didn't expect the pantheon to follow a mortal. But what was she supposed to be representing if they didn't at least listen to the Broken sometimes?

Maxim didn't care about mortals. He'd forced himself to not care about them, to distance himself from the pain they caused every time they died.

His disinterest informed the rest of the gods, and it informed the way he interacted with Vola. He didn't listen to her because he didn't care.

So what would make him care?

Greater Virtue of Strength and Loyalty. Vola's lips curled. He had a follower who embodied both those virtues more than anyone else Vola had ever met.

Somehow, she had to get Sorrel into Maxim's path. The halfling was exactly what Maxim looked for in a follower. And she carried his Warhammer. If anyone could convince the Greater Virtue to care, it would be Sorrel Thornbough.

"I think we should introduce Maxim to a monk I know," Vola said.

The best part about working with a goddess was that the Broken followed her train of thought better than anyone, except for maybe her team.

A slow smile spread across the goddess's face. "That's not a bad idea."

"Think he'll go for it?"

"Coming along to the mortal realm? Oh, definitely not. He hasn't manifested to anyone in centuries. Every paladin thinks he'll be the next one Maxim speaks to directly, but they're all wrong."

Vola pursed her lips.

"But…I'll work on him," the Broken said. "There was a time he enjoyed swinging a sword alongside mortals. If he was ever going to get out of this rut of his, now would be it."

SEVENTEEN

VOLA REAPPEARED on the lava field in front of the mess tent, scaring the crap out of a boy carrying a pot full of stew.

He shrieked, and the stew went flying. Bits of meat and potatoes pelted the ground and the canvas of the tent.

"Shawn! You idiot, what's so frightening you're wasting good food like that? You know how difficult it will be to get more hauled out here?" One of the cooks came surging out of the tent, bearing a greasy ladle like a sword.

"It's the black paladin," the boy said, pointing. "She just-just appeared out of nowhere. I think she came up out of the ground after consorting with Mulgash."

"I did no—" Vola bit her tongue. The boy wasn't exactly wrong.

The cook seized the boy's shoulder and thrust him behind his wide bulk.

Vola sighed. "Mulgash doesn't live underground, anyway," she said. "He lives in his own realm." She strode off before Mulgash's rage could flicker in her eyes and prove his point.

Everyone had prejudices. It was nearly impossible to get to

adulthood without having some ingrained opinion that hurt someone else. It was just bad luck that Vola seemed to embody most of the usual ones.

That and breeding but she'd pay to see someone confront her parents about that.

She turned a corner, putting more distance between herself and the mess tent. Where to find the others? They had to have gotten back by now. From the angle of the sun, she'd been gone for hours.

She paused for a second to get her bearings. Mishap's Heroes usually set up in any space that was left near the command tent, so she could start there.

She stopped as shouts wound through the canvas walls of the camp.

Or she could follow the sounds of arguing. Because if there was a mess around, she'd bet money her teammates would be in the middle of it somehow.

Sure enough, there was a knock-down, drag-out fight going on three rows over from the command tent, and several of the participants wore gray tunics.

At least it looked like Sorrel was trying to stop the fight. Not like she'd started it.

The monk held back two of her fellows, both of which stood several feet taller than her. But the halfling had her heels dug into the dirt and hauled on their tunics. The adversary seemed to be a small troop of Mistvalian foot soldiers.

Lillie stood to one side with her father, a couple of the scholars, shifting from foot to foot. Vola knew that look. She was trying to decide which spell to use.

Vola caught her eye and shook her head. *Save the spells*, she tried to say.

Lillie sighed and finally nodded. Then she gestured to the right where Talon stood, surveying the fight with crossed arms.

Vola signaled Talon to flank while she waded into the middle, yanking combatants off their feet.

"What the hell is going on?" she yelled. A little lightning bolt bounced from the tip of a spear on a nearby rack. "Do you want the War Princess over here to bring you all up on charges? 'Cause you're making enough racket to call her."

She hauled a soldier off his feet and set him back so the monks couldn't land a blow. Talon swept one's legs out from under him and made sure he stayed down.

Vola scanned the monks for the abbess and finally found the dwarf directly in the center of the fray. "Aren't you supposed to argue for non-violence most of the time? Save your energy. The enemy is out there, not in here."

"Believe me, we had good reason," Hazel said, her lips pulled back in a snarl. "Maxim would not thank us for backing down from an honorable fight."

From everything Vola had seen, Maxim wouldn't care. But since that was exactly what she was trying to fix, it seemed stupid to argue the point now.

Sorrel succeeded in hauling the other two monks back and now that the soldiers were mostly laid out on the ground, thanks to Vola, Hazel stepped back and adjusted her tunic.

"Now, explain this," Vola said.

Hazel and one of the soldiers started talking at once.

Vola held up her hands. "Never mind. Let's try again. First you." She pointed to Hazel.

The soldier snorted. "Of course, you'd hear out the orc lovers first," he muttered.

Vola turned on him. She could have snarled and shown off all the orc teeth since he seemed so interested in them. But she very deliberately kept her lips closed and raised a scathing eyebrow, the way the Broken always did.

The soldier fell silent.

"Now," Vola said. "What happened?"

Sorrel swept some loose hair from her brow. "Words were exchanged. There was some good-natured ribbing from what I could tell. But er, some of the remarks turned personal."

"He insulted Sorrel," Hazel said.

Vola glanced at Sorrel, who shrugged. "Must have been some insult," Vola said. "I've seen her keep her cool and her beer in the middle of an orc brawl."

"She didn't think there was cause for retaliation," Hazel said. "But I did."

"Someone might have implied that I was so short, there was no way you'd let me on your team. Unless sexual favors were exchanged."

Hazel's eyes narrowed.

"Hmm, and I thought simple skill would suffice," Vola said. "Maybe I should have held out for sexual favors."

Sorrel grinned. "Maybe. I'm probably not very good at them, though."

Vola caught sight of Imralen lurking at the edges. Her teeth creaked as her jaw clenched, but the Knight Commander remained silent and still.

"And what's your side?" Vola asked the soldier.

The soldier raised his chin. "We were just making conversation, and they jumped me. But I don't know what you expect from people who follow an orc. Violence is all they know."

There was a ripple through the crowd that had gathered, and many of the onlookers faded back as a whole division of orcs boiled out of the background and moved to surround them.

An older chieftain in his fur loincloth with leather bandoliers across his chest lowered his chin and glared at the soldier. "You'll want to be careful insulting our way of life, son," he said. "Since we're using that aggression to defend you and yours on the battlefield tomorrow." He glanced at Vola and cracked a grin. "Hiya, honey."

"Hey, Dad. Glad you could make it before we cleared everything out."

The soldier's eyes went wide, and Vola caught the little flick of movement where he checked with the Knight Commander.

Vola spun so she could pin the soldier with her gaze. And so Imralen lined up right behind him. She could talk to the one while glaring at the other.

"So, what's been going on here while I've been out there making sure this army has a place to advance to every day? Hmm?"

The soldier gulped and wouldn't meet her eyes.

"Picking fights with monks?" Vola asked. "And orcs?" She glanced at Lillie. "What about the scholars?"

The soldier didn't answer, but Lord Ephyra met her eyes. "There was some graffiti on our tent this morning. 'Go home, orc lovers.' Badly misspelled, too."

They were going after her friends now. Anyone who'd ever supported her. Imralen was waging a battle within the real war.

Vola checked on Talon, but the ranger kept her gaze lowered. If she'd been getting any harassment because of Vola, she wasn't saying.

Vola cursed inside her head. She was so busy running around trying to get through Anders's barrier, she hadn't had time to stop the spread of Imralen's poison back here. And now she was fighting from a weakened position.

"Go home," she said, suddenly weary. "Control yourselves. Or get out, because an army that's fighting amongst itself isn't any good to the War Princess or to the world. If you have so much of a problem with me that you have to attack anyone I've ever even had contact with, then you're too distracted to be a good soldier." She waved her hands as if she could magically be rid of them and stepped back, giving them all enough room to get out of her sight.

Talon helpfully reached down to lend a hand to the soldier on the ground.

"Get your hands away from me," he growled and staggered to his feet himself. He shuddered and spoke to one of his companions. "Did it touch me?"

Vola's hand shot out and wrapped around his throat. She lifted him with ease and slammed him onto his back against the lava rock. Then she placed her hand flat on his chest and held him there, making sure he could see how very little effort she expended in all of it.

"It's funny how no one notices when you're quiet and peaceful," she told him conversationally, ignoring the intake of breath around her. "They only notice when you get violent. So notice this and remember it. You want to attack me, you come after me. You go after one of them…" Her eyes flicked to her teammates one by one. "And I will show you the type of violence a black paladin is capable of. I'll show you what it's like to fight with all the fury of the Greater Virtue of Righteousness. Forget the Obstacle of Rage. He's a pushover compared to my lady."

She tapped his chest with her finger and pushed off of him to stand. She glanced around at the spectators still standing there, poised on the edge of something. Watching.

"I'm sorry. Did I say we were selling tickets? Move."

They scattered. Except for the orcs and the monks and the scholars. And Imralen, who just watched her with narrowed eyes.

She stared him down, daring him to say something, to attack her finally. To stop running around behind her back.

"How long before the princesses realize you're more of a problem than Anders is?" Imralen said. "You're taking us apart from the inside."

Heat beat in her chest. He was undermining her at every turn.

He was the one whispering lies and discontent and blaming it on her.

And the moment she retaliated, she became the very thing he claimed she was. She held her breath until black threatened to overwhelm her. But she didn't move.

Imralen shook his head. "I hope you come to your senses and withdraw from the field before you get people killed."

He stalked off with an air of sad superiority that put a blazing target on his back Vola had to fight to ignore.

"Oh my gods, I want to kick his ass so bad," Sorrel said as Vola finally sucked in a breath.

"A dagger in the ribs," Talon said. "He wouldn't even have to know it was coming."

"A fireball so big it knocks him clear out of camp," Lillie said.

They all looked at her.

"What?" She blinked. "Too much?"

"I take it I missed something big if Lillie is talking about blasting people." Rilla stalked into the cleared area, hands on the hilts of her daggers.

Vola cracked her neck and rolled her shoulders. "We're fine," she said. "Everything's fine." Except she was losing to Imralen, and she had no idea how to stop it.

Rilla opened her mouth, then stopped and squinted at the people gathered. "Holy crap, when did we recruit all these orcs?"

"When you put my daughter in charge," the orc chieftan said, rubbing his head.

"Hi, honey." A lithe human woman in a fur-lined leather bikini stepped out from behind the big orc. Faint traces of silver streaked her bushy red-brown hair.

"Hey, Mom. Thanks for coming."

"We were trying to find the commander in order to present ourselves and followed the sounds of fighting," Vola's father said. "That's usually the fastest way to find someone in charge."

"Well, I can help there," Rilla said.

"Mom, Dad. I'm not sure you ever officially met my boss, Rilla. Princess of the Dagger Throne. Rilla, this is Gorgo, chieftain of our tribe, and his wife, Lydia Battlemane."

"Lydia Battlemane…Wow," Rilla said, reaching to shake their hands. "I grew up hearing about your adventures. I even caught your bout at the friendship games where you trounced that minotaur."

Lydia giggled. "Oh, that was such a long time ago. You're making me feel ancient."

"Oh no, ma'am," Rilla said, pumping Lydia's hand. "Not ancient. Fit and sprightly and most welcome." Rilla's eyes flicked down to what Lydia was wearing for a split second. "And maybe you'd like to visit our quartermaster for some fitting attire."

"It's armor," Lydia and Vola said in unison.

"Sorry," Vola told Rilla. "Long argument. You won't win. We've all tried."

"Well, I can at least introduce you to War," Rilla said after a moment's hesitation. "She'll be happy to see you. The more fighters she can move around her board the better."

Vola gave her parents what she hoped was an encouraging smile and sent them off with Rilla. Then she rubbed her eyes hard enough to hurt.

She felt more than saw the rest of her team come to stand with her.

"How bad is it?" she asked them quietly, expecting the truth, though she knew they'd want to shield her from it.

"It's not good," Sorrel said. "They're coming after the rest of us now."

"Little things that we can handle," Lillie said. "Like you saw. The graffiti and picking fights."

"But how much longer before it's such a problem that the princesses notice?" Vola asked. "How much longer before he really hurts one of you? Or Anders wins because Imralen managed to take us down before we even started fighting?"

They didn't speak for a long moment. "We don't know," Talon said. "But we wouldn't be doing anything differently if we did, would we?"

The others shook their heads.

"This is where we're supposed to be, Vola," Talon said. "All we can do is keep going. And maybe the rest of them will see the truth before it's too late."

EIGHTEEN

THE NEXT MORNING, War sent the new battalion of orcs to protect them while they searched for the next illusion.

After their last encounter and Xavier's ambush, Vola was glad her parents were along. But she couldn't help noticing that War had chosen the group most loyal to Vola. The least likely to turn their backs on her or get her party killed just because she was a black paladin.

War had to know what was going on in camp. She knew Imralen was complaining about Vola. She knew the fighters were at each other's throats over it. But did she know how bad it was?

Maybe War knew better than Vola and that's why they were out here again, not in camp where the problems were the worst.

Lillie limped along ahead of them on the rough lava field with her own little contingent of orcs, looking for the next illusion to break. A couple of them remembered Lillie from Inga's stronghold. They remembered the way she'd helped free them and they greeted her with hearty claps on the back and little bows they'd obviously practiced.

The ones that didn't remember her hung back, seeing only

that she had the fair skin and pointed ears of the haughty elves and the regal bearing of a noble.

But their distrust melted as the wizard refused their help, scrambling over the rough terrain, even though it made her limp worse and Vola could see her wincing.

Orcs believed that pain made you strong. They believed that hardship wasn't something you hid from. And hiding your rage, your pain, and your suffering was unhealthy. So they respected Lillie's choice. And respected her more for making it.

Rilla, Talon, Sorrel, and Vola kept back a bit, giving Lillie room to work. The orcs ranged on either side of them in long lines, eyes alert for trouble. Gorgo led the left flank, Lydia the right.

Vola kept waiting for the undead to swarm or to rise up at their feet or come crawling over the horizon. But there was nothing for hours.

And then figures ambushed them from the low hills and hummocks of the lava field. But they didn't moan or shuffle. They screamed battle cries and rushed over the uneven ground.

Vola and her team drew their weapons, but there was hardly a need. Gorgo's fighters knelt and met the first wave with brutal efficiency, raising their weapons as the enemy charged. Lydia's group swept in behind to mop up the remaining survivors.

Vola and the others were left blinking, their weapons ready but no enemy to fight.

"Well," Rilla said, sheathing her daggers. "That was…anti-climactic."

"Anders must have sent a force for just the five us, not expecting any back-up," Talon said.

Vola stepped to join her father, who knelt beside one of the bodies.

"Did this seem strange to you, too?" he asked.

Vola crouched beside him. She turned the body over. "They're not dead," she said, looking down into the lifeless face of an elf.

Gorgo snorted.

Vola rolled her eyes. "I mean, they're not undead. They were alive. Until we killed them."

"Generally, that's how mercenary work goes," Lydia said, leaning on her battleax. "Things are alive until someone pays us enough to make them not alive anymore."

Talon and Sorrel joined them. "Maybe Anders's army isn't all zombies," Sorrel said.

"But who would fight for him?" Talon said. "Unless he's promising them something."

"Maybe part of the power he's stealing," Rilla said. "That's one of the big three. It's always money, sex, or power."

"Whatever it is, it's not enough," Vola said quietly. "These people weren't prepared to face us at all."

Gorgo sighed. "Bad press. There's always some well-meaning busybody ready to argue that mercenaries are vicious brutes because of this sort of thing."

"That's sort of funny coming from you, darling," Lydia said with a snort.

"I think before I swing my sword, thank you very much. I think 'gee, this guy's ax is headed for my head. I bet if I chop his head off first, I'll get to keep mine a little longer.'"

"We should move on," Lillie said. The circle of orcs around her hadn't broken during the attack. "We still have to break the illusion. And if Anders has more troops to throw at us, I think we'd rather be there than here."

"Good point," Vola said.

They moved on, leaving the mystery troops behind. It wasn't like they could bury them in the lava rock, even if they'd had the time.

For the first time in days, there was a break in the featureless expanse of rock besides the occasional skeletal tree. Half a house rose from the lava field, as if someone had attempted to settle the barren land and given up halfway through construction. Either driven away by the inhospitable terrain or by Anders himself.

"This is it," Lillie said as they approached the front door. It had been painted a bright cheerful blue, but the peeling plaster and bare wood created the opposite effect now and made Vola shiver.

"Of course it is," Sorrel said. "It looks like an ambush waiting to happen."

"Come inside, little mouse. I promise not to eat you," Talon muttered.

"Don't wolves normally eat herd animals?" Lillie asked as Vola pushed the door open and peered inside.

Warped floorboards creaked under her boots and a staircase led up to a second story open to the sky. The roof lay in collapsed timbers across the second floor.

"It's cozy," Gorgo said, poking his head over Vola's shoulder. "And it's backed up against the barrier." He gestured to the undulating magic that reflected through the empty windows at the back of the ruined house. "So it'll be easier to defend."

"Unless something comes through it you can't see," Vola said. "Keep that possibility in mind. If you stay far enough back, you won't get sucked into the illusion, too."

"Will do," Gorgo said, with a lazy salute. "Don't worry, Commander Lightless. We'll keep you safe while you're taunting bad guys."

"Thanks," Vola said, and just kept herself from calling him dad in front of his mercenaries.

She stepped across the rough gray floorboards, the rest of her team right behind her. The now familiar fog forms rolled up, obscuring the orcs around them as they moved toward the center of the house.

"You know, I'm starting to wonder if I'm ever going to get to hit Anders for real," Sorrel said as the peeling walls faded and the floorboards at their feet turned to cut stone.

Walls climbed up around them, opening onto a gray sky. Realistic wind blew sleet into their faces as they stood at the top of a tower open to the elements.

Johnson, Anders's mentor, stood in the center calling into the storm. Behind him stood the third man from the other illusion and Anders, who held Mariel's free hand. They all stared upward, faces pale and tight.

A crumpled form in crimson mage robes lay at their feet, as if they'd only just defeated Brindle the Butcher.

A scream echoed across the opening of the tower, and Vola threw up her hands to protect her aching ears.

Out of the gray clouds above fell a massive shape full of red and gold feathers and evil, curved claws. A giant raptor landed with a thump that shook the entire tower and opened its mouth to shriek again. Its talons dug gouges in the stones at its feet and its head darted back and forth, big black eyes fastening on the party before it.

"A roc," Lillie said behind them. Vola got the impression she'd meant to whisper, but the roar of the storm made her raise her voice to be heard. "A magical construct designed to —"

"Remember," Johnson yelled back at his team. "It will defend its master even in death. Either we die here, or it does."

The third man drew his hands together and whispered a spell. When he flung them out again, a purple glow settled around Anders and Johnson's weapons.

Johnson sprang forward with a cry. He swept the roc with his blade and dodged a buffet from its wing. He rolled up directly under it and slashed at the bird's wing, right where it attached to its body. The roc ducked its head, but it couldn't get to the swordsman underneath it.

Anders took the opportunity to lunge forward and slash at its eye. The roc screamed and threw him against the wall.

Vola tore her eyes away from the fight. What were they supposed to be doing here? Every other illusion had held something for them to fight. And those shadowy enemies seemed to be the key to breaking them from the memories.

A brilliant flash of light lit up the dark clouds and a column of white pierced through them, pinning the roc to the tower floor. Mariel stood with her hands raised and eyes closed as if she prayed the beam into existence.

"Anders, now!" the third man shouted. The spell caster kept his hand twisted, keeping the magic swirling around Anders's blade.

Anders thrust himself away from the wall and shook his head as if to drive off dizziness. He sprinted for the roc and vaulted from a broken table, his sword held above him for the strike.

The roc slithered and wriggled out from under the beam of light. But instead of meeting Anders's charge, it lashed out at the spell caster, alone at the back of the tower. In one mighty beat of its wings, it leaped across the tower and snapped the man in half.

"No!" Mariel screamed.

Anders landed badly and tumbled. His sword fell from his hand and lay naked on the floor, dull steel once again. He lay against the stone, his chest heaving as he stared at the remains of the spell caster.

The roc spun on its hind legs, beating its wings, creating a gale-force wind that threatened to sweep them off the tower.

Vola planted her feet and leaned into it. Could an illusion knock her from the top of the tower? What were their bodies doing back at the ruined house?

And where were the enemies they were supposed to be fighting?

She raised her arm to protect her eyes from the debris flung by the wind and glanced at the others. Sorrel and Talon squinted back at her while Lillie braced herself against the wall and stared aghast at the pitiful remains of the spell caster.

"Lillie," Vola called. "What are we supposed to be fighting?"

Lillie shook herself and met Vola's gaze with a bleak look. "I don't know." She peered into the empty corners of the tower. "I haven't seen anything, have you?"

Johnson was the first of Anders's team to recover from his shock. "Anders," the old mercenary called. "Cover Mariel. We've got to pull out all the stops now."

Anders scrambled for his sword and flung himself in front of Mariel while Johnson lunged to distract the roc.

Mariel flung her arms wide and threw back her head, her lips moving in time to a single word spoken over and over again.

Johnson cut at the roc's feathered breast, but his blade barely nicked the bird now. The roc beat at the man with its wings and he staggered back. A huge claw swiped at the mercenary and Johnson fell heavily, face down against the floor.

Anders screamed as the roc stood atop his mentor, claws cutting deep into his body.

Vola winced.

"What is the point of this again?" Sorrel said. "Are we really just supposed to sit here and watch this happening?"

"We're supposed to break the illusion," Vola said. "Whether that's by finishing it, or fighting, I don't know." There still weren't any other enemies for them to take care of. And the ones from the other illusions had all been faceless. Just figures to cut down. This roc seemed more real than some of the monsters they'd fought in their own travels.

Anders raced forward. He couldn't connect with the giant bird, but he ducked and dodged, making it chase after him instead of Mariel while she wove her spell.

She clasped her hands, whispering a name, and light filled the space between her palms. Then she threw it at the roc. The spell filled the fearsome creature, spilling from its mouth and eyes, and out from under its feathers.

It shrieked and thrashed, catching Anders across the chest and flinging him into the tower wall. Mariel raced forward and its claws tangled in her skirt, dragging her down under its convulsing beak and claws while it died.

"No!" Anders struggled to his feet, then collapsed. Finally, he crawled forward as the roc lay still amid a mess of feathers and blood.

He gathered Mariel's limp body into his arms.

Vola tried to breathe normally and found she couldn't around the lump in her throat. She'd held each member of her team, sometimes thinking they were dead, and it had nearly broken her. How much worse would it have been if she hadn't been able to heal them?

Anders's lips moved, and Vola realized she could hear him in the silence. The storm whistling above had died abruptly in the face of the roc's death.

"Please, please, please," he was saying.

Rilla watched, her face still as stone. Lillie held her hands over her mouth, eyes full.

Mariel didn't stir.

Anders threw back his head. "Maxim!" he cried, voice ragged. "She's one of yours." He pulled Mariel close and bent over her once again. "She's one of yours," he whispered. "Maxim. Please."

Finally, a single shadowy figure crept from the back of the tower, where a set of stairs led down. One, after all of that. It slunk toward the grieving Anders.

Vola ignored the ache in her throat and stepped to intercept the enemy. She didn't even try to sneak up on it. What was the point, anyway? This was just a memory. Nothing she did would affect the outcome.

As her sword cleaved the shadowy figure in two, a familiar shiver started at the top of Vola's head and swept down to her feet, and the tower faded around them, dissolving into a smear of black and white and gray.

"Well, that was uniquely horrible," Sorrel said.

"What is this for?" Lillie asked, scrubbing at her eyes. "What is he hoping to accomplish by making us watch all this?"

"To feel sorry for him, obviously," Talon said.

"Everyone's lost someone," Rilla said, sharply. "That doesn't excuse him from trying to drain the world of magic. My dad died when I was eight. You don't see me terrorizing entire countries."

Vola rubbed her forehead, trying to erase the after images of Anders's grief and failing.

Sounds came to them first as the rest of the world smeared into existence like watercolors running together.

The clash of weapons and calls of wounded soldiers slipped down Vola's spine, and she settled her shield more firmly.

"Heads up," she said. "We're coming out hot, apparently."

They circled up, keeping their backs to each other, and Vola kept her ears open as the colors shifted and gathered and finally solidified into the real world once again.

Orcs circled them, weapons drawn. They guarded the windows and doors of the ruined house as sounds of fighting drifted from outside. Vola found the familiar figure of Gorgo just outside the front door, and she raced to join him.

"We're out," she called as she stepped across the threshold. "What do you need?"

Gorgo glanced at her with a frown and kicked an enemy in the knee. He cut the man down as he staggered.

Then the world fell strangely still, and the orc chieftain wiped his brow. "Nothing, apparently?" he said. "It's just been little feints like that. Testing our defenses. I'm more worried about them."

Vola raised her gaze and her breath froze in her chest. Ranks of people stood in a solid wall just twenty yards from the ruined house. Just standing there, staring.

These weren't undead. These were fully fleshed humans, mostly. With a scattering of the other races represented.

"What are they doing?" Vola whispered.

"Exactly this," Gorgo said. "Every now and then a little group attacks, but it's more for show than anything. The rest are waiting for something. Before you went in, our backs were to the barrier at least. But now it's gone, we're too exposed."

Vola followed his gaze. The barrier had retreated once again, now that they'd broken the illusion. It shimmered quite a ways away, but it seemed much smaller now than before. Vola even fancied she could see the looming bulk of the volcano through the curtain.

"I don't like these," Gorgo said. "They're strange."

"I know our village is small," Vola said with a grin. "But surely you recognize humans."

"Smartass. That's not what I meant. These are acting odd. None of them want to talk."

Vola surveyed the enemy. Gorgo was onto something. For one, they looked nothing like soldiers. Where was the armor? And weapons? They carried rusted swords and pick axes. Like they'd picked up any old thing lying around. A blank-eyed woman nearby even wore a kilted-up gown covered in flour, as if she'd just walked away from her baking.

Something about her stare stirred in Vola's gut.

"Oh," Vola said. "Oh crap. Lillie!"

Lillie popped her head through a window.

"They're controlled."

Lillie's mouth dropped open, and she stared at the pressing enemy. "Oh." She said. "Oh crap." She wove her hands together and cast a shield around a group of them.

The subverted villagers blinked. Then one by one they toppled to the ground, eyes closed as their minds tried to recover from what had been done to them.

"Mind control?" Gorgo said. He whistled to Lillie. "Can you do that to all of them?"

Lillie stared around at the enemy army. "Not any time soon."

"Hey!" Lydia called from the left, where she stood with a line of orcs. "Hey!"

Vola spun to see a large man with raggedly cut hair and a beard that hadn't been trimmed in ages try to push past her mother. He wore the remnants of a knight's surcoat, but it had been so badly stained Vola couldn't even see what color it was anymore.

The man pushed again, and Lydia shoved him back. She roared in his face and launched herself at him, battle ax raised.

The man screamed and rolled away. The subverted villagers remained frozen, waiting. But this one had desperation in his eyes as he fought to get through Lydia.

"Lillie!" he called. "Lilliara!"

Lillie's head whipped around and her lips parted on a name. "Innis."

Vola charged forward and snatched the man away from her mother's ax blade. She hauled him to his feet and yanked him into the center of their circle, keeping her hand clenched on the back of his neck.

Lydia growled and followed.

"Just a second, Mom," Vola said. "I want to hear what he has to say."

"I can't kill him?"

"Depends on what it is he says next."

The man blinked wide blue-green eyes up at her. All four Ephyra children had inherited their mother's eyes, but Vola wasn't going to be swayed by how much Innis looked like his sister.

"You," he said, voice hoarse like he hadn't used it in a long while. Or like he'd spent a lot of time screaming. "You protected her."

Vola's eyes narrowed. True, the last time she'd seen this man, she'd done a pretty good job of keeping Lillie alive. But also, the last time she'd seen him, he'd been banished for treason.

Innis shook himself. He didn't try to pull away from her grip, but he did try to draw himself upright more, throw his shoulders back, and at least stand like a real knight.

"Lillie," he said again.

Lillie tumbled through the open window of the house and stopped short, keeping a good ten feet between herself and one of the brothers who'd betrayed her.

"Innis," she said, voice steady without inflection. "What are you doing here?"

"I came to warn you." He coughed and tried to clear his throat. "Anders. He helped us escape your prison, but…he's trying to take all the magic out of the world. He subverted all these people, just like he did to Kellan. And…and he's convinced Xavier this is all for the best."

"We know," Lillie said. "We saw Xavier already. He tried to kill us. Again."

Innis's shoulders slumped. "Lillie, I'm sorry."

"Might be a bit late for forgiveness, boyo," Sorrel said, leaning on her staff in the doorway.

Innis's eyes flashed. The first bit of defiance Vola'd seen since he'd disappeared through the portal to another plane. "I'm not saying it because I want forgiveness," he said. "I'm saying it because it needs to be said." He turned to Lillie. "I was wrong, and I'm sorry. I'm sorry about Xavier, I'm sorry I supported him for as long as I did. And I'm…I'm just sorry."

His eyes flicked to Vola, then Rilla, then Sorrel. "I'm not asking for forgiveness. I'm not asking for a pardon or exoneration. But I am trying to make up for my actions now. I left Xavier. I left Anders. And I came here to warn you."

"Warning would have been nice before we were surrounded," Gorgo said with a huff.

Innis shook his head. "This isn't the worst of it. Anders has a new commander on the field. She's out there right now. She holds the reins for these troops. They'll follow her mindlessly into the slaughter just because she tells them to."

Vola stiffened, eyes unfocused, while her lips thinned. "This commander. I take it she's a half-orc. Spell caster. Carries a staff and thinks she knows everything."

"Goes by the name Inga," Talon said.

Innis looked between them. "You're not surprised," he said.

Vola closed her eyes, drew a deep breath, and then released it with all the pent-up rage and exasperation she could carry. "Not even a little."

NINETEEN

A SHUDDER WENT through the ranks of subverted villagers, and Vola took an involuntary step back.

"To the house," she said as calmly as she could.

It didn't matter. The others picked up her urgency and turned to race for the ruined house. Its walls were crumbling, but it would be better than nothing.

Vola kept her grip on Innis and threw him through the open door as the sea of subverted villagers surged forward, covering the twenty yards between them in less time than it took to smash an egg.

Vola slammed the door shut behind them and leaned on it.

The entire house shook as the bodies hit the walls at the same time.

Several orcs rushed to take her place against the door, the rest guarding the windows, shoving bodies back through the openings.

"Um, so what's the difference between these guys and zombies again?" Sorrel asked as Vola raced to join her team upstairs. "Because these look about the same."

"We can get rid of these," Vola said. She leaned out a second-story window to stare down at the milling heads. "At least cut them off from Inga's spell. Lillie, we're gonna need a bigger shield."

Lillie bit her lip. "If I do that, Inga and Anders could learn how to counter what I'm doing. It will be that much harder to break their mind control the next time."

Talon joined Vola and Sorrel at the window, bow ready in her hand. On the floor below there was a violent crack, and they heard Gorgo call out to hold them back.

"I don't think we have another choice. Not if we want to get back to our own army. Are you ready to make your last stand here?"

Lillie's mouth firmed.

There was a ripple in the ranks below them, and Vola held up her hand to wait. The subverted villagers around the front door pulled back, leaving a clear path leading from the front step.

Vola followed it with her eyes and her gaze latched on the figure at the top of the bare hill beyond. She was tall and shapely, with gray-green skin almost a perfect match for Vola's, and she wore a blue gown split up her leg. Her hand curled around a gnarled staff.

Vola inhaled.

"I'll do it," Lillie said flatly, pulling her spellbook from her satchel. "Give me as much time as you can. And don't let her get in your head."

Vola set her jaw and signaled the rest. "Let's go."

"Right, racing down the path the bad guy has paved," Sorrel said, following Vola down the shaky stairs. "Throwing ourselves into her waiting arms."

"Do you have a better idea?" Vola asked.

"Nah, it sounds fun. Just because we know something is a trap doesn't mean we don't have to throw ourselves in feet first."

"It means exactly that," Talon said as they paused at the front door. "We could choose not to rise to her bait."

"Sneak out the back while she expects you to walk out the front," Rilla said.

"I don't think we could get everyone out before she noticed," Vola said. "It's not like there's a lot of cover out there to hide fifty orcs."

"There's not a lot of cover in here to hide fifty orcs," Gorgo said. "But we're making it work. You going out there?"

"I am," Vola said.

"I'm going with you," Lydia said.

"What?" Gorgo said.

"The last time Vola faced this monster, she nearly killed me," Lydia said, baring her teeth. "I would like to return the favor."

"You stay here and wait for our signal," Vola told Gorgo. "Guard Lillie and when the subverted villagers go down, you can join us."

She swept up to the door. The orcs holding it shut took one look at her face and stood back. Vola raised her boot and kicked the door open.

"You know it was unlocked, right?" Talon said.

Lydia cast Gorgo a concerned look, but Vola ignored it. Her rage was firmly in check, held on a tight leash, ready to be released when it would do the most good.

Talon and Sorrel's expressions were set. Rilla just looked determined.

Sorrel poked her head out the door, checked that the way was clear, and then waved them through.

Vola stalked through the door, between the ranks of subverted villagers, and up the lava rock that rose outside the ruined house. The figure at the top stood tall and straight with a little smirk that crawled up Vola's spine and lodged in the back of her head, making her seethe.

Vola stopped about fifteen feet away and planted her feet. "You look pretty good for a dead woman, Inga," she said.

The half-orc's skin was as firm and clear as it had been the last time they'd seen her. She didn't look particularly undead.

"I feel like you should be falling apart more," Sorrel said, tilting her head. "And hunched over. You need to work on your corpse shamble. Anders has a lot of undead that can give you some pointers if you like."

Inga's lips twitched wider. "That would only be helpful if you'd actually succeeded in killing me," she said.

"How did you survive, then?" Talon said. "I seem to remember you getting thrown out a window."

"I had friends in high places. Or don't you remember?"

"Mulgash," Vola growled. "Funny how he forgot to mention you were still alive when I talked to him two days ago." And she'd be bringing it up the next time she saw him, for sure.

"He definitely seems to have developed a thing for you." Inga examined her nails. "I don't really like people who come and steal my patron out from under me."

"I don't really like people undoing all the work I've done. I just cleaned up this mess."

Inga's eyes flashed. "Oh, don't get me started. You stole my patron. You stole my purpose. And you stole my magic. Without Mulgash…" She closed her eyes and took a deep breath before opening them again. "He saw something in you he liked. The Obstacle of Rage dumped me and chose a paladin. A white knight."

Vola lifted her shield. "Not so white, now, you might recall."

Inga rolled her eyes. "Oh please. You and I both know that means nothing with the Broken standing at your shoulder."

Vola stiffened. "The Broken?" she said carefully. Inga knew Cleavah's secret?

Inga snorted. "Yes, the Broken. How long did it take you to figure it out?"

Vola ground her teeth. If she'd doubted whether this was the real Inga or not, it was gone now. The woman had always had a way of getting right under Vola's skin, like a splinter. She wriggled and wormed her way into her mind, knew exactly what she was going to do before she did it, knew exactly what to say to make Vola doubt herself.

"How did you get your magic back?" Sorrel said, swinging her staff idly. "If Mulgash dumped you."

"What makes you think I did?"

Sorrel raised an eyebrow and indicated the subverted villagers around them as if to say "duh."

Inga sighed. "Point to you. The process is very similar, at least, even if the source is different."

Inga hadn't been born with magic. Like Anders, she'd been born with less than so many other people. She'd tried to go to the universities like Lillie. She'd tried to learn the magic she hadn't been born with. But her orc heritage had put her at a disadvantage. The authorities had kept her out, and Inga, full of bitterness and hate, had made a bargain with the Greater Obstacle of Rage.

Mulgash had given her magic and in return, she'd served him. Now without Mulgash, she'd be magicless once again.

Unless, of course, there was someone nearby with excess amounts of it who would be willing to lend her some. Someone who didn't have any scruples about stealing magic in the first place.

"So what did you promise Anders?" Vola asked. "What are you giving him in exchange for power?"

Inga grinned and gave Vola a look that said, "clever." "The usual," Inga said. "It's not complicated. He gives me the power he's collected, and I use it to further his cause. All the years with Mulgash gave me the skills to use it. Anders is ambitious, I'll give him that," she said. "But he's inexperienced. It would be like handing over all this power to you." She pointed to Lydia. "And wielding magic isn't like swinging a battle ax."

"I'd like to see you swing this," Lydia muttered.

Inga cocked her head. "But what are you trying to accomplish here?" she said. "Why all the questions?"

Vola exchanged a glance with Rilla while Sorrel raised her chin. "What do you mean, what are we trying to accomplish? You blocked us into that house. Then clearly you wanted to talk to us so we came out to oblige."

"But you haven't even tried to kill me yet," Inga said, folding her arms and tapping her chin. "And after trying so hard last time —and nearly succeeding—I just expected more from you. Unless…"

Vola's gaze wanted to crawl toward the second-story window where Lillie had to be working, but she didn't let it.

"Unless you're stalling for time," Inga concluded. Without even pausing for breath, she shot a ball of black fire at the window.

"Lillie!" Vola screamed.

A roar drowned out her cry as Innis surged from a hiding place among the subverted villagers. He leaped upwards and the ball of black fire burst against his chest. He fell with a heavy thump.

Vola sucked in a breath. She jerked her thumb over her shoulder, and Lydia scurried to check on him. The rest spread out around Inga without her having to say so.

Inga just shook her head. "You should know better by now, Vola. I'm always one step ahead of you."

Vola set her teeth and raised her shield. "Charge," she said.

She rushed for Inga, ready to bash the smirk from her face, but Inga disappeared with a wink.

Vola skidded to a stop on the top of the hill, narrowly avoiding a collision with Sorrel.

The half-orc reappeared on a distant hilltop. She cupped her hands around her mouth. "I learned a couple of things from Lilliara the last time I was in her head."

The crowd of subverted villagers who had stood silent and still turned in a circle to face Vola and the others.

"Charge," Inga called.

Vola whipped around, sword ready, as the villagers raised their makeshift weapons and rushed forward.

Light flared from the second floor of the ruined house, and it burst out across the sky, falling down to cover the army arrayed against them. As the light touched each villager, they fell into place. One by one they toppled, some falling over those in front until piles of villagers lay still, as if sleeping.

Sorrel and Talon turned to the window to give Lillie matching grins, but Vola was already sprinting in the opposite direction. Toward Inga.

Inga shrugged. "A setback," she said. "But nothing serious. I have no idea why Anders wants to meet you so badly, but he was very specific about not killing you. So…"

Vola brought her blade down and the edge whistled through empty air as Inga disappeared yet again.

Vola roared in frustration, but Inga didn't reappear to meet her challenge. There was nothing around them. Nothing but the house, fifty-some odd orcs, an unconscious army, and Innis.

Vola stood there for a moment, fists clenched around the hilt of her sword and the grip of her shield, fighting against the red that washed across her vision as the others raced for Innis. She was needed. She was the healer, but all she could do was stand there and try to breathe without screaming.

"Vola," Sorrel called.

Vola turned, fighting away the last bit of red, and sprinted back to the others.

Innis lay against the rough lava rock, his breath coming raggedly through his lips.

Lillie burst from the house and fell to her knees on the rock, gathering him into her arms. Vola knelt beside her, hands reaching for Innis.

The knight's chest was black and caved in. Vola couldn't even find the edge of his surcoat within the charred mess.

"Lady bless," she whispered, reaching for the well of healing within her that connected her to the Broken.

Light flared between her and Innis, and she poured the power into him, pulling flesh and blood and bone and organs back into place. An ache started in her own chest, mirroring Innis's wounds. But the harder she pulled, the more the healing resisted. The blackened bits of skin receded bit by bit, but not enough. Not nearly enough.

Vola continued to pour the power into Innis, but he soaked it up without getting any better.

What was wrong? This was bad, worse than anything she'd ever healed before, but she should at least be making it better.

Vola's mind raced over the last few minutes. Talking with Inga, the black fire racing toward the house.

Inga's power came from Anders. And Anders had stolen a piece of the Broken's power.

And she used the Broken's power to heal. But it wasn't enough, apparently. Perhaps a god's power couldn't counteract itself.

"I'm sorry," Vola whispered, shoulders sagging as the light faded between her fingertips.

"Lillie," Innis gasped out.

"I'm here." Lillie's voice was thick, and Vola could hear her swallow.

"S-sorry," he said, the word a bare puff of breath between his lips.

Lillie choked. She took Innis's hand and held it against her cheek.

"Sorry."

In the next moment, he was gone.

TWENTY

THEY CARRIED Innis back to camp between four orcs who acted like they didn't even notice his weight. Lillie's face remained pale and stony as she limped beside them.

Vola nearly outpaced them several times, the seething anger under her skin driving her faster and faster. She couldn't fight this threat. Inga had run away instead of facing her. And Anders didn't seem to be hurt by the progress they were making breaking down his barrier. Which left Vola feeling penned in and useless. Like a sheep being herded against a fence. She couldn't fight back. She turned to bite and found nothing to hurt. All she could do was keep running forward.

Anders was taking everything she'd worked for, everything she'd accomplished in the last year, and stripping it away. All her work was being unraveled beneath her feet, and she felt like any second now she'd tear through that thin foundation and start falling.

And what could she grab onto?

The camp was packing up by the time they arrived. War must have an innate sense of when they were about to return with good news. Or she just had someone monitoring the barrier to send word when they could advance again.

Without saying anything, Lillie led them to the camp's temple, which was only two rows from the scholars. And without saying anything, the orcs followed her.

The acolyte manning the tent hadn't done more than break down the benches and altar inside. He didn't complain when they laid Innis's body inside out of the way with his hands crossed over his chest.

Vola sent Gorgo and Lydia off with the other orcs after a quiet word. Gorgo cast a worried glance at Lillie. But the wizard didn't notice, and Lydia drew him away gently.

Lillie found Ephyra and Kellan inside the scholars' tent, packing their things.

"Lillie?" Kellan said, stopping dead in the middle of the tent when he saw his sister. "What's wrong?"

"You two should come with me," Lillie said quietly. "There's something…someone you should see."

Ephyra and Kellan exchanged a glance before following Lillie.

One of the scholars looked up, brow drawn down. "Wait, we have all this to get done before—"

"Let them go," Vola growled. "It's a family matter."

The scholar looked like he would argue, but then he glanced at Vola's face and snapped his mouth shut. He stared down at his feet.

Vola instantly regretted her tone. "I know what you're working on is important. But it can wait a few minutes."

"What *are* you working on?" Sorrel asked.

"Plan B," the scholar said. "In case Plan A doesn't work out."

"Um, what's plan A, then?" Talon said.

"Break through the barrier and bash Anders's brains out?" Sorrel said.

"Sounds about right," said Vola. She stepped back to get out of the way as one of the scholars carried a box bursting with papers out of the tent. Vola couldn't imagine how annoying it had to be to haul all the books and papers with them every time the army moved, only to have to unpack and repack everything a day or two later. But they were still working to understand Anders's draining spell, and that seemed a lot more important than the inconvenience.

Normally Vola and the others should have gone to break down their own campsite, but they'd already done that this morning before they'd left. After the last few days, it seemed prudent to pack up their tent and belongings and load them on the swamp monster ahead of time. The hostlers kept begging them not to leave it with them, but they couldn't drag the thing out in the field with them. Rilla had finally put her royal foot down and convinced them to handle the swamp beast without complaining. Vola suspected bribery had been involved.

Raised voices drifted between the tents, and Vola was too weary to be surprised. Squabbling seemed more usual than it should be now.

Sorrel cast a glance at the rest of them, her eyes resting on Vola for a moment, before she said, "I'll go sort them out. I thought I made it clear last time…" She scampered off towards the bickering.

Vola took a breath and tried to clear the tension in her chest, but it stayed there, heavy and oppressive. She couldn't help feeling like she was responsible for all the fighting, even if she wasn't the one here to start things. Or end them.

A shadow blotted out the dreary late afternoon light, and a down draft ruffled her hair.

Vola threw up her hand to shield her eyes.

"Looks like the contingent from Firewatch finally got here," Rilla said with a grin.

A huge turquoise dragon circled lazily down from the clouds

to land on the north end of camp where there was plenty of flat space. Several other massive shapes followed her, as well as a swarm of smaller horse-sized figures.

A bit of the tension bled from Vola's shoulders as she stared at the beautiful creatures. "Shall we go say hi to Listrell?"

It took longer than Vola anticipated to make their way through the frenetic packing. They had to reroute entirely around the mess tent, which had been brought down and laid across two different pathways. And someone had stacked about a million crates in the middle of a third.

Over all the chaos they could see flashes of colorful scales and broad heads big enough to swallow a cart, horse and all.

Finally, they broke out past the last line of tents and found the welcome sight of six dragons waiting on the field. Each had a small army of figures climbing down from their backs, little draconic shapes that they knew from experience would stand even taller than Vola. The dragons had brought their guardians with them. Fierce warriors bred to protect the dragons with their lives.

A whole herd of the smaller dragons, *draconis minimus*, swarmed around their landing site, each one about the size of a horse. Vola had often wondered if maybe the swamp beast was a mutant form of one of these, showing off only the awful bits of the species.

Vola hurried across the field, Talon and Rilla following. But as she moved, her heart sank. In the gray afternoon light, she made out a figure speaking to the big turquoise dragon. Listrell had her head bent low in order to hear Imralen and the poison he was surely pouring in her ear.

Talon must have heard her intake of breath.

"It's fine, Vola," she said. "Listrell knows you well enough to not listen to him."

It didn't stop her heart from racing and her steps to speed up.

They approached the dragons and more of them had their heads down, listening to Imralen now. Renvick, Listrell's lead guardian, stood beside her head, his rust-colored scales glinting with blue-green highlights.

Vola fought to keep her attention on Listrell and her friends, not the Knight Commander. But Imralen turned as she stepped up.

"Speak of the devil," Imralen said, a smirk breaking through his normal frown.

"Is it true there was trouble today, Vola?" Listrell asked, deep voice rumbling across the lava field. "Someone was killed?"

Vola felt something snap in the back of her head. These were her allies. These were her friends. People and creatures she'd fought to protect and earn their respect. Over and over again. From Water's Edge to Brisbene to Glenhaven to Deersford and Firewatch. She'd ignored the whispers. She'd ignored the flat-out insults and petty arguments. She'd trudged on and on, doing what she did best, helping people, hoping that one day it would pay off and people would look at her and see who and what she was.

And this man came along behind her and swept every deed, every calm word, every warm smile under the rug as if it had never happened.

She lunged forward and planted her fist in Imralen's face.

Imralen stumbled back, his hands going to his gushing nose as Rilla and Talon cried out. Several dragons reared up, and Renvick shot forward to hold Vola back.

He held Vola's shoulders as she surged against him, ready to finish Imralen. Finish him how she wasn't quite sure. She was angry enough to kill right now, ricocheting between protecting her allies and protecting herself.

Renvick's claws gripped her shoulders, leaving ten perfect scratches in her armor.

"Let me go," she growled.

"No, Vola. People such as us cannot react in anger the way others can. We are too big. Too threatening."

She hesitated and caught his glance. He stared down at her, slitted eyes hooded with sympathy.

"We cannot rage the way they can," he said quietly at her. "You know this. You have only forgotten it for this moment."

Her fingernails dug into her palms. "I'm tired of being the better person." Just once she wanted to hit the thing in her way. The prejudice and discrimination that had taken physical form in Imralen. She wanted to pummel him into the ground until he begged for mercy.

And that was made her step back. And realize that she wasn't thinking like herself.

Rilla and Talon dragged on her arms, hauling her back another step or two.

"What the hell are you doing, Lightless?" Rilla hissed.

Imralen glanced at his hands and saw the blood that had come from his nose. His lips curled in a snarl, but Vola thought she saw a glint of triumph in his narrowed eyes.

"This!" he cried. "This is what happens when you fail to contain your beast."

Vola surged forward again, but Rilla and Talon leaped to hold her back. Renvick stepped between them and placed a hand on Imralen's chest.

"Go, now," the big guardian said.

Imralen tried to straighten his clothes with a dignified yank, but the effect was ruined when he had to keep one hand up to stop the blood from spilling down his chin. "I've been telling you all this time, she's too close to Mulgash. A paladin connected to the god of Rage will ruin us all. Her violence will tear this army apart before we even get close to Anders."

Vola wanted to scream. He was the one tearing the army apart. He was going to ruin all their plans. But the others were all glancing at her, looking at her out of the corners of their eyes as if she'd explode all over everyone. Which maybe she already had.

Renvick crowded Imralen back, and finally the Knight Commander threw up his hands and stalked away.

Vola yanked herself out of Rilla and Talon's grip. Talon tried to step in front of her.

"Why are you listening to that bastard?" Talon said. "You've always ignored him before."

"Maybe I haven't been ignoring him," Vola said. "Maybe I've just been storing up every little thing he's said and realizing that ignoring him will never work. Maybe I'm tired of not fighting back. Letting him say anything he wants. Maybe it's time someone told him to hold *his* tongue."

"No one was accepting what he was saying," Listrell rumbled above them. She turned one golden eye on Vola, looking hurt. "We know you better than him. We would have defended you. If you had waited just one moment more."

Vola's lips thinned, and she looked away.

"Now you've just given him ammunition," Talon said, holding onto her arms as if Vola would rip away. Maybe she would. She felt like it. "He has all the proof he needs now."

Vola caught the quick look that passed between Rilla and Talon, but she couldn't interpret it past "what a mess."

Talon let go of Vola. "I'll handle the dragons," Talon told Rilla. "I've always been better with non-humans."

"I'm only half human," Vola grumbled.

Rilla shot her a sharp glance. "I'll handle Lightless," she said like she was taking charge of an unbroken horse.

Vola couldn't help swallowing. She didn't want to be the direct focus of the Dagger Princess's anger.

Rilla took her arm and dragged her away from the dragons. Vola got the impression that even if she dug in her feet and put all her strength into resisting, the rangy princess would win.

Rilla dragged her to a clear area outside camp, away from Talon and the dragons, away from the bustle of the packing camp, and Vola had enough presence of mind to think that at least this wasn't going to be a public dressing down.

"What. The. Fuck?" Rilla finally turned to face her. "What was that?"

Vola opened her mouth to answer, and Rilla waved a finger in her face. "No, wait. I'll tell you what that was. That was a tactical disaster. You're supposed to be smarter than that. I know you're smarter than that. But you just struck the Knight Commander, giving him everything he ever wanted."

Vola yanked her arm away from Rilla and paced exactly ten steps to the left, then spun and paced ten steps back.

"You know what he says isn't true," Rilla said. "You know the rest of us don't believe it."

"That doesn't mean he should get to say whatever he wants without consequence. I just gave him his consequences."

"I know this is stupid and hard but—and I can't believe I have to say this to you of all people—striking him in anger isn't the way to fix any of it."

Vola stopped and looked down at Rilla. The princess tipped her head back and stared back at her.

"How long am I supposed to stay quiet, Rilla?" Vola asked. "How long am I supposed to take the higher road? How long does it take to disprove the lies he spouts about me? Because none of that's working."

"Longer than four days."

"I've been rolling over for him for half my life!"

For once Rilla didn't answer. She just watched with calm, dark eyes.

Vola tried to run her hands through her hair, but her braid was tangled and thick with sweat and a little bit of Innis's blood.

"Knight Commander Imralen ran the academy," Vola said.

"He made my life miserable. For years. The only thing that made it worth it was Henri. And the thought that as soon as I graduated, I could leave, and I'd never have to see his looks or bear his snide remarks again. And then…"

"And then?" Rilla said.

"Then I graduated and found out that Imralen was just a representative of the rest of the world. He wasn't the only one who saw me that way. He wasn't even the worst. And I realized that my entire life was going to be one long string of convincing people I'm not what they thought."

"What changed?" Rilla asked. "You've been doing this half your life, you said. So what changed today?"

Vola slumped. "It's easier to fight him when I know he's wrong."

Rilla's mouth went tight. She reached out and touched Vola's arm. "You're not responsible for Innis," she said.

Vola found an outcropping of lava rock and let her legs collapse. She buried her head in her hands. "Maybe not. But maybe I could have done better."

"Or you could have done a lot worse."

Vola huffed a laugh, but she didn't lift her face from her hands. "He's right about Mulgash. The Obstacles might not be evil. But they are obstacles. And Mulgash just won't leave me alone. Even after Cleavah and the Broken. Learning to work around him instead of against him. He just keeps cropping up. And it's like all that work I did is just…gone."

Rilla rubbed the back of her neck and sat next to Vola.

"Everything we've done against Anders so far, he's reversing. How do you fight against that? Just do the same thing over and over again? How long do you beat your head against the wall before you admit the wall has won?"

"If the alternative is letting him win?" Rilla said. "Forever I guess."

Vola shot a glance at her. "Thanks for the pep talk, boss."

Rilla snorted. "You don't fight alone, you moron. That's the trick, I guess. Every time you come back, you have more people on your side. All those people you think aren't listening to you or aren't getting convinced are gathering. Until one day you have enough to topple him."

Vola's eyes swept the camp, taking in the flags still flying. The different countries who'd come to their aid. The dragons, the scholars. The monks and the villagers. The paladins.

"You were right," Rilla said, startling Vola out of her reverie. "We haven't been defending you the right way."

Vola shook her head. "I didn't mean —"

"Shut up. It's my turn. You were right. Just because we know Imralen's a liar, doesn't mean he should get to spout lies all over the place. No one's called him on his bullshit. Your entire defense has fallen on you and how well you keep silent. And that's not right."

Vola blinked, then stared down at her hands clenched over her knee. She didn't trust herself to say anything right then. It could have come out as tears of relief and gratitude or a bitter diatribe about how too late it was. But neither of those things was right or true to the wash of confusing feelings she was actually experiencing.

"I'll try to do better," Rilla said. "And I'll bet you have plenty of people like Listrell." She nodded toward the dragons settling down outside camp. "Like Talon and Lillie and Sorrel who are already doing better than me."

It was hard to forget the rare fire in Lillie's eyes anytime someone tried to convince her Vola was a monster. Or the way Sorrel laughed and mocked those who spat poison words. Or Talon, who barely said anything but stayed standing beside the family she'd chosen even when her own fears were dragged out into the open.

And suddenly Vola felt warm and small and ungrateful all at once.

"Of course, that doesn't mean we haven't made an unholy mess of all this in the meantime. Between our silence and Imralen's bloody nose, things in camp are going to be worse than they were before."

Vola winced. "I'm sorry. For what it's worth."

"Thank you. You lie low out here with the dragons. If Lillie's right—and I've learned never to bet against her—we only have one more illusion to break before we get to Anders. After defeating him, no one will be able to question anything about you again."

TWENTY-ONE

VOLA WAS glad to step out onto the lava field with her team the next morning, leaving the turbulent camp behind her. She'd apologized privately to Talon the night before, and they'd spent the night under Listrell's shadow with Renvick and the rest of the guardians. Sorrel hadn't joined them, and they assumed she was busy managing disagreements back in camp, and Lillie had remained shut away with her family.

"Are you sure you want to come?" Vola asked her now. This was the first chance they'd had to talk since they'd left Lillie with the Ephyras the day before. "We've got Rilla and—"

"I'm coming, Vola," Lillie said, sharper than normal. "You can't convince me not to, so don't try."

"I was just…" Vola blew out her breath, knowing it was pointless to argue. Lillie was grieving. She was allowed to be irritable, and it didn't mean that she was actually angry with Vola. No matter how much Vola was angry with herself.

"She just means you seemed busy," Sorrel said. "With whatever the scholars are working on."

It was at least part of the truth. Lillie had been head down in her notes when they'd collected her that morning.

"Plan B," she said. "Yes. But…That's what my family does. When we're sad or anxious, we bury ourselves in research. This…" She gestured, taking in the five of them as well as the rippling barrier ahead of them. "This is better. It feels more proactive. And…well, I'd really like to kill Anders or Inga or whoever gets in my way next."

Vola raised an eyebrow.

"Sounds good to me," Talon said. "Do you think when this is done, we can go back to regular adventuring?"

Vola swallowed away the lump in her throat. When this was over, would they even have a reason to stay together anymore? So much had happened…

"What is 'regular adventuring?'" Sorrel said. "I'm not sure I know anymore."

"It's…less than ideal quests pulled from a job board in a seedy tavern," Lillie said.

Vola shook off her melancholy and grinned. "It's getting paid in room and board because that's all the villagers can afford."

"It's thwarting kidnappers and bandits," Talon said.

"And rescuing princesses." Rilla cocked her head with a smirk.

"Huh," Sorrel said. "Sounds like we've had a pretty good run so far."

"Speaking of princesses," Talon said, and Vola turned to find War riding up the ridge behind them.

"What are you waiting for?" she said. "Get a move on. We're serving as your honor guard today." She jerked an elbow, indicating the ranks of elite Southglen guards behind her.

Vola's eyes narrowed.

War caught her look. "We're faster than we look. We'll escort you to the last illusion and watch your backs while you're in there. That'll give the rest of the army a chance to catch up so we're all in place for the final assault. Once that barrier goes down, I want our scouts in first. The rest will follow on their intelligence. I want Anders taken care of tonight."

Vola gave her a salute and signaled her team forward.

"That seems ambitious," Lillie said under her breath as they moved down the treacherous lava rock and started toward the barrier. "It's unlikely that Anders has just been sitting in his stronghold waiting for us to break through to him. He must have defenses in place."

"Like an undead army," Rilla said. "And anyone he managed to subvert into fighting for him."

"Inga did say he wanted to meet us personally," Sorrel said. "Maybe he'll make it easy."

"I don't trust easy," Talon said.

"Neither do I," Vola said. "Let's just get to the illusion and do our job. I'm sure War is worrying about the details. And we'll let the scouts handle what's behind the barrier before we go charging in."

Lillie led them unerringly to the edge of the barrier. It now contained only the volcano and the space directly around it, and they could just make out the shadow of the jagged mountain behind the shimmering wall of light.

The gray clouds seemed to press down on them as they stood contemplating the clear area at the base of the mountain. Vola glanced up at the sky, but despite the clouds, they remained dry.

War and her elite guard arranged themselves around them.

"This is the last one, right?" Vola asked Lillie.

"It should be," she said. "I will be monitoring the spell from inside. To make sure. But yes. The barrier had five anchor points. We've done four. Ergo this should be the last one."

"Thanks for the math lesson," Talon muttered.

"Did you just use 'ergo' in a sentence?" Sorrel said.

Lillie gave her a baffled look. "Yes. Why?"

"Keep your eyes open as we come out of it," Vola said. "These have all been ambushes so far, and I imagine the last one will be the biggest trap of all."

Sorrel drew her staff. "Let's do this, then."

"Is it really a trap if you know about it before and walk into it, anyway?" Rilla said, fingering the hilt of one of her many daggers.

"Yes," Talon said "Yes, it is."

The lava field and the elite guard dissolved into smears of gray and black. Rough pocketed stone replaced the open air, forming a large cavern made up of more lava rock. It climbed far above their heads to a jagged opening that let in bright sunlight.

Vola couldn't help whistling. They must have been inside the mountain their physical bodies were currently standing before.

"This cave would have been formed by a lava pocket hundreds of thousands of years ago," Lillie said. "Back when the volcano was still active."

A couple of pickaxes and some shovels lay abandoned in the corner and some of the rock around them bore evidence of rudimentary excavation. Someone had been chipping away at the interior of the cave, expanding the walls.

A single rough wooden table stood in the center of the cavern, where the light was best. A figure stood over it, studying some sort of diagram. Vola craned her neck to see and caught sight of the man's face.

Anders. Now with pain lines etched in the corners of his mouth and a few strands of silver hair threading through the black, but still recognizable from all the memories he'd forced them to watch.

Vola glanced at Lillie to see if she had any clue yet what they were supposed to be doing this time. Lillie had the frown she always wore when she was analyzing something, but she didn't meet Vola's look, so Vola let her concentrate.

"Nice place you have here," a voice said from behind them. "You need some curtains or rugs to make it homier, though."

The familiar sing-song voice sent a shaft of heat through Vola's limbs, and she whipped around to find a gnome standing in the wide opening of the cave, her hip cocked nonchalantly. She wore a tattered robe that fell to about mid-calf and carried a staff tipped with a clump of black feathers.

"Please tell me we're supposed to be fighting Nargilla," Sorrel said. "I want to beat the crap out of her. Again."

"Shh," Vola said.

Nargilla's large eyes took in the cave and its sole occupant, and her seamed brown face creased in a smirk.

Anders pushed off the table. "Welcome, Miss Pipwattle," he said. "I hope you didn't have any trouble finding the place."

"The golems at the door didn't seem to want to let me in but we had a little chat. I assumed it was some sort of test to keep the rabble out."

"Hmm," Anders said noncommittally.

"Anyway. They were much friendlier as a pair of frogs. Impressive armature," she said. "But there's always a weakness to transformation. Golems aren't nearly as scary once you've turned them into something you can squish."

"I'll keep that in mind in the future," Anders said.

"So what does an abandoned volcano run for these days?" Nargilla said, digging at the solidified ash with her toe.

"Plenty," he said.

Nargilla cocked her head. "And you still have enough to pay that exorbitant fee you advertised?"

Anders's expression remained serene. "I do."

Nargilla tapped her chin. "Hey wait, I recognize your name now. You were part of the team that took down Brindle the Butcher and his roc. Weren't you?"

Anders's mouth went thin and hard. "The only survivor," he said, turning back to the table.

Nargilla whistled. "No wonder you can afford all this, if you got the dead guys' shares as well."

He glared at her.

She held up her hands. "Oh, sore spot? Sorry."

He went back to the paperwork on the table, and Nargilla checked him out from behind, her eyes traveling up and down his form.

"So about that exorbitant fee," she said when he'd been quiet for too long. "I'll knock a couple of zeros off the price if you want to just stand there and let me look."

Anders turned to stare, aghast, and Nargilla wiggled her eyebrows.

"The fee stays the same," he said. "It depends only on whether or not you can do the spell."

Nargilla snorted. "Trust me, that won't be a problem. I can suck the magic out of anything."

"Anything?"

Nargilla gave him a sidelong look. "That sounds like a challenge."

Anders pushed off from the table once again and took a piece of paper with him. "I have some very specific needs for this project. You'll have support from the rest of my contractors, but I need to know that you can handle your part of the work. It's essential."

He held out the paper.

"All right, sexy, I'm listening." She took the page and scanned it. Then her mouth dropped open. "You want all this?" The fun had gone out of her voice.

"I do."

"For what?"

"That's my business."

"Hey, if I'm going to be going up against the gods to steal their power, I deserve to know."

"Are you afraid of them?"

She rolled her eyes. "Hell no. They sit up there doing nothing. But this is serious." She waved the paper in her hand. "This is world-ending shit if we get even the slightest bit wrong. I should know what I'm getting myself into."

Anders hesitated for a moment. "You're right." He held up one hand, palm out. "The gods aren't fit to carry the responsibility that they do. Someone I love trusted him—them. And they let her down. They didn't even try." He glanced away. "They don't deserve the power they have."

"And you think you do," Nargilla finished for him. She rolled the paper up. "Welp, that will do, I guess."

"You don't have any objections?" Anders asked.

Nargilla shrugged. "I don't care enough to have objections. You're paying me buckets of gold. As long as your reason is better than 'I want to be more powerful than everyone else in the world.' And it only had to be like a smidge better." She caught his questioning look. "Hey, I'm not a complete monster. Oh, and I needed to be sure I get to keep my magic, which I see you've already made a provision for." She gestured with the paper. "So I don't really care. Unless you want me to be a god too and reign at your side?" She batted her eyelashes at him.

"No," he said shortly.

She shrugged. "Worth a shot. I know you're going for terse, but I really like a man who can hold his tongue and look sexy while doing it."

"If you continue with the sexual harassment, I can always dissolve our contract."

"Fine, but I get to do whatever I want with you in my head."

Anders made a face.

Vola lifted her lip. At least now they knew Nargilla had

always been creepy. But what was the point of this illusion? No shadowy figures threatened the two conspirators. There was nothing for the barrier to be keyed to, as far as Vola could tell.

"Lillie?" she asked. "What's going on?"

"I'm not sure. I've found the anchor point in the spell," Lillie said. "But it's different from the others. Just completing this illusion will break it down. Except…" Lillie's eyes moved like she followed invisible lines through the world. "This one is connected to something."

"The barrier," Rilla said. "Weren't they all connected to the barrier? That's how we've been getting it to withdraw and shrink."

"This goes beyond that. I can't find where it ends." Her hands stopped moving, and her eyes went wide. "Oh. Oh gods."

"What?" A shaft of ice went down Vola's spine.

"Don't let it end! The illusion. Keep it going."

Vola lurched, but she didn't know what she was heading for. "How? Lillie, I don't know how to do that."

Around them, the illusion began to dissolve. The walls of the volcano faded and blurred to gray, and Vola reached out as if she could hold on to it, grip it between her fingers and keep it in place. Trusting Lillie, even though she had no idea what the wizard had seen.

But of course, it didn't work that way.

The scene fuzzed, but in front of them, the figure of Nargilla froze, her wide grin mocking them. Black and purple lights shot out from behind her, outlining her form in dark light until she seemed like a shadow within a shadow.

Then the dark light pulsed and a shock wave knocked Vola off her feet.

She hit the ground with a thud and the rough lava rock scraped her fingertips. She rolled over onto her elbows and shook her head, trying to clear it.

What the hell had just happened? Something bad. That was all she knew right now.

A musical tink tink tink echoed in her ear, and she realized rain pattered onto her armored back, matting her hair down.

The illusion was definitely gone now, replaced by reality. Vola blinked to bring the world back into focus and finally managed to lift her head.

Ahead of her, one of the elite guards of Southglen lay on his back, stunned. War sprawled just a little beyond, golden mail shining under a layer of rain.

Vola turned her head, her neck creaking from the strain. Her team lay around her, struggling to their feet. Talon, Sorrel, Lillie, and Rilla. All accounted for.

All arrayed around a single figure standing in the middle of their circle.

A gnome. Barely three feet tall and dressed in a tattered robe. Her coarse features were creased with a broad smile.

No illusion this time.

She stood there. Physically. On the field in front of Anders's mountain. Vola could see it now that the barrier had dropped, standing darker even than the clouds. A wide maw opened in the base, giving them a straight shot into Anders's stronghold.

But Nargilla Pipwattle stood in the way.

"Wow, you guys really do get into some trouble, don't you?" she said.

Vola scrambled to her feet, drawing her sword and shield. Sorrel pushed herself up using her staff.

"Oh my gods," Sorrel said. "Didn't we get rid of you once already?"

Nargilla put her hands on her hips. "What, you didn't want me here? That's your own fault, then."

"How?" Talon said.

"The illusion," Lillie said and coughed. Vola stepped across to help her up. "The illusion was tied to her."

"They all were," Nargilla said. "That Lord Arthorel really knows his business. And it's funny how you can attach just about anything to them when you have enough power."

"Your prison," Rilla started.

"Yup," Nargilla said. "Lord Arthorel's illusions, Anders's power, my prison. All connected so that every single time you broke one, it chipped away at my bonds just that much more. Until, poof. Here I am." She tilted her head. "I'm surprised you didn't see through the illusions. That was like, their sole purposed."

"Not their sole purpose," another voice said. "I might have linked up some other things as well."

A figure moved down the pale path that led to the maw in the base of the mountain, his feet crunching in the bleached lava rock. He stood tall with stark black hair. The rain stuck to it like little bits of starlight.

Anders looked much like his illusion self in real life, though a set of puckered red scars ran down his neck from the roc's claws. Like they'd never really healed properly.

"Oo, clever and sexy," Nargilla said. "I like it."

Anders's eyes locked on Nargilla. "Our arrangement has not changed, Pipwattle."

Nargilla shrugged. "It was worth a try."

"Well, now it's time to fulfill your contract. You'll find everything you need in the mountain. I trust I don't have to tell you to hurry."

"Nope. Army-leveling god power coming right up, Your Worshipfulness." Nargilla didn't even give the rest of them a second glance as she turned and trotted for the mountain.

Vola sucked in a breath. She was too far away, but they

couldn't let Nargilla leave. They couldn't let Anders start draining the world. She signaled Sorrel.

Sorrel planted her staff against the ground and used it to launch herself at Nargilla, feet first, aiming a kick at her head.

Anders barely glanced at her.

An invisible hand struck Sorrel in mid-air and sent her flying back into Talon and Rilla.

"Oh, nice one," Nargilla said. "You must have been practicing."

Anders cracked his neck. "It doesn't take that much skill once you get the hang of it. Go. I will rid the world of these nuisances."

Vola's grip tightened on her sword. Anders was a fighter, not a spell caster. But he'd just swatted Sorrel out of the air like the most adept wizard. He must have been learning how to use all the power he'd stolen.

Nargilla trotted away, calling over her shoulder, "Tell the gods hi for me. I appreciate their hospitality but it was getting a little constricting."

Anders turned to face off against them.

Vola glanced back. War was only just picking herself up off the ground, shaking her head while her elite guard groaned and tried to climb to their feet.

How much power did Anders have? How much had he stolen already? And how much of that was from the Broken and the other gods? Gods who should have been able to hang onto Nargilla and failed.

Anders raised his hand, and Vola lunged. She brought her sword down to strike his arm from his body, but her blade struck something solid. A magical shield flared and threw Vola back.

Anders brought both hands down and lightning crackled from the sky. Vola threw up her shield and sparks crackled across the surface, undeterred by the rain.

Rilla and Talon righted themselves and rushed for Anders

while he was distracted. Rilla went high and Talon went low. But his shield held, flaring.

Talon stumbled back, her hand over her eyes, and Rilla rolled away, holding her arm.

Vola's mind raced along several paths at once. How could they break the shield? It seemed similar to one Lord Arthorel had used, and that had just needed blunt force.

Vola signaled Sorrel again, and the halfling swung her staff. Maxim's Warhammer whistled through the air as she brought it down against Anders with a crack.

His shield flickered. But the moment it faltered, he flung up a hand.

Lightning hit Sorrel square in the chest, and she skidded along the ground to land at Vola's feet.

"Sorrel!"

The monk didn't stir.

Vola lunged for the halfling, her heart beating wildly in her throat, but power struck her between the shoulder blades and slammed her into the ground. The others fell to their knees, crying out in a chorus of pain and surprise.

Anders raised his arms over his head, and the clouds started to swirl. Flashes beyond the dark clouds made Vola's eyes go wide.

This was not good. Every avenue she followed in her head led to their destruction, or to a dead-end where Vola couldn't predict what Anders was capable of.

"Retreat," she tried to yell, but the crushing weight against her back turned it into a whisper. "We have to retreat."

Dust from smashed lava rock clogged her throat as she reached for Sorrel. But a flaming rock struck the ground between them, and she yanked her hand back. She twisted her neck to see meteors falling between them. If they stayed here, pinned to the ground, they'd be pummeled to death in seconds.

Across from Vola, Lillie managed to roll over, far enough to get her hands free. She whispered three words and a line of fire sprang up in front of Anders. He cried out and stumbled back a step.

The crushing weight left Vola's back, and she surged to her feet. Anders must only be able to concentrate on a spell or two at a time.

Meteors still fell around them, but Vola ducked her head and scooped Sorrel up to throw her over her shoulder.

"Go," she cried.

Talon went, walking backward to cover their retreat with her bow. Rilla stopped to help War, who turned and signaled her guard to get out.

Lillie took the chance to cast another spell and lobbed a fireball at Anders, who couldn't keep doing two things at once.

"Skill is more than just power," Lillie said. "It's knowledge and control. Concentration and—"

"You can lecture him later," Vola yelled. "Running now."

"I'm covering your retreat."

"Like hell you are."

Anders glared at them through the flames that flickered across the lava field, and the rock at their feet split. A meteor streaked in front of her nose, and Vola jumped back, stepping into a hole where a zombie was emerging. She cried out and kicked its head, her boot going right through its skull. But the creature kept climbing up, even without its head, and latched onto her leg.

Three more had hold of Lillie. The wizard set them on fire, but the undead didn't seem to care. These were more than just the normal zombies they'd fought so far. And they were cutting them off from their escape.

Lillie yelled in frustration and disappeared under the grasping limbs and rotting flesh.

Vola took a deep, bracing breath and let the rage rise in her chest. It felt a little too close to panic, but she'd learned how to control it, use it, focus it. The red seeped across her vision, narrowing what she could see, and she focused on the pile of undead that covered Lillie.

Vola roared and charged ahead. She flung bodies aside. Someone tried to clamp their teeth around her arm, and she shook free. A meteor sizzled past her ear, and she turned so it wouldn't strike Sorrel's limp form.

She kicked and dug at the undead until she found a pale arm with perfectly oval nails.

She yanked, pulling Lillie bodily from the pile. With one arm over Sorrel and the other around Lillie's waist, Vola glanced at the undead horde pulling themselves out of the ground. She glanced at the god-like being standing on the other side of the flames.

They were going to lose. They were going to die and the world would crumble with them. And there was nothing she could do.

"You have one more spell to get us out of here?" she asked Lillie. But Lillie's head lolled, her eyes unfocused, like she'd hit her head or used too much magic.

The rage sustaining Vola faltered. "Lady," she whispered, turning her head up toward the smoke-filled sky, letting the rain slide down her cheeks. "Lady, please."

Anders was right. There were so many gods who didn't care. Who thought that they could sit back and watch mortals in their conflicts and bet on the winner. So many like Maxim who thought that distance protected them.

But not all of them.

Not all. Right?

"Lady."

Arms closed around Vola, just as the first of the undead horde reached them.

"I have you," the Broken whispered in her ear.

And with a wash of clean, fresh air, they were away. Vola

closed her eyes against the sudden vertigo and the bright light that threatened to blind her.

After a moment that lasted an eternity she felt rock beneath her feet. And she opened her eyes to find herself standing on the ridge with War, Rilla and Talon, Gruff at their feet. Lillie and Sorrel were still clasped close in her arms. The remains of the elite guard sat or lay around them, too beaten to stand.

The Broken stood beside her, staring back at the mountain.

Clouds ringed the distant volcano and meteors flared, bright against the underside of the haze as they rained down around the stronghold.

A tug on Vola's arm prompted her to let go of Lillie. The wizard rubbed her face and took a step forward before falling to her knees. The orange and red glare of the meteors lit up against her skin.

Anders already had power enough to rival one of the gods. And now he had Nargilla to give him more. She was there inside the mountain, beginning the spell that would strip the rest of the world of magic.

Vola cast a hopeless glance at the others around them. War's face was streaked with soot, and her eyes seemed glassy with shock.

Talon and Rilla both looked back at Vola as if waiting for orders or an idea, or anything. And Sorrel lay limp, looking singed around the edges.

The rage had left Vola completely, leaving a ringing hollowness in her chest as she stared out over the lava field. Most of which was on fire now.

"We are so fucked," she said.

There was no lightning bolt. The Broken didn't even pretend to be offended.

"Fucked indeed," the goddess said.

TWENTY-TWO

They dragged themselves back through the deluge to meet the rest of the army. War gave the order to camp right there. They wouldn't be getting any closer to Anders's stronghold. Not with the meteor storm swirling over the place.

Besides, what exactly would be the point?

Anders had won. He had Nargilla. He had all his lieutenants. They were poised to drain the magic out of the world and set Anders up as a god to rival all the gods.

Lillie and Talon stood huddled together, watching as War and Rilla struggled to put up the command tent themselves. Soldiers and messengers scrambled around them, trying to organize the rest of the chaos. But in the rain and the dark with their leaders just as confused and frightened as they were, nothing was getting done properly. Everyone was just pitching their tents where they could and hunkering down to wait for orders.

Vola knelt beside Sorrel in a nook between the half-fallen command tent and the healers, who stood arguing over the ripped canvas of their tent.

The halfling still breathed, but it sounded ragged to Vola's ears and the skin across her chest and collarbone was streaked with black. As if some of Anders's lightning had crept through her veins.

Vola bent her head, ignoring the rain trickling down the back of her neck under her armor. She held her hands over Sorrel and spoke. "Lady bless."

Gods, what if this wound was just like Innis's? What if there was too much of the Broken's power in the lightning for Vola to heal it? She could only hope the magic Anders had used had come from somewhere else. One of his other thefts.

Light shone under Vola's palms and streaked into the halfling's skin, chasing away the darkness in her veins and leaving healing in their wake.

Sorrel took a deep, unfettered breath.

Vola sank back on her heels and rubbed her face as Sorrel stirred. The rain made the halfling flinch, and she finally opened her eyes.

"Welcome back," Vola said.

Sorrel blinked, her gaze flicking from Vola to the dark sky, to Lillie and Talon watching pale and silent from the shadows.

"All right," Sorrel said, rolling so she could get her elbows under her. "Tell me the bad news."

"We're screwed," Rilla said, coming up beside them and kneeling. The command tent sagged behind her. "That's the worst of it."

Vola glared at the ground as she slipped a hand under Sorrel's elbow and helped her sit. "Give her a second."

"No," Sorrel said. "I want to know. What happened after he hit me?"

"Lillie and Vola got us out of there," Talon said.

"But not without a lot of luck," Lillie added. "And some help from the Broken. Which I don't know if we're going to be able to count on again."

Vola's lips thinned as she stood and faced Anders's mountain. She could just about see the dim glow between the jumbled tents.

The Broken had ferried them to safety and then vanished. Again. The way she always did. Vola could feel her, just over her shoulder. That faint, comforting presence. But it wasn't the same as when she was here.

"So Anders just gets everything he wants?" Sorrel said, drawing her knees up with a wince. "He gets to be a god and there's nothing we can do about it?"

"What do you want to do about it?" Rilla said. "Go in there and get hit by lightning again? Or get pummeled by a flaming rock? That was just with the power he's already stolen. What happens when he starts to drain the rest of the world?"

"We all die," Talon said. "Then, as opposed to now."

"Well, I'm not going to just sit here and wait for it to happen," Sorrel said.

"You'd rather speed up the process?" Lillie asked.

Vola put her hands over her head to block them out and hunched down, folding her bulk into as small a package as possible. She felt like she was going to fly into a million pieces if she didn't hold on as tight as she could.

They'd thought Anders's illusions were narcissistic. An arrogant way to slow them down and funnel them into his traps.

But they'd been so much more than that. They'd been a clever way to get them to do his work. To free Nargilla.

And now to plant doubt. To wriggle that little worm of worry and question into a mind that had already seen too much of the gods.

Vola couldn't get the image of Mariel out of her head. Standing with her hands raised to the sky, calling on a god that couldn't be bothered to answer. Dying in Anders's arms while he prayed over and over to an empty sky.

The shadows overrunning Anders's family.

Maxim ignoring Sorrel.

All of them ignoring Vola. Ignoring her pleas, ignoring her warnings.

She knew what it was like to have a god who listened, one who stood next to her in battle and after. One who gave her strength and faith and hope.

But she also knew what it was like when that god disappeared. Leaving only the outline of her presence at Vola's shoulder.

How wrong was Anders?

And how much of what he'd become could have been prevented?

Vola's breath came faster. The rage rose inside of her and she let it. Held it simmering under the surface.

She'd learned to love Cleavah. And she'd learned to love the Broken just as much. But right now, she was angry. Angry at the pantheon for not listening to her. Angry at the pantheon for not listening to the Broken. And angry at the Broken for not pushing them and making them listen.

The time for politics was over. It had been over for a while; there were just some people too stupid to see it.

Vola unfolded herself and stood up straight to her full height. She didn't say anything, but the others fell silent, their bickering forgotten as they stared at her.

"Vola?" Lillie said. She stepped forward to place a hand on Vola's arm, fingers light. A reminder to anchor herself in the loyalty and strength of her team. "What is it?"

"It's the end," Vola said. She forced herself to focus and turned her gaze to Lillie's worried face. She put her hand over the wizard's fingers. "You guys want to come tell off some very important people?"

Lillie's eyes widened. Behind her, Talon cracked her neck.

Vola reached down and gave Sorrel a hand up. She handed

the monk Maxim's Warhammer, which had come with them from the battlefield. Miraculously.

Vola met Rilla's eyes. "Coming?" she said.

"I didn't know I was invited," Rilla said quietly.

"I guess that's up to you. Are you a Mishap's Hero? Or not?"

Rilla raised an eyebrow. "Will I get to stab things?"

"Almost definitely," Talon said.

"Well, then, how can I refuse?"

Vola stepped away from the healer's tent, which they'd finally gotten off the ground. She hadn't done this by herself before, only with the Broken. But she carried a good bit of the Broken's power within herself, and she had a connection to the goddess that transcended most of the rules of the world.

Vola closed her eyes and found that power. Found the connection that drew her to the goddess just over her shoulder. She wrapped it around herself and her friends. And then she reached for a bright, featureless hallway and a plane that connected to countless divine realms.

She pulled, and something in her gut lurched. But the air around them still smelled like wet ash.

She yanked harder, but that only made her feel dizzy.

Vola stopped. Walking with the Broken had never felt like pulling before, had it? It was always like a stroll.

She took hold of the power one more time and stepped. And her boot connected with pure white marble. Smooth walls rose on either side, neither solid nor exactly ethereal.

"Holy hell," Rilla said.

"Actually, I believe this would be the opposite," Lillie said, peering at the marble under their feet.

Sorrel scuffed at it with the toe of her sandal. It squeaked. Vola herself was still dripping.

"All right," Talon said, glancing suspiciously from one side to the other. "Now what?"

"This way." Vola cocked her head and started down the hall. Really, she had no idea what she was doing, just a burning anger and the belief that anything was better than what the gods were already doing.

It's not like any of them had anything left to lose by getting this wrong.

The wide room at the end of the hall seemed empty at first, or at least as empty as it had been the first time Vola set foot in it.

But voices ricocheted around them, echoes of shouts and arguments that seemed a million miles away one moment and just beside her ear the next. Little flits of color flashed in the bright air, indicating agitation somewhere that wasn't quite here.

Vola planted herself in the doorway, her boots leaving wet streaks across the marble. Today, black streaks climbed through the white walls, fracturing the little bits of opalescent color in the marble.

She cleared her throat.

Beside her, the air shifted, a puff against the hair on her arms, and Vesteral shimmered into existence. His long face pulled into a scowl, and his gangly limbs twitched in agitation.

"What the—How did you get here?" he said.

"I walked," Vola said. "Oh. And I brought some friends. Hope you don't mind."

Vesteral spluttered until Lillie stepped up all sweet eyes and beaming smile. "Vesteral, isn't it?" she said. "I've read so much about you."

Even the immortal wasn't quite immune to Lillie's smile and while he sucked in a breath and decided what to do with a pretty face and flattery, Vola stepped across to the center of the room.

"Ahem," she said as loudly as she could manage.

Around the room the tiers filled with angry gods, appearing as if trickling in from another plane. Colorful robes and gowns and heavy scowls faded into existence until she was surrounded by outrage.

Several of them looked familiar from her time here before—she recognized Maxim and Mulgash, Ona and Bierhel—but none of them were the Broken.

And then one last figure formed, on the floor next to her, coalescing into a slim woman with dark curls cropped close to her head, one arm missing, balancing on her remaining leg. She stood in the center of the circle, arguing against the rest.

The Broken started and turned to find Vola beside her. And Vola felt a stab of shame for having resented her for even a moment.

Their eyes met, and the Broken's scarred lip tilted in a lopsided smile.

"What is this, Broken?" Maxim said, climbing to his feet to point at Vola. "How is she here? Did you bring her here?"

The Broken tilted her head. "The funny thing about choosing smart, capable mortals is that they think and act for themselves."

Vola felt the rest of her team coming up behind her, arraying themselves around the center circle.

Maxim stepped down from his tier, each stride eating several feet, although Vola had no idea how physical distance worked in this plane of gods.

He stopped before them. "You dare come here after you failed? I admire your courage mortal, but now it could be read as stupidity."

Vola raised her chin, counting on the rage under her skin to bolster her. Maxim towered over even her, his presence oppressive and judging.

"We failed, yes," Vola said. "We failed to see the trap even though we knew there had to be one."

Maxim scoffed and turned.

"But you failed us before that."

Maxim froze.

Vola half expected the Broken to leave them to their argument, to go sit among the other gods, or to whisper to Vola to stop, to be careful. But she stood beside her, silent, back straight.

"Excuse me?" Maxim said, voice quiet.

"You failed to heed my warning. I told you Anders was coming for Nargilla. And you did nothing. You rested, content in your own strength and superiority."

"He used you to get past that strength," Maxim said. "And you let him."

"You failed us long before that," Vola said.

"You dare—"

"Do you remember Mariel Stillwater?"

Maxim hesitated, his mouth hanging open as his eyes went deep and blank. "What?"

"Do you remember the ones who pray to you? The ones who serve and give their lives to you? Or do you forget them as easily as you ignore them?"

Without prompting, Lillie began whispering and an image of Mariel formed on their left, hands raised to the sky, skirt whipping around her. Another formed in front of them. Mariel lying broken and bleeding in Anders's arms as he screamed without sound. And a third formed to the right. Anders standing over a table, alone in a mountain, plotting his bid for power.

"Do you remember her?" Vola said. "Because she's the reason for all of this. *You're* the reason for all of this."

Maxim stared at the young woman's face. "I don't...understand."

"Mariel was one of yours," Lillie said. "Your indifference to her convinced Anders to take your power. He thinks he can be a better god than all of you."

"I'm not certain I disagree with him," Rilla said.

Maxim remained there, staring. "I do remember her," he said.

"Anders is angry," Vola said. "And I'm angry, too. I'm tired of gods who sit absent and indifferent. Who cast one of their number out for trying to actually do something." She cast a glance at the Broken who returned it with a mildly raised eyebrow.

"The thing is, you have a problem on your hands. A problem you made. Anders has the power to strip you of your godliness. And I can't stop him. Not without help. And…well, I'm not sure I want to."

She'd fight tusk and nail to keep Anders from hurting the Broken, but she couldn't see a single reason to raise a finger to help these indolent, indifferent bastards. If only the whole world wasn't going to suffer for her choice.

Lillie let the images dissolve away.

Maxim blinked at Vola and the others as if seeing them for the first time, and his eyes latched onto Sorrel.

Vola could hear her gulp and didn't blame her. Vola had had plenty of time to get used to Cleavah's presence. Sorrel had never actually seen Maxim in person.

"You carry my hammer," he said.

"Yessir. Or well, part of it. The other bit's where you left it."

"And it works for you?"

Sorrel spun the staff in demonstration. It morphed from a staff to a bow to a sword and back to a staff again.

"You must have shown great strength and loyalty to have found it, halfling."

"Her name is Sorrel," Talon said. "Sorrel Thornbough."

"We're still loyal to you," Sorrel said, but her voice was quiet and even Maxim couldn't mistake the doubt in her eyes.

A flurry of expressions passed over his face, too fast or too complex for Vola to fully grasp. She saw anger and shame, yes, along with a whole host of other things.

"Damn you," Maxim said, gaze latching onto the Broken. "You know this will hurt."

"It's supposed to hurt," the Broken said. "That's how you know you're doing it right."

"Would you rather the mortals dealt with pain?" another voice said, and Vola saw Mulgash sit forward. "Puny beings who are less equipped to handle it?" He winked at Vola.

Maxim cast him a glare, but then he shook his head. He looked out over the assembled Virtues and Obstacles.

A collective shiver went through them, nearly silent except for the ripple of colors.

And then the gods started to dissolve, disappearing once again from this plane.

Five of them remained. The Broken and Maxim still stood in the center of the circle. And Ona, Bierhel, and Mulgash stepped down from the tiers to join them below. Representatives for the entire pantheon.

Maxim gave them a bow. "I know I have done nothing to earn your trust. But will you work with me now? To see what can still be done?"

TWENTY-THREE

It was still raining when Vola, Sorrel, Lillie, Talon, and Rilla appeared outside the command tent, trailing five gods behind them. The sun and the moon had long since set, leaving the camp in complete darkness. Here and there a few wizard lights sputtered valiantly, but it was clear no one had bothered to do more than fall into their bedrolls.

The only light nearby was the flicker through the canvas of the command tent.

Maxim squinted down as the rain pattered off his golden armor. "Ah. Precipitation. I'd forgotten this was a thing."

Vola exchanged a look with the other mortals and shook her head. Then she pushed into the command tent.

War stood over the table, her face still streaked with soot. The rain had made little runnels down her cheeks.

It looked like she'd convened everyone she could think of and squished them all in the tent together. Hazel sat shoved in with Lydia and Gorgo. Raven perched on a crate in the corner in his eagle form while Cyrano lounged below him. Renvick stood on the opposite side of the tent where the flaps had been pulled back far enough for Listrell to stick her nose in. Ephyra and Kellan stood along another wall, while Henri and Finn watched the openings. Knight Commander Imralen stood beside War at the table.

War shook her head when she saw them come in. "Shit, Rilla. Where have you been? We need to focus on damage control and you and your team go haring off after the battle?"

The Knight Commander looked up, eyes narrowed. Deep bruises still darkened the skin around his nose and under his eyes.

"Your Highness, I have to protest," he said. "You invited the traitor?"

"Blow it out your ass, Imralen," Rilla said, pushing through behind Vola. "No one is listening to your lies anymore."

"She's the entire reason we're in this mess now."

"No," Maxim said, crowding into the tent. "I am."

"I hope you don't mind," Ona said. "She brought friends."

Vola didn't know how to describe it since she'd been talking to gods in all their states for years now, but they did something when they were around other mortals which sort of hid their divine glory a bit. Probably so they didn't scare anyone right off the bat. They each had aspects they wore that glowed and pulsed with their power, but it was like they pulled a veil over that aspect. Keeping most of it hidden until they chose.

"Who are you?" War asked.

And Maxim chose to drop the veil.

The Greater Virtue of Strength and Loyalty's aspect was enough to take Vola's breath away, and she'd seen it before.

"Oh," War said, the word no more than a puff of air leaving her lips.

"This is...I don't—" Imralen started to say.

Rilla held up a hand. "Don't open your mouth again. We all know what you've been saying. And you're done." She turned to Vola. "Now, why don't you introduce your backup?"

"I don't think they really need an introduction," Vola said. "But this is War, princess of the Southglen War Throne. She's been spearheading our offense down here. Until—"

"Until you screwed it up," Imralen said.

Mulgash sidled up to the Knight Commander. "Hi," he said over his shoulder.

Imralen jumped and then glanced back at the Greater Obstacle of Rage, meeting his red eyes.

"Oh, I like you," Mulgash said. "You have so much more rage to overcome. And all of it so deeply ingrained. It's like you're holding onto it for dear life."

"Mulgash," the Broken said mildly. "Focus."

Imralen's eyes latched onto the Broken. She stood with Vola, still veiled, but she wore her Greater aspect underneath and there was no mistaking the scars and the missing limbs or the fire floating behind her. The gods might have thrown her out, but there were statues, paintings, and tapestries of the Greater Virtue of Righteousness everywhere.

Strange how standing next to her made Imralen seem small and insignificant.

"My lady," Vola said, giving the Broken a little nod. "Would you take the lead?"

War stepped back, leaving plenty of room for the Broken to stand at the edge of the table with the other gods splayed around her.

They frowned down at the disaster depicted before them. The map showed Anders's mountain and someone had drawn a ragged line around it to depict the meteor storm.

"Anders had enough power and smarts to get past the gods and steal Nargilla right out from under our noses," the Broken said.

Imralen snorted.

The Broken sent him a narrow-eyed look, but he wasn't actually stupid enough to open his mouth.

"With her, he now has the power to drain the entire world of magic."

"He has started," Listrell said, her voice a deep rumble against the ground. "I can feel them setting up their spell just as they did in Firewatch."

The Broken nodded. "Yes. We feel the land as well."

"Couldn't you just…" Hazel started, and then flushed.

Maxim fixed her with a stare. "You are one of mine, yes?" he said. "Say what you will."

"Couldn't you just pop in there?" She gestured to the mountain on the map. "And destroy his setup? I mean, you're gods."

The Broken's mouth went flat and hard. "A portion of the power he has already stolen is mine. It locks us out."

"And we are not what we once were," Ona murmured.

Vola glanced at her in question, but the Greater Virtue of Honor didn't meet her gaze.

"Well, breaking through the barrier and facing him head-on didn't work," Sorrel said. "What's left?"

A burst of furious whispering drew their attention to the side of the tent where Ephyra and Kellan stood. Lillie had sidled up beside them and had her head bent toward her father and brother.

"This seems promising," the Broken said.

Lillie looked up, biting her lip.

The Broken smiled. "You have earned Vola's trust, Lilliara," she said. "And therefore mine. Speak."

"Well, there's always plan B," she said.

War's gaze sharpened. "Will it still work?"

"What is plan B?" the Broken asked.

"We steal the power first."

Everyone in the tent blinked at her. Lillie's cheeks burned a fierce red, but she raised her chin.

"If we don't want him to take the world's magic, then we take it first."

Vola couldn't do more than blink for several moments. That was…ridiculous, dangerous…and possibly brilliant.

Rilla's mouth hung open. "This is what you've been working on?"

"We have a solid understanding of Nargilla's spell now. And we have Myron who designed the original bits that held the excess magic. And with divine help, it would go even smoother." Lillie nodded to the Broken and Maxim.

Talon shook her head. "Draining the magic killed those spots in Firewatch. Permanently. How is this a good idea?"

"Nargilla didn't care about killing the world. We do," Lillie said.

"That's what we've spent all this time making sure wouldn't happen." Ephyra's gesture included Lillie and Kellan and all the scholars not present.

"The power would need a vessel," the Broken said.

"Yes." Lillie spread her hands. "We would have to choose someone to receive the power. Or several someones."

"Wouldn't that just create another Anders?" Gorgo said from his seat. "We'd be creating our own thieving demigod."

"One of the reasons to have more than one, I would think," Cyrano said. "In case one goes rogue."

"They would have to accept the power with the understanding that it would only be temporary," Lillie said. "Until Anders is defeated. And…well, I think our champions would be our best bet for taking him down. Anders has been going after the magic in people, the magic in the dead, and the land, and magical objects like the Thrones."

"And the gods," the Broken said.

Lillie nodded. "If we took these first, pooled them into our choice of champions, they would be formidable enough to face

Anders head-on."

"Or we could lock them away and guard them," Ephyra said. "If all the power is locked away in one place, it will be easier to keep it out of Anders's hands."

Hazel's chin jerked up. "Only a coward would run from a fight that only they can win."

Ephyra shrugged, unfazed. "It is only one option."

"We would not run," Maxim said. "The gods will take on this burden and we will fight the threat and conquer it as gods should."

Mulgash snorted so hard he choked and spent the next few moments coughing.

Maxim frowned at him. "What?"

The Broken, Ona, and Bierhel gave the Greater Virtue of Strength and Loyalty pitying glances. Ona and Bierhel each then stepped aside and left the Broken to explain it to him.

"We fought an entire Divine War because you would not acknowledge my power over you," she said gently.

Maxim flushed, and Vola wondered if the Broken had ever actually had to say the words out loud before.

"Do you really think this fractured pantheon would look kindly on the five of us taking on even more power?"

"I'd like to think we learned our lesson the last time," Mulgash said, examining his fingernails. "But I'm not going to risk another Divine War on that gamble."

The Broken gave Maxim another sad smile. "I hate to say it but the power is safer in the hands of mortals."

"You're asking the entire pantheon to give up our power," Maxim said.

"I am." The Broken raised an eyebrow. "You're always going on about sacrifice. How you're willing to sacrifice yourself for the greater good. Are you willing to sacrifice everything in this way as well?"

"Damn you, again," Maxim said. "You know I can't say no."

The Broken spread her hands, a little smile playing on her lips.

"Then we must choose our champions," Listrell said.

"One for each," Ephyra said. "One to hold the magic of the living, one to hold the magic of the dead."

"The magic of the land," Listrell said.

"The Thrones," War said.

"And the gods." The Broken turned her head to look directly at Vola, where she stood with Talon and Sorrel. She cocked her head. "Funny how there are five of you."

Vola sucked in a breath. "Oh." She held up her hands. "Oh, no."

"I chose my champion a long time ago, Volagra. Are you going to refuse me now?"

Vola's mouth worked, trying to find an answer to that. But of course, there wasn't one. She'd decided to trust her goddess in a tight spot deep in Myron's laboratory. And she'd chosen the Broken again and again since then. She'd knelt before her in a temple in Southglen. She wouldn't back out now.

"No, my lady."

"Then you shall be my knight. As always."

"Now hang on," Imralen said. "Clearly the orc has tricked—"

The Broken's eyes flicked to Maxim, and she jerked her chin.

Maxim stepped to Imralen. "You were warned." The Greater Virtue of Strength and Loyalty picked Imralen up by the arms and carried him to the tent flap.

"You can't throw me out!" Imralen cried. "I'm the Knight Commander of the paladins. A holy warrior."

"Paladins must be kind as well as strong and just," Maxim said. "You are none of these. Learn better or do not bother returning."

He tossed Imralen into the rain and turned to dust off his hands.

"Any other objections?" the Broken said.

Hazel glanced around at the others gathered in the tent. "Nope. Honestly, we all like Vola. No one who knows her was really listening to him. But thanks for getting rid of him. He was really annoying."

Vola bit her lip and blinked rapidly. Apparently, she was the only one who'd been listening to him. The only one who mattered, at least.

"So Vola gets the power of the gods, obviously," Cyrano said, scratching his chin. "What about the rest?"

"Rilla will get the power of the Thrones," War said, casting a glance at her counterpart. "I know how much she hates being a princess so I'm not worried about her running off with the might of Southglen."

Rilla rolled her eyes.

"The magic of the land should go to Talon," Listrell said. "She is already in tune with the way it works."

"Same with the power of living spell casters," Ephyra said, face solemn. "Lilliara will handle it better than anyone."

"That leaves the power of the dead," Hazel said. "Which should go to Sorrel who will treat it with the respect it deserves."

Vola and the others looked at each other, and she noticed the same slightly glazed look in their eyes that said, "How did we get here again?"

"We shall have to do this quickly," the Broken said. "Anders already has a head start on us, and Nargilla has done this before."

"We have the gods on our side," Cyrano said. "How bad could it get?"

The Broken gave him a rueful smile. "You'd be surprised."

TWENTY-FOUR

BY THE TIME the sun rose, they had cleared a significant space in the center of camp. The rest of the army had packed up, and War stationed them around the ritual area, keeping watch in case Anders decided to interrupt.

This was their last chance. If Anders kept them from succeeding here, they would have lost the war. And the world.

After the council with the gods, War had ordered Vola and the others to sleep. They were the ones who would have to pull this off, and she wanted them at full strength. But Vola had spent most of the night staring at the canvas ceiling, and she knew for a fact Lillie had spent most of it rolling around. Ephyra and Kellan and the rest of the scholars knew what they were doing. And they had gods helping them out. But that wouldn't keep the wizard from feeling like she had to be there to keep an eye on everything.

They'd given up an hour before dawn and packed up the tent onto the swamp beast's back.

The camp was quiet, but definitely not still, filled with a frenetic sort of energy. Voices stayed hushed, but figures raced back and forth, following the whispered orders coming from the command tent.

There'd been a twitchy moment right after dawn when Myron had wailed that he couldn't make the tanks he needed out of thin air and why hadn't anyone told him he would need them.

Lillie calmed him down. "The tanks were only for storage, right?" she said. "To store the magic until it could be shipped to Anders? Well, we're not shipping anything anywhere. Your tanks are right here." She'd placed her hand on her chest. "We're the tanks."

After that he'd been perfectly happy puttering around, muttering about people doubling as tanks and possible uses in the future.

Vola hoped there would be a future where he could test his theory to his heart's content, though this might not be the sort of thing they'd want to attempt twice.

Vola, Talon, and Sorrel mostly tried to stay out of the way while Lillie flitted from the scholars to the gods to the princesses, trying to make sure everything was lined up just right. Vola didn't follow any of it. She just knew there were anchor points like Nargilla's original spell, which the gods had spent much of the night ferrying around to magically important places in the world. And there were representatives for each of the different types of magic that were needed for the ritual.

Rilla spent the time finalizing arrangements with War. Vola wasn't quite sure what those arrangements looked like. No one knew what would happen to the world if this failed.

"Blow up," Sorrel said when Vola asked the rest of them what they thought.

"The whole world?" Talon said.

"Figuratively or literally?" Vola asked.

"Both."

"You can't have both," Talon said. "You could look at any kind of trouble and say 'yep, I was right, the world 'blew up.'""

"Is this a competition now?" Sorrel asked.

"Maybe." Talon chewed her lip. "I want metaphorical. If this doesn't work, the world will metaphorically 'blow up.' That just leaves you with physical."

Vola buried her head in her hands. "You guys aren't making me feel any better."

"Were we supposed to?" Sorrel said.

The rain tapered off to an unpleasant drizzle around the same time Lillie finally came for them.

"We're ready," she said quietly. Anyone who didn't know her would think she was calm, but Vola noted the way her eyes shifted constantly and her bottom lip was raw from worrying at it with her teeth.

Vola decided not to call attention to it and just followed Lillie out of the tent into the gray dawn. The air was cool but heavy against their skin and the damp seemed to muffle what little noise came from the rest of the camp.

Around the cleared space, the scholars had arranged the different representatives, the channels that the spell would use to funnel all the different magics into their chosen champions. The Broken for the gods. Listrell for the land. War for the Thrones. Ephyra for the living spell-casters. And Myron had summoned a shambling zombie he named Fred to represent the rest of the dead.

Lillie nudged Vola into position beside the Broken and chewed her bottom lip some more. She tapped Vola's breastplate. "Maybe take this off. For now."

"Why?" Vola said even as she reached for the straps.

"Um. Just in case."

"Just in case of what?" Vola asked, but Lillie had stepped away to find her own spot in the center of the circle.

"Just in case we blow up," Sorrel said. "Don't want any shrapnel."

"No one is going to blow up," Lillie said from beside her father. She made a face. "I don't think. I just don't want the metal to serve as a conductor."

"And roast Vola alive inside her armor," Sorrel finished for her.

"We're all going to die," Talon muttered.

Sorrel sighed gustily. "But what a way to go."

Lillie gave the signal and there was no more time to worry.

There wasn't much to see here, but Vola knew that around the world the gods were activating their pieces of the spell. Beginning the process that would hopefully disrupt Anders's plan.

Vola blinked and squinted up at the gray drizzle. She could have sworn there was a change in the feel of the air on her skin. A shift in the state of the world itself. It crackled across her like little fizzles of lightning.

Pebbles danced across the ground as it rumbled. The land Nargilla had drained near Firewatch had turned black any time she cast her spell. The lava rock here was already black, so not much difference there, but Vola could make out lines of gray snaking out from the center of their circle.

And then a fist of power struck her in the chest, and she fell to her knees. The others thudded to the ground as well. But Vola's entire focus was pulled inward to the point where the Broken poured all the divine power of the gods through her skin, into her heart and mind, filling up every space in between.

Shit, Vola couldn't help thinking, even though she knew the Broken would be able to tell. Shit, shit, shit. They hadn't prepared for this. They'd done nothing, and Sorrel was right. They were going to explode. No one was built for this type of power. She was going to split down the middle and every drop of divine magic would go splashing out, spilling all over, and Vola would be dead. As dead as Fred.

She choked on a hysterical giggle and struggled to breathe, concentrating on her chest and the air moving in and out.

"Do not fear," she heard. A voice like the rushing of wind. "I'm still here with you."

The power sizzled along her veins, and she clenched her fists, worried it would spill out of her fingertips if she wasn't careful.

Slowly, she realized that the ground didn't tremble under her palms anymore. And the roaring in her ears hadn't gotten any louder. It remained constant, as did the hum in her chest.

She blinked, staring at the porous rock between her hands. Was it over? Or was this still the beginning? Fire filled her veins, burning from the inside. And maybe she'd be trapped in this sizzling state forever.

"Vola?" Lillie's voice sounded in her ear, louder than the roar. "Vola, are you all right?"

"Should it have hit her harder than the rest of us? Is that normal?" Sorrel said.

Talon snorted. "Is any of this normal?"

"The power she's holding is divine," Rilla said. "It makes sense it would hit her harder."

"Vola." Cool fingers under her jaw finally made her raise her head. Lillie's blue-green eyes met hers. "Are you all right?"

"Fine," Vola grated. Her voice sounded hoarse and used, like she'd been screaming, except she couldn't remember screaming. "I just feel like I got hit in the chest with a flaming battering ram."

Lillie's lips tipped in a relieved smile. "That appears to be a side effect, yes."

"You sort of get used to it," Sorrel said, rubbing her own chest.

"It worked, then?"

"Yeah," Rilla said, voice subdued. "Yeah, it worked."

She and Lillie gave Vola a hand to her feet, and Vola saw why she didn't sound terribly happy about that.

Every person around them, human, dwarf, elf, halfling, and dragon alike, had fallen to their knees or flat on their faces. Only a couple had enough energy to struggle upright again.

The land beneath their feet was already lava rock and made up of every shade of black and gray, but the air itself seemed to be dimmer, less vibrant. Just like the dead spots near Firewatch.

"Is it like this everywhere?" Vola whispered.

"Rand says yes," Lillie said. "As far as he can see. I think it's safe to assume it worked."

The Broken was on her hands and knees in front of Vola. They'd seen her like this once before, and it gave Vola an unpleasant wrench in her gut to realize she was the cause this time.

The goddess raised her head with obvious effort and gave them a wan smile.

"The rest is up to you now, Mishap's Heroes."

TWENTY-FIVE

THEY HAD TIME NOW. Not a lot, but enough to grow used to the power surging beneath their skin. Enough to establish a plan. And enough that the army could slowly drag themselves to their feet and grow accustomed to the way their limbs felt leaden and lifeless.

Vola remembered the feeling. She almost preferred it to this. Almost.

She touched the wall of the command tent by accident and it burst into flames under her fingertips.

Lillie put it out with a little cloudburst, making the canvas sizzle and smoke.

"Oops," Vola said.

"That would be a bit of my power," the Broken said wearily from the corner of the tent. War had handed it over to them after they'd talked tactics. She was next door, trying to stay upright without looking like a toddler learning to walk again.

"If you try to toss something across the room and it ends up halfway across the world, that's Maxim's strength. The trick is to keep it stuffed under your skin," the Broken said.

"Easier said than done," Vola muttered. Lessons from long ago kept flitting through her head. She'd had the entire pantheon and their different areas of interest memorized once. And if she concentrated, she could feel their heat and light tangling and unwinding beneath her skin. Ona's honor, Bierhel's joy, Erthand's determination. Every single one stuffed inside her.

With the entire pantheon at her beck and call maybe now she'd be able to counter that bit of the Broken's power that resided in Anders.

The others were having their own sorts of troubles. The ground tended to roll as Talon walked across it like it was rising to greet her. Rilla crackled with bits of lightning that twirled around her arms and legs. And Sorrel kept rubbing her ears like she could hear a million whispering voices at once.

Lillie was the only one who seemed to be taking this in stride. "I'm used to flinging fire when I'm angry or afraid," she said. "I guess I've already developed techniques for keeping it under wraps."

"Any suggestions?" Vola asked her.

"Think of your skin like a dam. Or a net, holding everything inside."

"I think my problem isn't about containment," Sorrel said, hitting the side of her head like she was trying to knock water out of her ear. "It's about distraction. Is this what necromancers feel all the time?"

"It's temporary," Vola said. She stripped out of the shirt she'd slept in and traded it for a padded surcoat she could wear under her armor. "We're giving it all back as soon as we get rid of Anders."

Lillie's lips thinned. "And what if we can't?"

"Way to instill us all with confidence right before battle," Talon said.

"I don't like this plan," Lillie said, lifting her chin. "The part where we all get to the mountain and kick Anders's ass, that's all right. That's normal. But I don't like Vola going down the middle with the army while we sneak in the sides."

"We don't have a ton of other options," Rilla said. She pulled a strap on her leather harness, checking all the little pockets and sheaths.

"She's making herself a target," Lillie said with a frown. "If we die, the power we carry is released back into the world. Anders has to know that if he kills any of us, he can scoop that power up. And Vola's just going to go striding out there with only the army to protect her."

"More like I'm protecting them," Vola said. "And that's the whole point. I'm going to make his life so miserable he won't even have time to wonder where you four are. The army is going to be way under-strength, yes, but so will Anders's undead horde and subverted forces. Hopefully," she added under her breath.

"You agree with this?" Lillie asked Sorrel. "Aren't you supposed to be her second in command?"

Sorrel regarded her solemnly. "It plays to all our strengths," she said.

"And she won't be alone," the Broken added. She seemed tired, but she was at least upright and didn't have a problem moving around like the mortals. Some of the other races were dealing with the draining better as well. The dwarves of the army were doing well, as were the dragons. The broken had said their magic might have been drained, but their natures remained the same.

"I don't want to talk about this anymore, Lillie," Vola said quietly. She knew the plan was solid. She knew this would give them the best chance against Anders. But she also knew just how fragile it was. They might hold the power of the world. But they were still mortals. And Anders just had to kill one of them to increase his power and make it that much harder for the rest of them.

Lillie's mouth snapped shut and her eyes went bleak. Like she knew what Vola was avoiding thinking about.

"I need to get ready," Vola said.

"I can help with that." Henri pushed through the tent flap and gave them all one of his radiant smiles. "It's been a while since I've been anyone's squire."

Lillie subsided back, giving him space.

Vola spared her a glance and opened her mouth, but she couldn't think of anything else to say. All her reassurances fell flat in the face of her own worry.

Henri stepped forward and took up her breastplate.

"You don't have to do that," Vola said. "I've been armoring myself since I graduated."

"What if I want to?"

Her lips twisted in a smile. "Then I guess it would be mean to not let you."

He helped fit her into the plate, tightening the straps expertly. And there was something soothing about his presence. He'd always had that calm air. When she'd been his student, she'd gotten the impression that he'd seen everything, so nothing surprised or worried him anymore.

He seemed subdued now, but his fingers were still steady. In fact he was the most normal-seeming human in camp so far.

"How's Finn?" Vola asked.

"You know teenagers. They're made of rubber," Henri said. "Finn's stronger than he looks. He'll serve as a full knight before too long."

"If he survives this," Vola said quietly.

Henri flicked one of her pauldrons so it rang in her ear. "None of that now."

Vola gave him a look. "How are you so cheerful? Does nothing frighten you?"

"Very little."

Her eyes narrowed. He moved a little slower than usual, she thought, but he didn't seem to be dragged down by the very air like everyone else. He was acting more like the dwarves and the dragons.

Her eyes flicked to the Broken.

And the gods.

"Thank you, Henri," Vola said as he tightened the last strap on her greaves and straightened.

"You're welcome."

"I don't just mean for this," she said, raising her arm. "I mean…for everything. All those years you taught me. Everything I know about being a paladin I learned from you. Not from Imralen and the others."

He cocked his head.

"And you've always been honest with me."

"I have."

"You're not…fully human, are you?"

He didn't seem surprised. Only amused. His gaze flicked to the Broken who shrugged.

"I told you she'd figure it out sooner or later," she said.

"I didn't doubt it," he said.

"I'm right, aren't I?" Vola said.

Henri shrugged. "If we're being completely honest, I'm not at all human. It's just a whole lot easier to serve my lady if I appear as one."

"What are you, then?"

"Let's just say I've been training knights for my lady since the beginning. And you are the first one she's chosen since her fall." He pulled her in close and kissed her on the forehead. "I'm very proud of you, Volagra."

He handed her her sword and shield, and then turned to leave. For a moment he stood silhouetted against the sunlight outside. It lined his shoulders and glowed like a pair of bright, iridescent wings.

Hazel brushed past him into the tent, and the moment was gone.

The stocky dwarf held a fabric-wrapped bundle under her arm, and she seemed tired but upright. "Is Maxim in here?" she said, glancing around.

"No," the Broken said. "But he can be."

A whisper of air and the Greater Virtue of Strength and Loyalty appeared under the peaked roof.

"How did you—" Talon said, jumping. "Your magic is gone."

"But not our nature," the Broken said. "We might not have magic, but we are still immortal with all the—let's call them perks—that come with it."

"Was I needed for something?" Maxim said. "I think the army is about ready for the charge."

"This won't take long, sir," Hazel said. She held out the wrapped package. "I sent for someone to bring this from the monastery. If we're ever going to use it, now would be the time." She flipped back the fabric to reveal a stone bigger than Maxim's two fists put together, carved all over with whorls and leaves. One side was flat and solid, the other came to a nasty point, sharp enough to pierce armor. There was a recess in the middle.

The air in the room grew brighter and sang, as if the stone called to something outside of itself.

The staff on Sorrel's back began to glow.

"Oh," Maxim said, soft and reverent. A million memories crowded his eyes as he reached out to touch the head of his Warhammer.

Then his smile tipped in a rueful grin. "That's funny. It's not looking for me."

He glanced at Sorrel, who waited with wide eyes.

"I guess you could just stand there, if you like," he said. "Or you can come take what's yours."

She skipped forward a step, but still didn't reach out for the stone. "I'm not really sure it's mine, sir."

"I left the two pieces here well protected, with Jodin Battle-called. He established various tests to ensure only the right person bearing the qualities I honor would be able to get to them."

"She recovered both of them," Hazel said. "Even though we put her through a lot of pain denying that fact."

Sorrel held out the staff on both palms and offered it to Maxim. He took it and weighed it in one hand. Then fitted the end into the slot on the stone.

The Warhammer rang like a gong, complete at last. He held it out to Sorrel.

"Uh, I'm not really a warhammer sort of girl," Sorrel said.

Maxim grinned. "I know. But your friend there already has a weapon from her god. And I'd prefer to give this one to one of my own."

Sorrel blinked, then bit her lip before she reached out to take it from him. In her hands, the weapon rippled and morphed, and instead of holding a warhammer, she held a long polearm, tipped with wickedly curved blades at both ends.

A double-headed glaive.

"Oh, wonderful," Talon said. "Let's make Sorrel even more deadly."

Rilla elbowed her in the ribs. "Be nice."

"What? I meant it."

Sorrel gave it a spin and everyone in the tent ducked.

Rilla lunged in to catch the weapon's haft. "Save it for Anders."

"Does that mean you're ready?" War asked, stepping through the tent. "'Cause it's time."

Vola's stomach dropped, and she glanced at the others. "Give us another minute," she told War and the two gods. "And we'll be out."

Thankfully, they took her meaning without her having to explain fully, and War held the flap open so the Broken, Maxim, and Hazel could duck out.

Vola swallowed, tucking her hands under her armpits so she could ignore how they shook. They were out of time, and this was where they had to split up.

She wished she could wipe away the look of pain on Lillie's face, but she'd said everything she could say. Someone had to draw Anders's attention. And she'd spent the last year keeping these women safe. She couldn't do anything else now.

But they were more than friends. More even than family. Her soul knew them and loved them, and the thought of walking out of this tent and sending them off without her made something ache just below her left ribs. The thought that she might not see them on the other side…Anders had already proved to be smart and powerful. Even with the gods' power flowing through her, she was still mortal. And she was painting a target on her back as well as leaving them defenseless.

How did you say good luck without it meaning goodbye?

"I…I don't even know what to say." She tried meeting each of their eyes. "There isn't a word for…for how I feel about you guys. I'm not me without you. Not anymore."

And this could be the end of that. But she couldn't say that. Not to them, and definitely not to herself.

"We know, Vola," Sorrel said, her normally cheerful face solemn. "Believe me, we know."

Trust Sorrel to prop her up. Who knew a halfling would be so essential to the stability of a half-orc?

She nodded, clearing her throat. "Right. That's it, then." She had to leave. War was waiting, but also, she couldn't stand here just looking at them anymore without the knot in her throat turning into something ugly.

She turned to the tent flap.

"Vola!" Lillie cried.

Vola paused and looked back, keeping her eyes carefully on Lillie's soft boots and not on her face. She couldn't see her face right then and keep any semblance of calm. And she couldn't defend their plan one more time if Lillie decided to test it again.

"Don't you dare die before meeting us at the mountain," the wizard said.

Vola's eyes flashed up to hers involuntarily. Lillie stared back, gaze fierce and full of worry but also pride and wonder and hope.

Lillie surged forward before Vola could leave and wrapped her arms around the paladin, armor and all.

Vola closed her eyes. She could feel the power rippling under Lillie's surface, responding to her emotions, and the matching power under Vola's skin.

Another set of arms joined her, wrapping her below the waist. And another from behind. And another over all of them. Vola allowed herself this one moment, encircled by trust and care and fear.

Slowly they drew back, but Vola didn't feel like they left her alone. She felt like she carried them with her. Maybe they'd given her a little bit of their power in that embrace. Or maybe they'd been giving her little bits of themselves all along. Entrusting themselves to her the way she'd entrusted herself to them.

"Don't worry." She could say it now. Say it and mean it. She flashed them a real smile as she held back the tent flap. "I'll meet you at the mountain."

Outside the camp in front of the entire army, War waited on a white charger. The horse tossed its head and stamped. War reined him in with a firm hand. Dark circles ringed the princess's eyes, but she held her spine straight and kept her chin up.

The corners of War's mouth pulled down, and Vola stepped up to her, armor perfectly adjusted with her sword and shield crossed over her back.

War looked her up and down. "Are you planning on walking into battle?" she said.

Vola opened her mouth and then closed it. To be fair, she hadn't really thought that far.

"I usually do," she said.

"You usually fight skirmishes," War said. "This is different. You'll need the height. Especially if you're going to be a figurehead. The army needs to see you. As does Anders."

Good point. And she'd had plenty of training on horseback back at the academy.

There'd been a time when she'd dreamed of riding to the rescue on a white charger. That image of herself had been as much a part of her as her sword arm.

The dream had since faded. She liked to think she'd grown up since then and had a much healthier mental image of herself.

Still. Some dreams never quite died.

"I'll have to borrow one," Vola said.

War snapped her fingers and a weary-looking hostler stumbled away from the gathered army, back to camp.

The Broken stood beside War. For the first time since they'd been in the lava field, the clouds above had finally broken, leaving bright blue sky and glaring sunlight. The wet ground began to steam.

The bright sun hid the flames behind the Broken's shoulders, making the flickers look even more ethereal and wraith-like.

"You all right?" the Broken said quietly.

Vola felt a lot better. The shakes and the fear had dissolved from her limbs, and now she could stand there calm.

"I am," she said.

Vola took the chance to survey their troops. This was nearly everyone. Everyone besides Mishap's Heroes. Southglen's elite took up the middle with their allies from Mistvale and Elfhome flanking. Behind them ranged an assortment of others. The monks, the villagers who'd come to defend themselves, the battle mages.

Gorgo stood at the head of a phalanx of orcs. He might have been a little slower than normal, but he didn't show any exhaustion or struggle as he stood with his troops. Lydia paced beside him, swinging her arms to stretch. They each caught Vola's eye and gave her an encouraging smile.

Far, far to the right, Cyrano and Raven stood with the dragons, who waited for the signal to take flight.

And arrayed near the front, in full plate with the sun gleaming from all their shiny bits, were the paladins. Kinght Commander Imralen was nowhere to be seen, but ranging up and down the line of holy warriors was a bright figure in gold-washed armor. Maxim checked their weapons, their stances. He called out to hold the line steady. And when he saw her looking, he raised his sword in salute.

Henri stood with them, Finn safe and strong in his shadow.

A squeal made Vola frown and turn.

"Oh," she said flatly. "Oh, no."

The hostler had returned, dragging a long lithe shape covered in green and blue scales. Slime dripped in its wake. Far behind them a soldier slipped and fell and took his entire platoon with him.

"Sorry, ma'am," the hostler said as Vola glared at the swamp monster. "This is all we have left."

"What?" War said. "We brought an entire line of extra mounts to serve as pack animals."

"Yeah, it ate at least half of them and scared the rest away."

They all stared at the swamp monster, which chewed malevolently and glared back at them, its crest wobbling with fury.

"At least it's fitting," Vola said.

The Broken stepped up to take the lead rope from the hostler, who turned and sprinted in the opposite direction.

The Broken ran a hand down the thing's neck and murmured in its ear.

"Of course it likes you," Vola said.

"Oh, she's not that bad," the Broken said.

"She?"

"She's actually descended from dragons, you know." The Broken leaned back a little to eye the creature up and down. It spat, and the lava rock sizzled. "Although she's a little far from the family tree now."

"You think?"

The Broken closed her eyes and laid her forehead against the beast's neck, stroking down its slimy scales with her palm.

The swamp beast's scales shimmered, and Vola had to blink. The bright light made her eyes water and she winced away. When she could focus again, wide glistening wings extended out from the beast's flanks. Gossamer tissue stretched from each delicate rib, looking like bat wings in the sunlight.

"Holy shit," War said, her charger prancing back a pace.

The swamp beast shook its head, spraying slime in every direction and looking very smug about it all.

The Broken cocked her head at the swamp beast, looking almost as smug.

"Lady, Anders should be just as scared of you without magic as with."

"I only called to her nature, and she responded."

Vola sighed. She wasn't getting out of this no matter what, and War was tapping her knee in an annoyed little pattern.

Vola swung past the swamp beast's head, avoiding the teeth and climbed onto its back behind the wings. Her feet hung down, so they almost dragged on the ground. The creature wasn't really that tall.

War winced. "I was going to say that's better, but I'm not sure it is. I guess it'll have to do."

War turned to catch the attention of her commanders, her arm raised in readiness.

The swamp monster turned its—her—head and tried to nip Vola's boot. She yanked her foot out of the way and flicked the creature's ear. "Focus," she said. "There's plenty for you to eat out there."

Vola pointed the beast's nose at the battlefield. Ahead of them stretched the lava field. Undead swarmed the rock plain, shambling between the fiery impacts of meteors.

The Broken rested her hand on Vola's knee.

Vola swallowed. "Wish me luck, lady."

The Broken smiled up at her. "I don't have to. I will be with you the whole way."

She faded even as the feel of her presence grew stronger. Like a friend standing over her shoulder.

And War gave the signal to charge.

TWENTY-SIX

VOLA KICKED the swamp beast into motion. She squealed and reared up, wings flapping, sending a wave of fishy stench back at Vola. And then the beast launched herself forward, carrying Vola down the ridge-line, straight into the horde of zombies.

The army roared behind them and the ground shuddered with the sound of thousands of feet charging ahead. War's horse drew even with the swamp beast and neighed at the top of its lungs. The swamp beast shrieked in reply, and Vola would have sworn the creature grinned.

Well, if the intention was to draw Anders's attention, Vola couldn't think of a better way to do it. The swamp beast's wings glinted in the sunlight, and while she never really took off, she did carry Vola over the heads of the enemy in leaps and bounds no normal mount would have managed.

Their forces clashed with the undead, meeting in the center of the field with a roar Vola could feel in her chest.

She struck down a zombie who tried to pull her from the swamp beast's back and the swamp beast leaped six feet up to carry her to safety before falling on the next enemy with her teeth bared.

Vola caught a blow on her shield and heaved while another zombie landed at the swamp beast's feet where the creature could trample it to death. Or, well, more dead than before.

A wall of orcs marched beside her, pushing through the ranks of undead. Using their superior strength to keep the line moving forward.

Vola remembered what she was supposed to be doing and urged the swamp beast ahead. She was the figurehead. The shining object the rest of the army was trying to follow.

Their job was to engage Anders's forces. And Vola was supposed to draw his attention. All so the rest of Mishap's Heroes could get through without challenge. As long as they made it to the stronghold, nothing else mattered.

Vola kept an eye out for Listrell and the other dragons. They were supposed to give the signal when Sorrel and the others were off, but closer to the mountain, the dark clouds still circled, belching forth meteors that pummeled the lava rock.

A whistle made the hair on the back of Vola's neck stand up and the swamp beast twisted out of the way as a flaming rock struck the ground where they'd just been.

Vola breathed out a sigh of relief. She could get used to this unusual partnership, given enough time and evidence like that.

But also, the surrounding army was getting struck as well.

Normally this would be Lillie's job. Vola wasn't a spell caster, just a field healer. But Lillie wasn't here, and Vola was filled with so much power it crackled along the edge of her sword when she wasn't paying attention.

She tried to focus her concentration on the clouds above them, thinking "clear skies" really, really hard. But strangely enough, that didn't seem to work. How did Lillie do this?

"You're not Lillie," the Broken's voice said in her ear, sounding like the rush of wind through tree branches.

"Yeah, I noticed."

"Don't think how would Lillie do this. Think, how would Vola do this? We gave you our power for a reason."

That was less than helpful. Vola didn't do weather. She smashed things. She stood between her team and the bad guy.

She glanced down at her sword. It was worth a shot.

Vola urged the swamp monster up and the creature leaped into the air with a massive beat of her wings. She focused all her attention on her blade for those few seconds as they hung in the air, concentrating the Broken's fire along its edge and Maxim's strength into her sword arm.

Then she slashed along the bottom of the clouds, which split with a shriek of released air.

The spell protecting Anders's stronghold and sending meteors crashing to the ground shriveled up, the clouds twirling into a single point. That dark point exploded; bits of cloud scattered across the sky so the sunlight shone down unimpeded.

"Much better," the Broken whispered as the swamp beast landed again.

Now Vola could see the dragons twisting above in the complicated pattern that indicated Mishap's Heroes had left camp without incident and were making their way around the battle. According to the plan, Sorrel and Lillie would be striking out along the northern edge while Rilla and Talon took the southern.

Vola ignored the curl in her gut and waved her sword to tell Listrell and the other dragons that she'd seen the signal.

The bright, colorful figures broke up and circled to begin their diving runs. Listrell fell from the sky first, snapping her wings out at the last second and flaming an entire row of zombies.

Hurren, gleaming red and gold, led the smaller dragons to harry Anders's forces from the sides.

In that moment she was distracted, Vola's skin tightened and the hair along her arms tingled as the air grew close and hot. She flung up her shield just as a bolt of lightning gathered in the clear air above her and snaked down.

It cracked against the bright wings of her shield and she winced. But her shield held and the only effect she felt was her hair trying to stand on end.

Vola's lips peeled back as she bared her tusks. She'd pissed Anders off apparently.

Good thing she'd spent all that time around Lillie and her spells. Vola shook the feeling of lightning off as she drove the swamp beast forward.

The ground split and fire gouted ahead of them. Vola didn't even have to use the power of the gods this time. The swamp beast swerved around the flames, leaving the rest of the army to deal with it. Hopefully, none of them fell in.

As they ran, the lava rock rumbled beneath their feet, and even the swamp monster staggered in response. Vola gripped her sword and resettled her shield, glancing about to see what Anders threw at them next. At least she knew now that the plan was working. He wasn't throwing any of this at the rest of the army. Or off to their flanks, where Mishap's Heroes crept.

The rock ahead of them bulged into a massive hillock, and the swamp beast danced back a couple of steps. The black rock crumbled and rolled away from a mound of flesh that twisted and pushed until a giant bald head burst from the ground. A patchwork of skins, all different colors and textures, reared up out of the hole, tossing its head to fling bits of rock everywhere. Vola threw up her shield and let the gravel ping across it.

Flesh golem, Vola thought distantly. Too bad Myron wasn't here now.

The giant monster patched together from a motley selection of corpses lumbered forward.

Vola ducked and the swamp monster leaped forward under the clumsy swing of the giant. Vola slashed at the back of its bulbous leg, trying to find the knee.

Her sword flared with flame as it scored the flesh golem's hide, and the monster bellowed. But it didn't go down.

Listrell raced by overhead, blotting out the sun with her wings, and a shape jumped from her back.

Renvick landed on the golem's head with a roar and swung his warhammer. The golem reached over its shoulder to grab at the guardian. Renvick smashed its hand and leaped away, rolling across the broken ground as Vola moved in.

Flesh golem, flesh golem. How had they dealt with this the first time? Sorrel had smashed it over the head with a divine weapon, hadn't she?

But Renvick had already tried that, and the Broken had chosen her for a reason. So, what would Vola do?

She yanked the swamp monster in close to the golem's feet, keeping them behind the reach of its arm. Then she strengthened herself with Maxim's might and imbued her sword with Velvain's fury. The Goddess of Mourning hated undead.

Her next slash cut across the thing's back and fire sprang out of the wound. Each cut she made severed a piece of the spell holding it together. Blow by blow she slashed at the magic keeping it upright until it wobbled on its feet and then toppled, splitting apart as it did so until it lay in a pile of corpses.

"Bleh," Vola said.

The swamp monster spat a wad of slime onto the pile, which hissed and sent up a plume of foul-smelling smoke.

"You are the most disgusting dragon I've ever met," Vola said. "And I kind of love you for it."

Renvick gave Vola a salute with his warhammer and turned to join the rest of the fray.

"Watch yourself!" the Broken cried. And Vola had just

enough time to bring up her shield before she was struck from above.

No spell this time. No meteors or fire or necromantic constructs.

Just pure, unadulterated power fell from the heavens and smashed Vola into the ground. The swamp beast squealed and struggled underneath her, wings stretched out on either side.

The pressure let up just long enough for Vola to draw in a breath, and then it slammed down on them again.

Vola cried out as the power ground against her, shoving her cheek into the rough lava rock and trapping her left leg under the swamp beast.

She tried to pull her sword arm free to slash at whatever was holding her down, but she couldn't move.

What good was all this divine power if she panicked and couldn't use it when she needed to?

She tried to pull Maxim's strength into her limbs again, but too much of her brain was preoccupied with not being able to breathe. She thought about using the Broken's fire to sear away Anders's attack, but would that smother her in the process?

The pressure let up again. And Vola acted as quickly as she could, bringing her sword up and around so that when it struck her again, she stabbed at it, point first.

But her sword twisted in her hand, wrenching her wrist and she was slammed into the ground and the sharp edges of the swamp beast one more time.

This time she was left staring at the sky. The dragons ducked and wove, turquoise over red, green around yellow.

It meant something. That pattern. They'd agreed on it for something.

A signal.

The rest of Mishap's Heroes had made it into the stronghold.

And they were waiting for Vola to join them if she could. If she hadn't already perished on the battlefield.

She didn't have to beat Anders here on this battlefield. Alone. She just had to get away. To join the others and they could face him together.

She carried the power of the gods, and the gods were connected to the world. She just had to draw on that connection.

Vola closed her eyes and waited. One more second. Two more. Until Anders pulled back the pressure, ready to strike one more time.

And in that space of breath, Vola concentrated. She pulled the divine power out of her center and reached into the world, finding that connection. Then she leaped, aiming for Sorrel, Lillie, Talon, and Rilla.

Vola and the swamp monster winked out of existence.

TWENTY-SEVEN

ON THE OTHER side of a darkness that was both very short and infinitely long, Vola popped back into the world on top of a very angry, very flat swamp monster.

The world spun around them, and she tried to hang onto something while at the same time registering rock walls and the chance of threat.

No threat, but familiar faces stared down at her anxiously.

The swamp beast writhed underneath her, making her wince, and Vola struggled to roll off onto the floor.

The cavern echoed with the creature's fury, walls stretching above them. A chandelier of wizard's fire far overhead lit the whole room and high windows up near the ceiling let in the daylight.

The swamp monster finally managed to buck her off onto the floor and the ungrateful thing launched herself into the air and flapped once, twice. She reached the windows and with a scream of triumph, she crashed through the glass and winged away into the sun.

Vola shaded her eyes, but she couldn't see the swamp monster any longer.

"Thanks," she called. "You were really great…for like a half an hour."

Vola finally tilted her head back far enough to see Lillie, Talon, Sorrel, and Rilla. They all stared out the broken window. Gruff panted beside them, unfazed.

"Soo, I feel like we missed something," Rilla said.

"Was that the swamp monster?" Sorrel asked. "It looked like the swamp monster."

"Long story," Vola said. She tried to push herself to her feet, but her whole body ached and her wrist collapsed when she tried to put weight on it.

She pushed Maxim's strength into her limbs and stood. Rilla darted in to lend her a shoulder.

"You all right?" the princess said.

"Sure."

Lillie bit her lip.

"I'm fine," Vola tried again. "It's just, I did exactly what the plan said. Drew Anders's fire."

"And you're still alive," Sorrel cried, throwing her hands in the air. "Hooray."

"Celebrate later," Talon grated. "He knows we're coming."

Vola glanced around. The cavern seemed to be an antechamber carved out of the mountain. A wide opening under the windows led back out to the battlefield.

Heaps of metal lay in a circle around the cavern, and Vola squinted. Finally, she realized they were piles of armor, golems like the ones that protected the palace in Glenhaven. Sorrel and the others must have slipped inside and taken them by surprise while Vola kept Anders busy.

A part of her wanted to fling her arms around them, but Talon was right. This wasn't the time for celebration. And Vola wasn't the only one preoccupied with the tunnel opening up in front of them. Dim light bounced off the rough walls, and Vola thought she heard voices beyond.

She took a few seconds to pause and heal the bruises and strains Anders had left her with. She didn't want to go on at anything less than her best.

"Ready?" Sorrel asked her.

"Ready," Vola said.

"Are we going to be clever about this?" Talon said. "Or go straight through the front door?"

"We know what's in there," Sorrel said. "And they know who's out here. I say we kick down the door."

Vola checked the others. Rilla and Talon were nodding. Even Lillie's face was set as she met Vola's eyes.

"Time to end this," she said.

Vola settled her shield on her arm. "Sorrel, take point. Talon and Lillie be ready with ranged attacks. Rilla and I will cover you."

Sorrel disappeared down the tunnel, and the rest of them followed.

Twenty feet later, the passage opened onto the large central chamber of the mountain. The one they'd seen in Anders's last illusion. High above, a jagged hole opened in the ceiling, letting daylight stream down to the floor.

Clearly, Anders had been hard at work since that memory had taken place. The dimly lit rubble was gone, replaced by rows of tables along a wall cut out of the rock. In the middle of the room stood a group of tanks, just like the ones Myron had worked with back in Brisbene. Like the ones Nargilla had used in Firewatch.

These however were empty. Because the power that was supposed to be filling them was walking around inside Vola and the others. And the rest was inside Anders.

Five figures waited for them in various poses of forced relaxation around the room. Lord Arthorel, a skinny man with squinty eyes and chewed fingernails, fidgeted from the corner on the left. Xavier glared at Lillie, his arms crossed over his chest, the sunlight bringing out the deep honey highlights in his hair.

Inga lounged on a bench, her gown artfully arranged around her as she examined her fingernails. Nargilla sat on top of one of the tanks, rocking back and forth as if in rhythm to a tune only she could hear.

And Anders stood behind them all, his gaze trained on the passage.

They didn't look weighed down by the absence of magic.

Vola forced herself to breathe. She couldn't afford to pass out from lack of air here at the very end.

"Gah, finally," Nargilla said and rolled her eyes. "I was starting to think you didn't actually want to fight us." She swung her legs and jumped down from her position, landing with an "oof."

"I never doubted this moment would come," Xavier said. "They can do nothing else but be drawn inevitably to their foretold deaths."

Nargilla rolled her eyes toward the ceiling. "Lighten up, Mr. Doom and Gloom. Otherwise, this will be no fun."

"It's not supposed to be fun," Lord Arthorel said. Vola hadn't remembered how nasally his voice was, but now that she heard it again that seemed just right. "It is revenge. It is justice. They took my title. My lands, my power."

"Your god?" Inga said mildly.

Lord Arthorel frowned. "Well, no."

"Then let's not argue about who they've screwed over the worst," Inga said, smiling so her tusks glistened. "You would only lose."

"I'm just saying," Nargilla continued. "If you can't enjoy your work, then what's left?"

"Oh, don't worry, I will enjoy it immensely," Xavier said. He cracked his knuckles.

"Any requests, boss?" Nargilla said over her shoulder to Anders.

Anders's eyes narrowed a fraction. "Kill them."

"Well, yes. Obviously," Nargilla said, planting her hands on her hips. "Only way to get the power back. I was looking for something a little more original."

Vola was done waiting. Done bantering. This was the end and none of them were leaving until the other side was dead.

She flicked her hand so her sword tip flashed, and Lillie hit them with a fireball.

The smoke cleared, revealing Arthorel and Xavier coughing while Inga waved a lazy hand in front of her face.

Nargilla cracked her neck. "That's more like it."

Xavier threw himself forward.

Vola stepped to intercept him, hoping to throw him back with her shield. But he planted his feet and met her strength for strength.

He hooked a leg under her and tossed her on her back. She braced to take his next attack, but Xavier leaped over her, stabbing at Lillie.

Lillie disappeared between one breath and the next, reappearing halfway around the room.

Rilla slid in front of Talon, covering the ranger as she loosed an arrow, which arced above them. At the peak of its trajectory, it flared, splitting into a myriad of deadly projectiles which whistled as they fell on their enemies.

One struck Xavier, piercing the joint between his pauldrons and his breastplate. Nargilla dissolved into the rock at her feet to avoid the volley, and a shield flashed over Inga, protecting her.

So they still had their magic, Vola thought. Anders's power

must have protected them when Mishap's Heroes drained the rest of the world.

Rilla and Sorrel converged on Xavier and Lord Arthorel, while Vola climbed back to her feet.

Fog figures unfolded from the ground, stretching up until they formed very familiar faces.

Illusory copies of Vola, Lillie, Sorrel, Talon, and Rilla stared back at them. Gorgo and Lydia readied their weapons. Cyrano and Raven and Hazel and Renvick and Listrell. So many they knew and loved.

Vola just sighed. They'd already seen this trick before.

"Don't you have anything new?" she asked Arthorel and lunged to stab her mother through the heart.

Arthorel frowned before Sorrel smacked him in the side of the head with her fist and followed it with a slash across his chest with Maxim's new and improved Warstaff.

Vola went after the illusions as Lord Arthorel defended himself against Sorrel. These were clearly here just to distract them. Rilla was engaged with Xavier while Lillie peppered Inga with spells, and Talon chased Nargilla about the room. But there were so many illusions in the way it would be easy to mix up friend and foe and accidentally try to stab the real Rilla or Sorrel instead. Gruff wove between them, teeth flashing at illusory ankles and hamstrings.

Vola lifted her shield to take an attack from the fake Talon and under its protection, she breathed out with forced calm.

She reached with the divine power still resting in her chest and found the point of magic within each illusion. The bright heart that held them together. And she tied them all together, linking each one to the next.

Then she surged to her feet, throwing back the fake Talon and slashing Cyrano. She took his head from his shoulders in one blow, and the chained illusions all fell to dust at their feet.

Vola glanced around to find Arthorel, but something tickled her ear and she ducked. A whisper and a giggle made her whirl, but she couldn't see anything. The cavern around her faded into splashes of bright colors that hurt her eyes, and she squinted against the pain, trying to see through to where the real world was trying to kill them.

Shit, shit, shit. She couldn't see. She couldn't even hear past the silky whispers in her ears. Anything could sneak up on her.

A hand grabbed her shoulder, and she cried out, spinning to strike with her blade.

"Vola!" Talon said. "It's me."

The air left Vola's lungs in a whoosh as the cavern faded back into view.

"What happened to you?" Talon growled.

"Arthorel's illusions."

Talon glanced across at Arthorel, who had pressed himself up against the wall. Sorrel stood in front of him, slack-jawed, her gaze focused on something that wasn't there.

"You go left, I'll go right," Vola said.

Talon didn't wait. She slipped off to the side. Vola made a show of growling and charging for Arthorel from the right, keeping his attention on her.

He managed to throw up a shield to deflect her blow, but he didn't see Talon coming from the other direction.

She stabbed him. As her blade sank into his neck, his form flickered sideways, and Vola realized he was an illusion himself.

Talon stumbled back and crashed into Sorrel, who fell with an oomph and blinked up at the ceiling.

"Snap out of it!" Vola said. "Where is he really?"

Lillie had a spell that showed her magic and could see through illusions, but she was busy keeping Inga and Nargilla occupied. Vola didn't want to distract her.

Wait, she was imbued with the power of the gods. And there were plenty of gods who dealt with magic.

Vola reached deep and called up the power of Gava, Greater Virtue of Perception, who hated deception and tricky illusions more than anything.

Vola scanned the cavern, ignoring the flashes and bangs of other magic, looking for Arthorel.

And found him looming over Sorrel, who was still reeling from whatever illusion he'd cast on her.

She gasped. "There!" she called to Talon.

Talon charged and leaped. And Sorrel being Sorrel rolled out of the way to let the ranger fly past.

Talon landed on Arthorel, daggers sinking into his chest. His real chest this time.

The illusionist hiccuped and stared down at himself as Talon yanked free and stepped back. Arthorel staggered. And fell, becoming nothing more than a heap of arrogance and magic and broken vows.

Vola looked up to find Anders staring at her from across the room. She raised her chin as if to say, yes, we're coming for you.

Rilla called out, and Vola spun in time to catch Xavier bearing down on her.

She blocked his swing badly and fell to one knee.

An enraged scream rang from the cavern walls, and suddenly Lillie was there behind her brother. She placed both palms on the back of his breastplate and sent lightning flashing across his body.

He cried out and dropped to his hands and knees.

Lille stumbled back, chest heaving.

Xavier pressed a hand to his face. "How many times do we have to go over this, Lillie? You're supposed to be the smart one."

Lillie's jaw clenched. "You don't have to do this, Xavier. You don't have to work with them. Anders is taking everything and turning it to ash. Magic, nobility, chivalry. Inga killed Innis. Don't you care?"

"Innis made his choice. He could have had protection. He chose something else."

"He chose what was right." Lillie swallowed. "I remember when I was small. When I was too little to play with Innis and Kellan, but you sat with me and showed me the stories in your books. The stories about knights who defended Southglen from evil. You always wanted to be one of those knights. You showed me their banners. Told me their stories."

"Boring," Nargilla said, head popping up from the rock where she'd been lurking. "When I was a kid, I dreamed of world domination."

Sorrel launched herself at the gnome, forcing her back into the rock.

"You can still be one of those knights, Xavier," Lillie said, holding out her hand. "You can still do the right thing. Father and Kellan miss you."

Xavier stared up at her, eyes so alike. "Really?"

Lillie smiled. "Yes."

Xavier reached for her hand and yanked her toward him, sword out.

Lillie whispered a quick word, and a blast of air threw Xavier off his feet.

"I guess I've always been more like Mother in that regard," Xavier said, climbing to his feet and brushing himself off. "You wouldn't remember but she chose to rise above messy things like emotions."

"I met her, Xavier. And she wasn't 'above' anything. She was just busy and selfish with no regard for anyone else," Lillie said. "And you can't pretend this isn't about emotion."

"Very well, I won't." He lunged for her again, having learned nothing.

Lillie blasted him with fire, and Vola ducked through the last of the flames to strike him with her shield. He grunted and staggered back a couple of steps.

Nargilla chose that moment to erupt from the stone behind them. Sorrel spun and slashed at her.

Vola was nothing more than a preoccupation for Xavier, who tried to lunge past her to get at Lillie.

Vola caught his blade on her cross guard and planted her boot in his crotch. He huffed in pain and turned his shoulder into her. She grimaced and slashed him across his arm.

Flames licked out from the slice, white-hot and flickering against his armor. The pale light cast shadows across his stubbled jaw and sharp nose. Now that she'd met both Ephyra and Shereille, she could see the planes of Shereille's features poking through Ephyra's softness in Xavier's face.

Xavier stomped on her foot and backhanded her across the face.

Vola stumbled away.

Talon dropped her daggers and held her hands over the ground. Then she clenched her fists and yanked up.

The rock under Xavier's feet heaved and wrapped around his legs, trapping him in place.

Nargilla surged upward, standing half in and half out of the ground as she tsked. "Nice one," she said. "But we can't have our big, strong knight pinned down now."

She pulled at the ground, and the rock crumbled away from Xavier. She glanced at Inga. "You gonna help at all?"

"You seem to have it handled," Inga said, tilting her head. "I'll pick off what's left at the end."

"Right, well, it's not like I'm not used to doing all the work," Nargilla grumbled as she subsided back into the rock.

"Oh, fine," Inga said, and waved her hand in Xavier's direction.

The knight began to glow.

"Oh, for Maxim's sake," Sorrel said, and she leaped at him, Warstaff flashing. The light caught the curved blades, turning them into streaks of lightning through the air of the cavern. And then real lightning began to flash from the ends of the blades.

Vola realized the halfling was muttering to herself as she whirled. Things like, "Yeah, yeah, I'm trying" and "you could help me out, you know, since you know all about it." And with a jolt, she realized Sorrel was talking to the dead. She carried their power, and they were arguing with her about how best to use it.

With a series of slashes, Sorrel drove Xavier back, one step at a time. The knight raised his blade to block her, but her glaive slashed down and sheared his sword off at the hilt. She slashed across his chest, and his breastplate fell to pieces around him with a clatter.

Xavier held up his empty hands, his eyes wide and frightened, and Sorrel took the briefest moment to check with Lillie.

Lillie didn't hesitate. She spoke a word that made the air shiver and the ground rumble. Xavier screamed. Then he collapsed to the ground, eyes blank and lifeless.

Nothing had touched him at the end, save Lillie's voice.

"All right, so that just happened," Nargilla said. She pulled herself out from the ground and stood with her hands on her hips, staring at Xavier. "Did you know she could do that?" she asked Inga.

Inga shook her head. "She couldn't the last time I was in her head."

Vola signaled the others. Rilla and Talon on one side, Lillie and Sorrel on the other. And forward.

"Damn, I would not want to be a part of the Ephyra family." Nargilla eyed Lillie, who approached her side of the cavern.

"Well, I guess there's just one thing left to do," Inga said.

"Kill them? Yeah. Duh."

Vola gripped her sword. "You know we won't make it easy, right?"

"Good." Nargilla stepped forward, then stopped.

The gnome frowned and glanced down at her chest. Lines of light threaded through her veins, creeping down her arms and legs, illuminating her with a network of light.

The magic spread to Inga, whose mouth fell open.

Nargilla's eyes went wide. "Oh, no." She spun to point at Anders, who still lurked behind them all. "No, don't you dare!"

Vola shrank back, eyes narrowing. What was he doing? She followed the lines of light with her gaze, racing to interpret this new threat.

He was filling them with all of his stolen power. Stuffing them so full they wouldn't be able to hold it. And as soon as they reached the tipping point…

Oh gods.

For a brief second, Nargilla and Inga lit up so brightly, they left images flickering across Vola's sight. She had time to throw up her arm to protect her face. But not enough time to think about how to protect her party.

Nargilla and Inga exploded with a roar of wind and light, and Vola ducked as wave after wave of heat struck her with a physical force. Her sword vibrated in her hand.

Instead of receding, the explosion intensified, getting louder until it rang in Vola's ears.

Her sword shattered, and the force flung her back against the cavern wall.

Pain blazed along her spine and the back of her skull as she fell to the ground and lay there slumped. She tried to shake her head, but the movement sent a stab of white light behind her eyes.

She couldn't hear, couldn't see, could barely think or breathe.

But this was important. She couldn't just lay here. There were people to protect. And Anders was just standing over there.

Vola forced her eyes open. She blinked the water from them and squinted through the afterimages that flickered across her vision.

All she could see in front of her nose was rock. She rolled with a gasp and pushed up to her elbows.

A few feet away, Talon lay unmoving at the base of the wall, arm outstretched and empty.

Vola sucked in a breath and turned her head. Sorrel and Rilla lay on her other said, faces still and singed.

Lillie. Where was Lillie? Vola coughed and gasped and struggled until she could see the wizard crumpled and small against the wall.

Vola sobbed.

What had Anders done? He'd sacrificed Inga and Nargilla, and in the process, all the power he held had lashed out and reacted with the power the Mishap's Heroes held. There'd been no way to shield them because they were all the fuse to his bomb.

She tried to swallow around the ache in her throat. They couldn't be dead. They were just stunned. Knocked out. Dead would mean all the power they'd been holding would dissipate and flow back into the world.

Vola tried to crawl forward, dragging herself across the ground toward Lillie.

Just as she reached the wizard, a red glow gathered over her limp form. The same color as the fire she'd wielded so well in life. It grew stronger and stronger, just as the power from the Broken had when the goddess had destroyed the tanks in Firewatch.

Light flickered at the edge of Vola's vision, and she turned her head to see the glow above each of the others. Gray and blue and green. And it flowed upward and out over the cavern.

A world's worth of magic dissolving back where it came from.

TWENTY-EIGHT

"THERE," a voice said, and Vola recognized Anders as he stepped across the cavern. "That's better."

Everything seemed crystal clear, the edges of the tables and the rock walls sharp and crisp. But to Vola, it seemed like she was looking at it all through a pane of glass. She was over here and all that was…over there. At a distance.

Vola gathered Lillie into her arms, her throat thick and tight. Her eyes burned, but no tears fell. There was a hole in her chest that should have held grief and rage and pain, but there was nothing yet. And she embraced the nothing because she knew that what came next was going to hurt like nothing had hurt before.

"Bit of a waste, I guess," Anders said. He stared around at the destruction of the cavern. The tables and tanks remained intact since they'd been behind Anders, but everything else had been shattered, little shards of Vola's sword scattered across the rock floor. There was no trace of Nargilla or Inga. Not even a smear or a puddle. Everything had been burned away in that intense blast of light.

"You were pretty clever about it all. Shame to waste your

talents. But you absorbed the power I was after. And the only way to separate you from it was to kill you. Now it's free to be gathered once again."

He waved a hand at the colors flowing and shifting above them.

A voice of rushing wind and the ring of blades spoke in Vola's ear. "Don't worry, I've kept the power from dissipating completely. We can still keep him from stealing it all."

Don't worry? Vola thought. *Don't worry when the others all lay dead, and she'd failed to protect them, to keep them alive?* Her fingers tightened on Lillie's arm.

She was not looking at the wizard's face. She wasn't looking at any of them. Her gaze remained fixed on the rock walls.

"Now, I just need yours."

So he could be a god. So he could do a better job than them. And was that really so wrong? The gods hadn't been able to keep the others alive. They wouldn't even have been interested in what was happening here today if Vola hadn't forced them to be.

"Vola," the Broken said.

Anders drew a sword, movements sluggish as if time had slowed.

Vola bowed her head.

"Vola."

Anders was *right*. That though burned in her mind, a white-hot pain.

"Vola."

Except *he'd* killed the others. He'd destroyed them so he could have their power. Lillie, Talon, Rilla, and Sorrel. They were dead because of him. Not because of the gods.

And the Broken had helped her protect them. For months now, Vola had healed them and kept them safe using the Broken's power. And the goddess had never been stingy with it.

And in the end, she couldn't abandon hope just because she

was alone. She'd been alone before, and she'd always found someone to help. Someone to hold on to.

She drew Maxim's strength into her arm and called to Sorrel's Warstaff. It answered, whether because it recognized her from the times she'd held it before or because she carried Maxim's power.

The double-headed glaive smacked into her palm and transformed into a sword the spitting image of the one the Broken had given her. A greatsword that she could wield in one hand.

She threw up her arm and blocked Anders's blow as it fell toward her neck. The sound of their blades rang against the walls of the cavern, and Vola pushed Anders back and surged to her feet, grabbing up her shield.

"You killed your people." Vola slashed at him.

He blocked and lunged. "Necessary," he said. "Just like killing you."

"You used them to destroy us."

"It should have destroyed you, too."

But her sword had absorbed the shock and shattered instead. The Broken protecting her, even when she didn't have the power to protect anyone anymore.

Vola ducked and swiped at his legs. Anders spun back and countered the blow with a quick slash up her breastplate. The tip of his sword shrieked against the metal and nicked her cheek.

She pulled the Broken's power up, and the cut healed in a split second. Maxim's strength bolstered her sword arm and Mulgash's rage battered at the inside of her skull, turning her vision red. She didn't dare feel anything else right now. Not until this was over. Not until she'd destroyed Anders once and for all.

Mulgash's rage gave her strength and purpose when her strength and purpose had bled out along with her friends.

She feinted right and then kicked Anders in the knee when he followed. Instead of falling back in pain, he ducked his shoulder and shoved, sending her stumbling away.

Vola paused to catch her breath.

Anders was as good a fighter as she was. And this wasn't a time to push it to see who was better. If he won…if she died here, the world was lost.

But she carried the power of the gods.

She pulled the Broken's fire into her blade and lunged in for the attack.

She was fast enough to score a hit, the edge of her sword slashing across his chest. But instead of the feel of metal on flesh, there was a flash and a bang and the force of it blasted her back a few paces.

Vola resettled her grip as Anders checked himself. There was no wound. Only a line of thin pale fire that sputtered and went out as they watched.

Anders looked up with a grin. "That won't work, you know."

Vola huffed through her nose. Of course. He had some of the Broken's power as well. He'd used it to destroy his minions and her team. And now he was using it to protect himself against her.

Well, she had more than just the Broken.

She pulled Maxim's strength forward and attacked with that, driving him back and trying to smash him beneath the weight of a god's might.

He just laughed and thrust back with the Broken's power.

Vola gritted her teeth and tried something else. Tirza, goddess of Magic and Discipline, lent her the force of a gale. With every slice, she sent forth a wave of magic.

And Anders's power cut through it.

Vola staggered back, panting. She was imbued with the pantheon's power. But she could only use them individually. And each one was countered by the Broken. Who was the most powerful of them all even if they wouldn't recognize it.

The fractured pantheon wasn't nearly as strong as it needed to be.

She could hear the Broken's voice in her memory. "Don't let them fool you the way they've fooled themselves. They are not united. They might be working together, but they are not united."

"Lady," Vola whispered.

"I'm here."

"I can't beat him. Not when he holds a part of your power."

She could feel the Broken's regret and frustration ring through her and wished she'd phrased it differently.

"I need to unite the pantheon," she said.

The Broken was silent.

Anders eyed her across the way. "You can't win this."

He surged forward to attack. Vola countered with only half her attention. She was thinking. Concentrating on something else.

She blocked a blow, but he swept her feet out from under her and pressed her to the ground. She dropped her sword and gripped his blade with her bare hands to keep him from cutting her throat. Maxim's strength and the Broken's healing shielded her palms, but only just. Anders shoved against the power, making it bend and warp.

"This is why the gods have to go," he said, so close he spat on her face. "They're useless, powerless apart."

Apart, yes. They'd been apart ever since they'd kicked the Broken from their midst. Since they'd rejected her, they'd been fractured. The Virtues and the Obstacles. Maxim and Bierhel and Ona and Mulgash and Cleavah and so on across the board.

Together. Together they'd be a true pantheon. They'd be united under the Broken the way they were supposed to be. And maybe with all of their power resting in Vola right at this moment, Vola could do that.

But using the gods' power against one of their own, that's

what fractured them in the first place. That's what sundered their bond and maimed the Broken and shattered the pantheon.

If she united their power and then used it to break the piece of the Broken that Anders carried, what would happen? Another fracturing? Another Divine War?

She gulped. Anders's sword pressed against her shield. Her strength was failing, and the blade crept closer and closer to her throat.

He was immune to her power the way it was now. The Broken's power in him made him immune to the divine power of the gods.

But not the magic of the world.

She turned her head a fraction so she could see Lillie's limp form out of the corner of her eye. Sorrel and Rilla lay beyond. And Talon on the other side.

"The magic hasn't dissipated," the Broken whispered, following her train of thought. "I hold it ready."

She could pull it into herself. If she united the gods' power, she'd be able to replicate Nargilla's spell without any of the casting or preparations. Without the circle or the representatives.

She could pull it into herself and cast him down.

But she would do it alone.

She closed her eyes. There was always a cost to healing. She had to pull wounds into herself and heal them from the other side. Sure, she carried divine power. But there were limits. And death was usually a pretty big limit.

But she carried the Broken's power. She knew the depth of it, even without the bit that Anders had stolen. And how much more could she do if the gods were united. Just enough?

Anders leaned on his blade. The shield protecting her cracked, and the edge of his sword cut into her palms.

She swallowed, gathered all the divine threads within her, all the Virtues, greater and lesser. And all the Obstacles, greater and lesser. And wove them together.

Light and dark, a mess of colors so bright it burned the inside of her eyelids as it roared through her. It swelled inside her mortal being and seared her from within.

Anders's eyes went wide. Maybe he saw something that warned him. Maybe he could see the colors behind her eyes.

He growled and shoved down, fighting to cut her head off. Vola's hands wouldn't grip anymore and her arms shook with fatigue.

Lady, I need a second. Just one second.

A shriek and a blur of murky green made Anders jerk.

The swamp monster dove through the opening in the roof and swiped claws across Anders's scalp.

Anders cried out and pulled away, slashing at his new opponent. The swamp beast ducked and dove, gossamer wings wafting a fishy stench into his face as he screamed at her.

Vola rolled and reached out her ruined hands toward her team.

"Lady bless," she croaked.

Divine power roared through her, scorching as it went. But she knew if she held it back even a little, this would never work. She blew out her breath and let it go, let it surge through her. It took the death, it took the damage the others had suffered and transferred it all to Vola, giving her their wounds, giving her their pain and their death.

Black crept across her vision. This was new. Usually, it was red and accompanied by a surge of strength. This came with bone-deep weariness. There was already pain. It seemed like she was made of pain. But now exhaustion numbed the rest, and all she wanted to do was close her eyes.

But she couldn't yet. There was one more thing she had to make sure of.

One. More. Thing.

The power swirled above her, hesitating.

The others lay still, unmoving. And the black flickered, threatening to take Vola with it.

Then Lillie stirred. Then Talon. Sorrel. Rilla. And above them, the magic of the world speared back down into them. The Broken had saved it for them. And now that they were back, it found a familiar home in their forms.

Shadows danced, and Vola fought to keep her eyes open to watch as Sorrel climbed to her feet, glanced around, and advanced on Anders.

Rilla and Talon joined her. Lillie pulled lightning and fire and little flickers of green and white into her hands.

Anders tried to duck away, seeing his fate in their faces, but Sorrel was far too fast to let him escape. She struck, and he fell.

Lillie called down a swirl of lightning and fire to pin him to the ground. And Talon and Rilla converged on him.

And Vola let herself go.

TWENTY-NINE

VOLA OPENED her eyes and found herself standing in a field of wildflowers, the bright sky stretching overhead and a playful breeze cooling her face.

She wasn't even lying down. Which was a bit of a surprise. When you died flat on the floor, you definitely didn't expect to wake up standing.

Vola felt like there was more than one thing wrong with that statement but wasn't quite sure she should poke at it hard enough to figure it out. There was a lingering ache in her body that she shied away from. An unpleasant memory best ignored until she had her feet under her again.

Feet. She glanced down. Her bare toes scrunched in the grass. Huh. Those weren't exactly how she'd left them, either. She was pretty sure she'd been wearing boots. Some sort of armor.

Nope, not thinking that hard.

Whatever she'd been wearing before, it was gone now. She wore a pair of dark trousers and a linen shirt. Simple. Comfortable. The type of clothing that said you have nowhere to be and no one to impress.

She held out her hands. The backs were criss-crossed with scars, and she shoved them behind her before she could think too hard about that as well.

"Everything is still there," a voice said. A voice like the rushing wind, though the breeze across Vola's face remained gentle. "You're not missing any pieces, I promise."

Vola looked up to find a woman standing beside her in the tall grass. She wore her dark curly hair short, almost like it had been burned off at some point. Probably in the fire that had left all the scars on her face. She balanced on one leg because the other was missing from the knee down, and when she scratched her nose, Vola noticed she only had one arm as well.

Flames flickered behind her like massive wings, and when she spoke, Vola realized the rush of the wind was actually the sound of wings beating the air.

"Is this the afterlife?" Vola asked. That nagging sense that she was forgetting something was starting to get on her nerves.

The Broken laughed. "No. Can you imagine how boring it would be if it were? I just thought this would be more soothing for you after…"

After Vola had died. The pleasant fog of forgetfulness tried to take over again, to urge down the rotten memories, but Vola shook it away, choosing instead to remember everything. The good with the bad.

"They're alive?" she said, her face twisting as she remembered Sorrel leading the others in a final charge.

"They are," the Broken said gently.

Vola closed her eyes, cherishing that image in her head as she fought to breathe without choking. They were alive. There was no reason to cry, no reason to mourn.

When she could finally blink her eyes open again, the Broken was still there. Keeping her company, as always. But her image flickered a little.

Vola tilted her head. First, she focused on the Broken, with her scars and her strength. But the next thing she saw seemed to be Maxim's face with its sharp nose and broad jaw. His black hair and brooding features morphed until Mulgash stared back at her with his red eyes and pale skin.

"Are…are you all right?" Vola asked the figure she thought was the Broken.

"Better than all right," she said, and her voice was comforting in its familiarity. "We are whole. You united us."

"Then you really were broken," Vola said. "Fractured."

"They thought we would be better separate. That we would be more powerful with more autonomy." Her lip tilted in a rueful smile. "I disagreed. So they cast me out, and I fell in flames. They never realized they were tearing out a piece of themselves. And every time I tried to return to reunite the pieces, they turned away, choosing isolation and brokenness."

The Broken's mouth thinned, and she turned her face away for a second in pain. "So I took the flames of my fall and made them my own. I claimed their power for myself and kept going. I kept working. The gods had stepped back from the world, but that didn't mean I had to give up on either of them. I never actually thought we could be fixed. Not truly." She smiled ruefully at Vola. "I doubted. I guess there are many reasons I am called the Broken."

"What was your name before we called you that?" Vola hadn't even realized she was going to ask the question before it popped out.

The Broken stared up at the sky for a moment. "I don't know. I took that and made it my own as well."

Vola squinted up as well, but there was nothing up there but an endless expanse of blue. Not even a cloud.

She wanted to ask, "what now?" But she had the feeling that

didn't really concern her anymore. Still, she wasn't used to not getting a say.

She took a deep breath and held out her arms to look at them. Scars covered her skin, turning her gray-green coloring into a patchwork of remembered pain. Every slice Anders had inflicted on the others, every bruise and cut and blow she'd taken onto herself, showed. The worst being the ones she couldn't see. The death blows that had taken their lives. She'd stolen those away as well, and now she stood here in a field of wildflowers instead of where she should be.

"I knew what I was sacrificing," she said, her voice thick. "I know the price of what I do, and I knew what it would do to me. I made that choice, and it should all be worth it as long as the others survived. Four lives for one seems like a pretty good trade."

"But?" the Broken said, staring at her.

Vola sucked in a breath. "But for once I want to be selfish. I wish it was five lives."

"Vola," the Broken said.

Vola winced.

"You are not stupid."

Vola glanced up in surprise.

"You know what you have done. For me and for the pantheon and for the world." She gave Vola a brilliant smile. "You have only to ask, my knight."

Vola fought hard to look at the choice logically. To give it a fair process.

Early retirement. Rest. No more sideways glances. No more blatant mistreatment because she was an orc. No more pain. No more worry.

Or…she could go back to all that. To the pain and all the rest. Except all the rest came with laughter and love and the wholeness of protecting the ones who meant the most to her.

She met the Broken's eyes. "Please?"

The Broken reached for her face and the scars that marred it, and Vola jerked back.

She touched the lines creeping up her cheeks. "I'd like to keep them. To remember," she said.

"You'll remember without them," the Broken said. "Trust me on that."

Vola felt herself flush. She would know. "Four, then," Vola said. "Let me keep four of them. I'd like to take the flames and make them my own."

The Broken didn't smile, but her eyes shone. "Very well."

The goddess reached for Vola, and this time, she didn't flinch away. The Broken folded Vola into her arms, hand pressing the back of her head. Her voice was the rushing of wings in Vola's ears as she said, "Lady bless."

Vola opened her eyes and found herself flat on the floor, her limbs leaden, her armor smoking and blackened, and she thought to herself, "This is more like it."

She tried to move and hissed in pain. The Broken might have fixed whatever it was that had sent her to that not-afterlife, but there was plenty left over to remind her she'd done some very stupid things before that. For instance, her hands were killing her.

Sorrel popped into her field of vision, which mostly consisted of the cavern roof with its hole. "She's not dead," Sorrel said, her voice an octave higher than usual. "Oh my gods, I was wrong. Vola's not dead."

Then she did something very un-Sorrel-like and dropped her head onto Vola's chest and burst into tears.

Vola struggled to lift a hand and patted the halfling's head.

Rilla came into view somewhere near Vola's feet, and Talon sat beside her head. Lillie took a position opposite Sorrel. It was a lot to take in right at the moment, but she needed to be able to see them and wouldn't have had it any other way.

"How are you feeling?" Lillie said.

Vola took stock. "Not dead," she said. That was about as good as it could get, all things considered.

"Um," Talon said, casting a glance at the sobbing Sorrel. "Were you? Or were we just imagining that?"

"No, you weren't."

"Don't you ever do that again," Sorrel said, lifting her head.

"Sure, as long as you don't ever make it necessary again."

Sorrel's mouth fell open, and she blinked.

"Deal," Lillie said. Her hand crept into Vola's, and Vola's fingers tightened on hers.

"Wait, we died?" Sorrel said.

"You don't remember that?" Rilla said, as Vola tried turning her head so she could peer between Lillie and Talon.

"I was really hoping that was a bad dream induced by head trauma when I hit the wall."

The swamp monster snuffled the ground across the cavern, her wings folded against her back.

"Where's Anders?" Vola croaked.

"There were too many pieces to find all of him," Talon said, grimly.

Vola winced.

The swamp monster caught sight of Vola and gave a little squeal. She galloped over to them, and Vola held up her free hand.

"Hey. You were actually really helpful," she said.

The swamp monster stopped and hawked a wad of toxic spit at Vola. It sizzled against her breastplate.

They all groaned.

"Its helpfulness does not exceed how gross it is," Rilla said.

THIRTY

VOLA NEEDED help standing and staggering out of the mountain. Everything seemed to be in working order, and Vola trusted the Broken to put her back together in one piece, but her limbs seemed to have trouble believing it for the first hour or two. Rilla supported her on one side and Talon on the other. They'd tried to drape her over the swamp monster's back, but the creature had tried to take a bite out of her, so they opted for something less fraught. Now the swamp beast followed them, ears pinned to her head as she glared at them.

The antechamber where they'd met was still scattered with broken glass, and they shuffled through to the entrance where they could see daylight shining through.

Had it really only been a few hours since they'd left the army? Vola felt like it should at least be dark or like a week later. Not the same day, with the same sunlight pouring down.

She winced away from the light after the dimness of the cavern and had to blink spots out of her eyes. Ahead of them stood War. She waited in the center of the battlefield, the point of her sword drooping to rest on the ground. Bodies, both undead and golems, littered the ground around her.

The rest of the army staggered behind her. Some were still on their feet, but many had fallen to hands and knees to rest among the dead. Vola caught sight of Cyrano supporting Raven off to one side. Monks were scattered among the soldiers and here and there an orc supported a human, keeping them on their feet.

The dragons flanked the army on either side, waiting.

War saw them and lifted her chin and her sword. She stepped forward, though from the way she wove, she was ready to collapse, too.

"Gods, I'm so glad it's you coming out of there," she said, wiping her brow. "These all finally fell, and no more rose to take their place so we assumed...well, we knew something had happened, just not what."

"Anders is dead," Rilla said, adjusting Vola's arm around her shoulders.

"You're sure?" War asked.

Sorrel raised her hand. "Witnessed."

"He wasn't immune to the magic they carry," Vola said, her arms tightening around Rilla and Talon involuntarily. "And the pantheon is whole now. I doubt they'd let him survive."

War blinked at her. The others all stared.

"The pantheon is what?" Lillie said.

Vola sighed.

The wind shifted across their faces, and Vola recognized the feel of a downdraft, like wing beats descending from the sky.

And the Broken appeared on the rock beside War. Figures stepped out of her form, like shadows detaching themselves from their progenitor, and Vola recognized faces. Hundreds of greater and lesser gods, Virtues and Obstacles alike, arraying themselves around the five of them and War. And standing at their head was the Broken, with Maxim on her right and Mulgash on her left.

The Broken placed her hand over her heart and bowed from the waist. The rest all followed her example.

And as they froze in their obeisance, Rilla and Talon both shuddered under Vola's arms. When Vola glanced at Lillie and Sorrel, they had gone rigid.

Power flowed out of them, streaming up into the air, dissipating back into the world.

It hung there for a few moments, glowing and catching all sorts of colors in the sun before it exploded out, streams and eddies of magic shooting away over the hills, down into the ground, and falling on the army in sparks and waves of colored dust.

Cries of awe and relief rang out across the exhausted army. Soldiers who had been prone on the ground leaped to their feet, laughing and staring at their hands as if they were made new.

Vibrancy came back into the world. The air itself felt wholesome and clear again instead of thin. Colors deepened, edges sharpened like coming out from underwater and seeing the world the way it was supposed to be seen.

War straightened, her eyes shining. Light crackled along her gold-washed mail and flashed over the army as the power of her Throne returned.

Raven morphed into a great eagle and winged out over the army, circling in tighter and tighter spirals, joined by the dragons as they trumpeted their joy to the sky.

Those who hadn't already leaped to their feet climbed upright and helped those around them. Spell casters all across the battlefield gathered sparks in their palms and fire gouted into the sky. Fireworks, bright splashes of lightning, and sparks of color decorated the battlefield as magic and life were celebrated by the survivors.

As the Broken straightened and the other gods faded back into her figure, she winked at Vola.

The party lasted the rest of the day and most of the night. War pitched their camp directly east of Anders's mountain where the field was flat and no one would fall into any crevices or gorges in a drunken stupor. Because Vola was pretty sure everyone was drunk that night. Except her, of course.

"I didn't even know we brought this much alcohol," she said, covering her mug as the cook and his assistants went through the hastily pitched tents with another round. They hadn't even bothered with tables. They'd just pitched their tents and sat on the ground like a massive picnic. It was kind of cozy.

Rilla gestured with her drink and ended up spilling at least half of it. "I think War built a portal special to bring in some celebrea—celebrit—celebratory supplies." She turned to Cyrano and leaned across to him, where he was wrapped around Raven. "Hey. Hey, say that five times fast."

The night sky lit up with more spell casters making sure their magic really was back, and Vola turned her face up.

Lillie gave her a really sappy grin and leaned her head on Vola's shoulder.

"I thought you only drank wine?" Vola asked her, nodding to the mug full of something too yeasty to be a good vintage.

Lillie made a face. "Hey, we died today. I'll drink whatever the hell I want." And to prove that point, she took a swig that knocked her over.

Vola chuckled and pulled the wizard's head onto her lap so she wouldn't wake up with a crick in her neck in the morning.

Across the way, Sorrel was still on her feet, with her arm slung around Hazel's shoulders. They sang a hymn double the normal tempo, at the top of their lungs, and completely out of tune.

Vola glanced behind her to check on Talon, who sat in the shadows at the back of their tent, Gruff wrapped around her. "How are you managing?"

Talon raised her mug as if to toast Vola. "Do you think I could get a little umbrella for this?"

Vola laughed. She was still working through the half a mug she'd been given, just to be polite. The last time she'd had a drink, she'd passed out and woken up on a ship sailing to Glenhaven, so…

Although she might welcome oblivion this time, if only to avoid the sight of her parents making out in the opening of the tent next door.

Vola shifted Lillie to a more comfortable position, and while she was distracted, the cook came and refilled her mug before she could protest.

The swamp beast wandered through the party, dribbling acid saliva on anyone too drunk to get out of the way.

Vola held out her mug. "Here. You earned it."

The beast slurped it down and then turned to aim a burp right in Vola's face.

Vola coughed and when the tears finally cleared from her eyes, the swamp monster had wandered off, and Renvick hunkered down next to her. Bursts of light overhead splashed across his scales, making patterns that glowed in the night.

"Do guardians drink?" Vola asked.

"Not if they can help it," he rumbled.

Vola raised her mug, which was melting from the swamp beast's spit. "Hear, hear."

Sorrel stumbled over and tripped into Renvick's arms. He caught her and helped her upright.

"Hey, Renvick," she said. "We have a conversation we need to finish."

His claws played with the end of a tent cord. "I thought you'd forgotten about that."

Vola had thought Sorrel had forgotten as well. Or made her decision without him.

"I've been busy saving the world," Sorrel said.

"And now?"

"Now I'd like to figure out what we are."

Vola cleared her throat. "What happened to Hazel?"

"She couldn't handle the last verse of 'Maxim Be My Vision.'" She gestured across to where Hazel was staggering away with the help of her fellow monks. "They're putting her to bed."

Vola tucked her mug away where it wouldn't hurt anyone.

Sorrel yawned.

Renvick picked up the halfling and stood. "Let's talk. Then I can be your pillow. I do not have to sleep."

Sorrel narrowed her eyes and then shrugged. "Oh, why the hell not?"

Vola glanced in Sorrel's discarded mug. "I'm not sure I've ever seen you leave a drink half-finished."

Sorrel waved a hand as Renvick carried her to the next tent over. "I'm not leaving it. I'm just taking a break. I'll come back to it later."

And she snuggled down against his scales.

Vola closed her eyes only for a moment. But when she opened them again, light brightened the horizon and dew dampened the tents around them. Soldiers snored where they lay, oblivious to the rough rock beneath them.

Vola shifted Lillie over and stood up to stretch. Rilla lurked in the shadows just outside their tent, giving no indication that she'd spent the night celebrating.

"You look fresh," Vola said.

Rilla gestured to the rest of the camp. "I think you'll find there's not a hangover to be found this morning. Some sort of miracle I'd wager."

That proved true as the camp stirred and groups began pulling down their canvas and packing it away. The majority of

Southglen's army would stick around to clean out Anders's mountain, but their allies had families and lives to return to.

Gorgo and Lydia stopped by to give Vola a hug.

"You're coming home for Yuletide, aren't you?" Lydia said, holding her daughter at arm's length. "All of you?"

Vola glanced back to see Renvick bidding farewell to a sleepy Sorrel, and Talon climbing out of the tent.

"Sure, Mom," she said.

"We'll see you around, Lightless," Cyrano said, his arm around Raven's waist as they passed on their way back to their tent. "I imagine there will be plenty of trouble to partake in wherever you're headed."

Vola gave him a mock frown. "What makes you say that?"

Raven gestured at the mountain in the distance. "You know. Evil kidnappers, tricky illusions, bad guys with god complexes. Just experience, Vola."

Soon after Renvick had taken his leave, the dragons lifted off from the edge of camp and swept low overhead, spouting fire in one last triumphant goodbye.

"You and Renvick?" Vola asked Sorrel, who stood beside her, shielding her eyes with her hand.

"Yeah," Sorrel said. "We'll see how it goes. He's got to stay with Listrell, but I'll see him around. And we each do love a little differently from the rest of the world. So at least it should be interesting."

Vola raised her arm to salute the dragons as they went by.

Sorrel moved to help Talon fold the tent, arguing softly about who did it better.

As Vola dropped her hand, Lillie slipped under her arm. Then she turned it over, her fingers tracing a scar across Vola's palm.

"This is new," Lillie said.

Vola ducked her head. The Broken had kept her promise. Vola

had four new scars to go with all the others she'd earned over the years. The one on her right palm she liked to think of as Sorrel's. Fitting, since she'd never accomplished anything without the monk backing her up. The one on the back of her left hand was Talon's. There was one across her temple, stretching up into her hairline, that belonged to Rilla.

And the last one was stark and clear over her heart.

"For remembering," Vola said with a smile for Lillie.

War walked down the aisle between the tents as people took them down. She'd left the golden mail behind today, but there was a look in her eye that Vola recognized well.

She stopped beside them and raised her chin. "Did you get enough rest?"

Vola saluted.

Rilla wasn't nearly so polite. Or patient. "Spit it out," she said. "What's happened now?"

"A town on the coast," War said. "They've sent word to the Thrones in Glenhaven that they're being attacked by swarms of mechanical creatures. Started just yesterday."

Rilla pursed her lips. "Could be another baddy filling the void now that Anders is gone."

"That didn't take long," Sorrel said.

War met Rilla's gaze. "Falls under your jurisdiction as the Dagger princess," she said.

"I'll take care of it. Meet you back in Glenhaven to debrief."

War nodded and turned on her heel.

Vola waited, watching Rilla. The others watched Vola.

"Well," Rilla said. "Are you coming? Or are you taking early retirement?"

Vola scratched her nose and glanced at the others. Sorrel swung her Warstaff across her back and cocked her head, making her choice clear. Lillie beamed. Talon hoisted the packs without a word. And the swamp beast grazed nearby. There was no grass. Vola was pretty sure it was eating rocks.

"Retirement does sound nice," she said slowly.

"What?" Lillie cried.

"Peaceful. We could open a tavern. Sorrel would serve drinks, Talon could bounce."

"I'll bounce you," Talon muttered.

Vola bit her lip, then grinned. "Yeah, you're right. Might be a nice retirement plan. But we've got a lot more trouble to get into before then."

Thank you so much for reading!

The Mishap's Heroes might be done (for now…) but if you enjoyed the misadventures of a group of unlikely heroes, you might also enjoy the Mark of the Least books, a series of fairytales featuring epic adventure, a little romance, and characters with disabilities and a whole lot of attitude. Check out By Winged Chair!

Ever wondered what happened to Vola, Talon, Lillie, and Sorrel before they met? Sign up here to get the Mishap's Heroes prequel, Creation and Calamity, and read their origin stories!

And finally, if you loved spending time with Vola, Lillie, Sorrel and Talon, consider leaving a review so other readers can find more stories about heroes who don't look like heroes but save the day anyway.

ACKNOWLEDGMENTS

I started out thinking I was writing something fun and light and hopefully hilarious. But it turns out I can't just write fluff. Meaning creeps in from the sides and makes its home between the lines. And then someone likes it, and I have to write more, and more meaning forces its way in, and suddenly it's a whole "thing." I blame these people:

First, the Kickstarter backers, for making all this possible. And for believing in the series before I'd ever sold a copy.

Mom and Dad, for reading every book ever. And always asking where the next one is.

Arielle, Betsy, and Alison, for being the first inspiration for a group of inept heroes who have no idea what they're doing and manage to save the day anyway.

Miranda and Lacey, for sisterhood which looks a lot like party dynamics sometimes.

Kevin and Andrew, for inviting me to play this little game called Dungeons & Dragons.

Kyle, Mary, Amy, Clark, Tim, Greg, Lauren, and Dave, and a host of other party members, for providing endless opportunities for inspiration. These books are all your fault.

Lucy Lin, for all the amazing cover art. I don't think anyone else could have brought Vola and the others to life the same way you did.

Fiona McLaren, for copy edits and flexibility. And for

enjoying my humorous fantasy as much as my slightly more serious stuff.

Kristin James, for giving the series a voice. And for nailing every punchline, making me giggle uncontrollably.

And Josh and Abby, for endless support. Especially when I decided to launch a series the same month I was supposed to have a baby.

ABOUT THE AUTHOR

Books have been Kendra's escape for as long as she can remember. She used to hide fantasy novels behind her government textbook in high school, and she wrote most of her first novel during a semester of college algebra.

Kendra writes familiar stories from unfamiliar points of view, highlighting heroes with disabilities. Her own experience with partial paraplegia has shown her you don't have to be able to swing a sword to save the day.

When she's not writing she's reading, and when she's not reading she's playing video games.

She lives in Denver with her very tall husband, their book loving progeny, and a lazy black monster masquerading as a service dog.

Visit Kendra at
www.kendramerritt.com

facebook.com/kendramerrittauthor

goodreads.com/kendramerritt

instagram.com/kendramerrittauthor

tiktok.com/@kendramerrittauthor